all i want

Alabama Summer Series, Book Two

New York Times bestselling author

J. DANIELS

All I Want
Copyright 2014 J. Daniels.
All Rights Reserved
ISBN-13: 978-1-970127-04-1

Interior Design & Formatting by:
Christine Borgford, Type A Formatting

Cover Design by:
Sarah Hansen, Okay Creations

This book is a work of fiction. Names, characters, places, events, and other elements portrayed herein are either the product of the author's imagination or used fictitiously. Any resemblance to real persons or events is coincidental.

No part of this book may be reproduced, storied in a retrieval system, or transmitted in any form, or by any means, electronic, mechanical, photocopying, recording, or otherwise, without prior permission of the author.

To the lovers of love, and all the heartache that sometimes comes with it.

This is for you.

all i want

Alabama Summer Series, Book Two

tessa

Two Months Ago

No.

No.

No.

Jesus. Fuck, no.

There are absolutely zero good-looking men at this thing besides Reed, who disappeared an hour ago with some giggly brunette, and the man I refuse to acknowledge. Weddings are supposed to be a breeding ground for nameless hook-ups, and I'm shit-out-of-luck at this one. So, instead of getting drilled in a concealed corner somewhere, my dress bunched around my waist as a stranger becomes familiar with my sounds, I'm having to find other ways to pass the time.

Eat cake.

Hit up the open bar.

Eat more cake.

Dance with Nolan.

Get cake with Nolan.

Steal Mia away from Ben.

Watch Mia get carried off by Ben.

And now this.

Sitting at an empty table, watching as Ben, Mia, and Nolan all slow dance together. Nolan's in between them, rubbing

Mia's growing baby bump, while Ben can't seem to keep his eyes off his new wife. I'm crazy happy for them, but right now, I can't watch them share another perfect family moment in front of me. I need a break from this. Just a few minutes to get some air.

I step out of the tent and head across the lawn toward the Estate House. I'm walking aimlessly, not having any destination in mind. I need to get away from all the love for a second. Love is great when you're with someone. It's better when it's reciprocated. But it fucking sucks when that shit is one-sided.

And that's the only way I've known it.

I walk down the side of the building and turn right to go around the back. As soon as I round the corner, I see him.

He's leaning against the building behind some shrubs, head back, eyes closed, lips slightly parted. His sandy-brown hair is cut shorter than normal, almost buzzed completely, and it does really annoying things to his face. Like show it off more. Those ridiculously gorgeous features of his are on display for my eyes right now, and I don't have to avert my gaze because he doesn't know I'm watching. He has no idea I'm staring at his sharp, angular cheekbones, the fullness of his mouth, or the bump at the bridge of his nose that I see as this perfect imperfection.

God, I fucking love that bump.

His face tenses as his arms move to the front of his body, and I let my eyes roam to the reason for this change.

The blonde, I recognize from the wedding, is on her knees with his cock lodged in her mouth, deep throating it until she gags. His hands are in her hair, encouraging her, pulling her closer until she practically swallows him whole. I lift my eyes to the face I was just secretly admiring seconds ago. It's no longer tempting to keep my presence unknown. Because there's no way in hell I'm going to let this shit happen right now.

Fuck him, and his face.

I step in front of the bush and make a fist, clearing my throat into it. Luke's eyes shoot open and he grabs the blonde's head, sliding her off his cock. She releases it with a pop and a grunt of disappointment. Apparently, she isn't finished. But she looks pretty fucking finished to me.

Luke tucks himself away quickly. "What the fuck, Tessa? What are you doing?"

I look from him to the blonde. "Oh, sweetie. You might want to go disinfect. He's got the herp."

Slutty blonde parts her lips as if she's waiting for another cock. She stands and wipes her mouth with the back of her hand, glaring in Luke's direction. "Oh my God. Are you serious? You have herpes?"

Luke's wide eyes train on mine. "What? No, I don't!"

"He's really sweet about it though," I say, looking sympathetically at the blonde. "He pays for my Valtrex every month." I turn my eyes to Luke, letting out a swooning sigh. "So romantic."

Blonde shoves against Luke's chest. "You're disgusting."

"I don't have fucking herpes!" Luke adamantly vows as he tightens his belt.

I watch, basking in my victory, as blonde trudges through the grass, getting her heel caught in the process. She stumbles a bit, glares at Luke over her shoulder, and disappears around the corner.

"I can't fucking believe you just did that," Luke says, prompting me to whip my head around to look at him. He buttons his suit jacket up and steps closer. "What the hell is wrong with you?"

You.

What happened between us.

And the fact that you've obviously moved on without any difficulty.

I close the gap and he freezes, his hand flattening against his jacket. My gaze flicks from his crotch to his face, and I mask all the hurt of seeing this asshole with another woman behind the fakest smile I've ever worn.

"There's absolutely nothing wrong with me. You, on the other hand, might want to go to the clinic. If you didn't have an STD before that whore touched you, I'm sure you have one now."

I turn and storm away before he can give me a comeback. But more importantly, before he can see the smile fading from my lips.

FUCK. I AM *desperate for some dick.*

I hit the enter key, and wait. Graphics flash across my screen.

Welcome to Ignite. It's how hot people meet.

Is it? Is this really how hot people are meeting?

Twelve months, Tessa. It's been twelve months since you've gotten laid. You need this.

I stare at my computer screen, having finally gotten up the nerve to visit the online dating website that Mia gave me. Her aunt has apparently been extremely successful on here, finding her current boyfriend after only having to go through two duds. And by the looks of the happy faces smiling at me on my screen with the little conversational bubbles above them, informing users like me of their amazing experiences with Ignite, I might actually get lucky on here.

Please enter a username. It's the first step in the direction toward your destiny.

"My destiny, huh?"

My dick destiny?

I decide on something simple and quickly type in my selection.

TK12

Twelve, because if I'm on this stupid site for a whole month and come up with nothing, bringing my grand total up to thirteen solid months of no ass, I'm out. And, at that point, I have no idea what I'm going to do. Because I've exhausted all the other standard ways to meet guys. Bars. Clubs. My brother's wedding. I'm completely out of options here. Trying to find a decent guy in Ruxton is like trying to find a virgin in a whorehouse. I'm willing to give this a go, but only for a month.

I press the arrow and the page turns, taking me to a different screen.

Welcome, TK12. Tell us a little about yourself.

I'm going to assume that putting down *I'm looking to get laid by someone who isn't a complete asshole* will most likely draw undesirable attention. Besides, having sex isn't the only thing that matters to me. If it were, I would've been set with Luke Asshole Evans. Fucking was the only thing he cared about during our three wasted months together. And because he was stellar at it, I tried to convince myself, and anyone that asked, that I didn't need more than what he was giving me. Which, looking back, wasn't much. He was private about most stuff, except his body. That he didn't mind sharing. But personal stuff—stuff you normally share with the person you're dating, or whatever we were doing—that stuff was off limits. After three months, I hardly knew anything about him, besides what everyone else knew.

He was a cop.

He grew up in Canton, Alabama.

And he loved raw cookie dough.

Okay, so that last fact could be taken as something personal, but I only knew that tidbit of information because he always had packs of those pre-made, break-a-part, cookie dough squares in his fridge and he snacked on them when I was around. But that's it. The most intimate detail I knew about the man I was completely crazy about was that he didn't mind possibly contracting salmonella poisoning. Anytime I asked about his childhood or his family, he'd distract me with sex or dodge the question. But even though he kept me at a distance, I still felt more connected to Luke than any other man I'd been with. He'd give me this look, or he'd hold me a certain way, like he was scared I was going to bolt. Like he needed me as much as I needed him. Like he actually cared.

He didn't. He didn't care about me. Not like I did him.

Looking back on it now, I'm glad I had the pregnancy scare with him. It made me ask the important "do you ever see yourself having a family of your own" question. Which was what I wanted. And I thought I could have had one with Luke. But he hadn't wanted that. He hadn't seen himself having what my brother had. So I'd ended it, thinking I was pregnant but keeping him ignorant to that tiny detail. Hours later, when I'd discovered I wasn't, I wanted to feel relief. Relief that I wouldn't have to go through it alone. But I hadn't. I'd wanted that baby, and I'd wanted it with Luke.

And while I've been celibate, not by choice, for the past twelve months, he's been whoring it up around Ruxton, sticking his dick into anything with a pulse.

God, I hope his dick falls off. He deserves to never come again.

I rub my eyes and focus on the blank description box in the middle of my screen. It doesn't need to be lengthy. It can be short and sweet, like me.

I'm Tessa Kelly. Twenty-four years old and living in Ruxton, Alabama. I like sex, but I want it with someone who isn't just in it to get laid. I'm not looking for a one-night stand. If that's you, don't contact me.

There. Straight forward. No confusion. *Oh shit.* One

other important detail.

If your job requires you to wear a uniform, keep moving.

I click the arrow button and the next screen pops up, prompting me to answer a few simple questions. What gender and age group am I interested in? How far am I willing to travel? I type in my answers and click the arrow.

TK12, you're almost finished! Please describe your ideal mate.

Well, I'm not usually the type to sugar-coat anything, so why start here?

Marriage material, who would like to eventually have kids, and can fuck like a champion.

Yup. That should definitely catch someone's attention. Hopefully the right someone. I'm sure there is a surplus of weirdoes patrolling this website for potential obsessions, but that doesn't worry me. I can take care of myself. Just not in the way that is forcing me to create a dating profile.

Congratulations, TK12! Once you upload your profile picture, you'll be added to our database and users will be able to contact you. Please follow the guidelines listed below for file requirements.

I minimize the window and scroll through my picture folders. I have a ton on here with files going all the way back to high school. But I need a recent photo. And my most recent ones are the pictures I took at Ben and Mia's wedding. I hover the arrow over the folder, ready to click, when I see it.

The folder I forgot about.

I don't want to open it. I don't *need* to open it. But I do and I have no idea why. And then the photos are filling my screen. Ones of the two of us taken selfie-style, and ones that I took of him when he didn't know it. Those were always my favorite. That comfortable look of his, so different from the look he had when he knew I was watching him. When he knew *every* girl was watching him. He has this cockiness that plays on his features, and when I see it, it drives me completely insane with lust. I swear to Christ, that look is directly connected to my pussy. One glance and I'm on my back, assuming the position.

Luke Evans knows how attractive he is, and uses that to his advantage. He can sit back and wait for girls to come to him if he wants to, picking them off like fish in a barrel. But that look isn't the one that I liked to capture when I snuck pictures of him. It isn't the look that had me thinking about things I've never thought of with other guys. It isn't the look I'm currently staring at.

He's concentrating on something, the TV I think, while I sit next to him. His one hand is tucked under his chin while the other rests on my foot that's in his lap. His light hair is sticking up a bit, and he looks relaxed in a worn T-shirt.

It was this look that got me every time. This settled-down look that made me imagine him on my couch several years from now, doing absolutely nothing and being perfectly content with that. But this look was just another one of his lies. Another way to manipulate me into believing what we had meant something to him. And I fell for it, just like all the other stupid fish.

I close down the folder and right-click it, bringing up my options. And I don't hesitate. I click delete and confirm my decision, sending the folder out of my picture file.

I find a picture of myself that Mia took with my camera at her wedding. I'm smiling and it's remarkably genuine, which is surprising considering who attended that wedding, and how nervous I was about seeing him. My auburn hair is curling over my shoulders, half up in an elegant twist. I choose this one because it's the most recent picture I have of myself, and because I look really happy in it. Of course I was happy. My brother made my best friend a permanent part of my family that day. I'd never have to say goodbye to her again. She looked so beautiful with her finally noticeable baby bump that Nolan kept touching during the ceremony. And when my nephew didn't have his hands on her belly, Ben did. Protecting. Claiming.

It's how he'll always be with her.

Love. It suits the two of them.

I saw it in Mia's eyes when she tried desperately to ignore her feelings toward my brother at the beginning of last summer. When she tried to hold onto the hate she was so comfortable with feeling and not let herself feel anything different. And I would've supported that hate, but I knew Ben. I knew how great of a guy he had become and how perfect he was for Mia. I saw his affection for her. The way he looked at her like nobody else existed, and I knew that he would've done anything to prove himself to her.

Even going the friend route, which I honestly did not see coming.

But it worked. And once Mia got to know my brother for the man he had become, she opened herself up to all those other feelings that were brewing just beneath the surface. I knew it wouldn't take long. Not with the undeniable attraction the two of them had for each other.

You can hate someone until you're blue in the face, but that doesn't take away the desire that brews in your gut at the mere sight of him or her.

I know a little bit about that struggle myself. Luckily, I've managed to keep my distance.

I upload my photo and the screen takes me to a list of possible matches. I scan their faces quickly. Some look promising, but I didn't join this dating service to patrol for penis like some cock-whore. If someone's interested, they can contact me.

I'm still a lady, Goddamn it, and I'd like to be pursued.

Just as I'm about to log off and shut down my computer, a message pops up on my screen.

CaptainMike would like to connect with you.

Captain, huh? He looks good in his picture so I click accept, opening up his message.

CaptainMike: Hey, beautiful. Where the hell have you been hiding?

I sit back with a smile, pulling my knees up to my chest. Less than one minute online and I already have a potential date. And I was worried this would take more than a month.

Why the hell didn't I do this sooner?

I keep my response short.

TK12: Hi. It's nice to meet you, Mike. I'm Tessa.

The little bubbles pop up, indicating that he's typing.

CaptainMike: Send me a shot of them titties. You barely gave me cleavage in your profile pic.

I gasp and immediately begin typing my response, fury in each key-stroke.

TK12: Fuck you, asshole. Go stare at your own titties, which by the looks of your profile pic, are bigger than mine. I'm actually jealous.

I close the chat window and march away from my computer.

Why the hell didn't I do this sooner?

That's why.

"OH LOOK. YOU framed it." Mia runs her fingers along the edge of the picture hanging in my living room. It's of the two of us on her wedding day, and I loved it so much I had it blown up to an 11x15. She turns toward me, keeping one hand on her enormous baby bump. "You really looked beautiful that day. Pale yellow is definitely your color."

"Thanks. Unfortunately for me, I was totally outshined by the bride. She looked amazing and got all of the attention." I reach over and lay my hand across her belly, dying to feel some of the kicking she's always talking about. "Nothing. This kid must sense my presence and go into a power nap whenever I'm around."

"He was flipping around like crazy earlier today. Kicking me in the ribs and using my bladder as a punching bag. I had to pee four times when I was at the grocery store, and you know my thing with public restrooms." She scrunches up her face. "Gross."

We both round the couch and sit on opposite ends, Mia taking a lot longer than me to plant her butt down. Once it's accomplished, she lets out soft grunt. "I really hope I go a little bit early. I mean, look at me." She motions to her belly. Her very pregnant belly.

Mia's due in less than a month, and I know for a fact that she's been doing everything possible as of recently to move things along. I think she looks amazing. From the back, she doesn't even appear to be pregnant. The only weight she's put on has gone to her mid-section and her boobs. I gaze at them in appreciation and then drop my eyes to my own chest, which serves its C-cup purpose.

"I bet my brother is loving the extra room those are taking

up," I say, nodding at her ample addition.

"He is a bit more fascinated with them than usual." She stares off at the floor for a moment, and I catch the flush in her cheeks as some memory washes over her. "Oh!" She turns her face up to me with a beaming smile. "I almost forgot about your date last night. Tell me everything."

I groan and throw my head back onto the couch.

I've been registered on Ignite for nine days, and every guy so far that has contacted me has either been too old, too weird, or given off a rapey vibe from his screen-name alone. One guy landed on ClitMaster69 when he went through the tedious task of settling on a name. And then there was FingerBanger and ItsSmallButWorks. Seriously? I applaud you for your honesty, dude, but I believe my ideal mate is supposed to be able to fuck like a champion, and there is always a size requirement when it comes to my pussy. You must be this long to board this ride.

"Helloooo?"

I look over at my best friend with a forced smile. "Oh, he was a charmer. Not only did he bring me flowers when he came to pick me up, but he also brought his dirty fucking laundry."

"Are you serious?" she asks with a hint of laughter in her voice. "Did you go out with him?"

I grimace at the very idea of entertaining *that* insanity. "Hell to the no I didn't go out with him. I told him to take his dirty whites somewhere else, after I snatched my flowers out of his hand." I admire the bouquet of lilies that I had placed on my coffee table last night after sticking them in my one and only vase. "It was a real shame, too. He was crazy hot."

Mia leans forward with great effort, and smells the flowers. "Well, it's only been a little over a week since you joined Ignite. You have plenty of time to find *the one*."

I thought I'd already found him.

I blink heavily. "A month. That's all I'm giving this. It's a shame you're married to my brother now because come July, I might actually consider switching teams."

She giggles and shifts on the couch. Holding her hands out to me, she gives me a pleading smile. "Can you help me up? I gotta go pick up Nolan from your parents' house."

I stand and grab both her hands, pulling her to her feet. She leans back and places a hand on the small of her back, arching her belly out until it's touching mine. "Whew. That's my workout for the day. You know I can barely fit behind the wheel with this thing? Ooooh! Give me!" She grabs my hand and flattens it out against her belly.

And then I feel it. Finally. The quick jabs against my fingers followed by a rolling sensation against my palm.

I lean down and get eye level with her bump. "Hey, Mr. Stubborn. It's about damn time you let me feel you." I look up at my smiling best friend. "Still keeping the name a secret?"

She shrugs. "I just thought it'd be more fun this way. But I think Ben blabbed the name to Luke a few weeks ago so if you want to know, I'll tell you." I stand and her smile fades to a frown. "Oh, and he's definitely going to be there on Saturday."

I sigh in annoyance. "Leave it to my brother to want a co-ed baby shower. What the hell are the guys going to do at that thing anyway? Pass around onesies?"

Mia laughs and grabs her keys off my kitchen counter. "You know how Ben is. He's insistent on not missing anything involving this baby, and he thinks everyone's as excited about it as he is." She turns to me, giving me a weak smile. "Are you going to be okay being around Luke?"

"I'll be fine as long as I don't see him getting his dick sucked. That isn't one of the baby games we're playing, is it?" I sit on the arm of the couch, clasping my hands in my lap. I wouldn't put getting freaky with some random chick at a baby shower past Luke. But I swear to Christ, if I see it, I'm punching him right in his jewels.

She twirls her keys on her finger, shaking her head with a grin. "No, smart ass, it isn't." Stopping with her hand on the front door, she turns back to me. "His name's Chase. Chase Kelly."

The tension leaves my body at the sound of my soon-to-make-an-appearance nephew's name. I hold a thumbs up out in front of me. "I love it. And I know my brother picked it." She furrows her brow in confusion, her free hand now rubbing her belly. "Chase Utley. The baseball player. Ben loves the Phillies."

"Oh my God. No wonder that name came flying out of his mouth when we found out it was a boy," she says. "Humph. What am I going to do with him?"

"Oh, I'm sure you and those monstrous titties can come up with something," I tease, motioning towards her chest.

She sticks her tongue out in disgust. "Ugh. I *hate* that word."

"Titties? You would. What does Ben call them?"

"Tits. I can do tits. It's more . . . sophisticated sounding."

I throw my head back with a laugh. "Sophisticated? I just seriously pictured them wearing a bowtie and a monocle."

"And they probably have a British accent," she adds with a chuckle before opening my door. "All right, I gotta go. You're coming early on Saturday to help set up, right?"

"Yup. And I'm bringing the booze. I'm getting tanked at that shower." She shoots me a stern warning look and I smirk. "Kidding. I'll see ya."

"Later."

I get up and lock the door after she closes it behind her, watching out the tiny window as my best friend waddles to her car. Yes, she is waddling now, and it really is adorable to watch. Mia has rocked this pregnancy, making it look better than anyone I've ever seen. And it's been relatively easy for her up until now. She's hardly had any morning sickness, and had been able to wear most of her regular clothes up until a couple of months ago. That was when she really started to pop out. But unfortunately for me, every time I see her and that belly, my thoughts always wander to last summer with Luke.

Which sucks. Because I hate thinking about him.

I would've had the baby by now if I had actually been pregnant. And I'd most likely be raising it on my own. Which is another reason why I don't understand his presence at the shower this weekend. Why the hell would a guy who doesn't want kids of his own attend a baby shower? I don't care if he is my brother's best friend. Shouldn't he want to bail on a party that focuses on the miracle of life? The one that he never wants to experience?

Asshole. He's probably just attending to annoy me.

And who the hell had the brilliant idea of making it a pool party baby shower? I know it wasn't Mia. She refuses to wear a bathing suit right now, even if it is a thousand degrees outside. So, not only am I going to have to endure Luke Evans' presence during this two hour ordeal, but I'm also going to be struggling with the task of not staring at his glorious body in a bathing suit.

Shirtless.

Tanned.

All those tattoos.

Sweet baby Jesus. He's impossible to ignore when he's half naked.

I clamp my eyes shut and picture it, feeling the familiar tingling sensation tickling between my legs.

Fuck this. I need a distraction.

I walk over to my desk and boot up my laptop, logging onto Ignite. It's been a day since I checked for any messages and I'm praying to God that there is a new one. I will definitely be fingering myself in the next thirty minutes, but if it's to Luke's face, cock, mouth, or anything else involving him, I'll be angry and annoyed doing it.

The screen loads and my inbox envelope blinks the bright green color I was hoping to see. I click on it and open up the message box.

> *TylerTripp has left you a note.*

> *TylerTripp: Hey there, TK12. My name's Tyler. I'm twenty-seven years old, living in White Hall, Alabama, and I don't wear a uniform. You're really pretty and I like how honest you are in your profile. I'm not looking for a one-night stand either. If some lucky guy hasn't already scooped you up, send me a message. I'd love to chat.*

I click on his picture to blow it up and am stunned by the hot face that fills my screen. "Sweet Lord. You are delicious." And he's in White Hall, which is only thirty minutes away, so that's totally doable. I quickly scan his profile, noting some interests. Coffee drinker. Soccer player. Likes to surf. I click on the respond tab and begin typing.

> *TK12: Hi, Tyler. I'm Tessa Kelly. No lucky guy has scooped me up just yet. To be perfectly honest, I haven't had much luck on here. Glad to hear you don't wear a uniform. What do you do?*

The little bubbles appear in the window as I chew on my thumb nail and wait for his response.

TylerTripp: Tessa. I like that name. It's beautiful, like you. I'm a bartender at a local pub in town. It's easy money, and luckily for me, doesn't require a uniform. What about you?

I calm my blushing cheeks as I respond. What girl doesn't like to be called beautiful? It's nice to hear, considering Luke never once said it. *Shit. Don't think about Luke.*

TK12: I'm a medical transcriptionist. It's kind of boring, but I get to work from home and set my own hours. So I'm not complaining.

TylerTripp: That's cool. I'm surprised you're having to find dates on Ignite. But I gotta say, I'm really fucking happy that you are.

TK12: I've sort of exercised all my options. My friend's aunt had success on here so I thought I'd give it a shot. And I'm glad I did. :)

TylerTripp: I hope you're referring to me.

God. Isn't flirting the best? Especially with someone who looks like Jax from *Sons of Anarchy*. Seriously. This guy is insanely hot. Or his picture is, at least.

TK12: Maybe I am.

TylerTripp: Go out with me.

I stare at his command, because that's exactly how he worded it, and there's no hesitation in my response. I want this. I need this.

TK12: Okay. What did you have in mind?

TylerTripp: I'm working this weekend but I'm free next Saturday night.

TK12: Sounds perfect. There's this bonfire that I was going to go to. It's a lot of fun. Wanna do that?

TylerTripp: That. And possibly more?

Yes. Sweet Jesus, YES. More. I need more. At least one orgasm. I'm not greedy.

TK12: Absolutely. Here's my cell # 842–555–6997.

I stare at the screen, waiting for the bubbles to appear. But they don't. And then his name disappears from the chat as if he's logged off.

"What the hell? Really?"

This guy asks me out, and then bails mid-conversation? Who does that? Well, awesome. Now I'm horny *and* even more irritated. Not a good combination for me. I log off Ignite and close my laptop. Just as I'm about to head to my bedroom to handle business, my phone beeps somewhere in my apartment.

Shit. Where did I put it?

I look around the kitchen, scanning the countertop and even looking behind my electrical appliances. I'm one to toss my phone just about anywhere and completely forget about it. When I come up with nothing, I move to the couch and stick my hand between the sofa cushions. Nothing. It beeps again, coming from the direction of the kitchen that I just ruled out. And then I remember grabbing a water bottle just before Mia arrived. I open the fridge, and sitting on the shelf next to the milk is my phone.

Really, Tessa?

I look at my screen and see a text message from a number I don't recognize.

> *Unknown: Hey, it's Tyler. Just wanted to make sure you didn't give me a fake number. I've had that happen.*

I lick my lips and walk over to the couch, plopping down with my head at one end and my feet at the other. I type my response with a nervous energy after I add his number to my contacts list.

> *Me: I wouldn't fake number you. Unless you told me you liked to fuck animals or something weird.*

> *Tyler: Jesus Christ. You're something else. I prefer to fuck women, so I think you can rest easy there. Listen, I've had some shitty experiences on Ignite. People aren't always honest, and a lot of them use photos that are either not really who they are or are so old that they don't even resemble that person anymore. I'm not trying to be a dick, but do you think you could take a picture of yourself and text it to me? I'll do the same.*

Hmm. I guess he has a point. I hadn't even considered the possibility of him not looking like his profile picture. But I guess it's possible. I hold my phone above me and take a picture, liking the flirty smile I give him, and attach it to my message.

> *Me: Here you go. Is this proof enough?*

My phone beeps with a file attachment and I open it.

He's smiling, his shaggy blond hair hanging in his eyes, and it's definitely the guy in his profile picture. *Thank fucking God.*

Tyler: Christ, you are crazy beautiful. Are you lying on your couch?

Me: Yes.

Tyler: This is what it would look like if I were hovering over you. Do you have any idea how fucking hot this picture is?

Holy shit. Is this guy trying to sext with me? I am totally down for that if he is. This is way better than getting off on a guy I don't want to think about.

Me: Tell me.

I grip my phone in my left hand and slip my right down the front of my shorts. Wetness coats my fingers.

Tyler: You want to know how hard your picture made me? How thick my cock feels right now in my hand?

Holy shit. Yes. Please.

It takes a great effort to type with just the thumb of my left hand, but I manage. There's no way in hell I'm stopping now.

Me: Yes. I was going to get off anyway. Might as well do it with you.

I moan as my finger slides over my clit.

Tyler: You're a dirty girl, aren't you? Wanting a stranger to get you off. Touch yourself like I would. Rub your clit with your thumb and put two fingers inside that pussy I want to fuck.

"Oh God, yes."

Tyler: Are you doing it?

Me: Yes. Please keep going.

This isn't going to take long. Not with this apparent master of sexting. I stare at his words and read them over and over while I feel myself tightening around my fingers.

Tyler: Do you feel how wet I make you? Spread those legs for me. Finger yourself deep and pretend it's my cock.

I nearly drop my phone as I arch off the couch and do as he commands. It's only his face in my head. His fingers in my pussy. And his words getting me to the edge.

Tyler: I want to feel you come. On my hand. On my dick. In my mouth. Do it. Come all over those fingers and suck on them like I would.

"Tyler," I whisper as I come hard, my legs shaking as they fall open even wider. And I do it. I slip my fingers into my mouth as if he were here with me. Demanding it. Needing it.

This is the hottest solo session I've ever had.

Me: Wow. You're going to be fun next weekend.

Tyler: That was fucking hot. I can't wait to actually watch your beautiful face when you come for me. Gotta go clean myself up. Thanks for that.

I slap my hand over my mouth and squeal. He came with me. The thought of him jerking off hadn't even entered my mind. But now, it's all I can think about. He got off on the idea of me touching myself. How fucking hot is that? Now I have a new face to occupy my fantasies, and a chat that I can save for later use.

Luke Evans, you're no longer needed.

luke

TESSA KELLY IS a man-eater.

She's like medusa, but without the whole "freezing to stone" bit. Because that's not her style. That's not painful enough for her. She'd much rather draw you in with her blinding beauty, and then rip your heart out and eat it in front of you. And then she'll stand over you and watch you slowly die at her feet.

Cold.

Heartless.

Fucking ruthless.

This should be enough to make me not want her. To make me not think about her every second of the fucking day. And if her Queen Bitch attitude wasn't enough of a reason to hate her, the fact that she destroyed me a year ago should be. But there's one major problem.

I have a cock.

And he wants Tessa. He knows what it's like to be with her. He's had a taste of her, and no other pussy is good enough. Believe me, I've given him options. First, there was Brandie, who I wasted no time in satisfying my needs with. Or, at least tried to satisfy my needs with. Maybe it was a fucked up move to bring her to that concert for the sole purpose of making Tessa jealous, but I didn't give a shit. I wanted to hurt her, after what she did to me—dumping my ass out of nowhere and not giving me a fucking reason.

You don't want this anymore? Fine. You need more than what I can give you? Whatever. I didn't care what the reason was; I just needed one. But she wouldn't talk to me. She wouldn't give me anything. And then I find out she broke up with me thinking she was pregnant with *my* baby.

Fuck her. She keeps something like that from me? I had a right to know.

Her reasoning behind the break-up, using my words to her as an excuse, was complete bullshit. How the fuck was I supposed to know she was fishing around because she thought she was pregnant? Tessa and I never put labels on what we were. And I liked that. I didn't need anything other than what she was giving me, and I don't need anyone getting too close. Except for Ben, but that shit's different. He's my partner. We have to trust each other completely, and you can't trust someone if they keep you at a distance. I'd risk my life for him, but that is my choice. And it's a fucking selfish one. He's my best friend, and I don't want to miss him. I don't want to miss anyone. So I don't let anyone else in. I can't. I saw what it did to my dad, and that's not happening to me.

He didn't just love her. He lived for her. She was everything to him, and for nineteen years he was a better man. But when you love someone like that, when they become your only reason and they're taken away from you, a part of you dies right along with them. And nothing can fill that void.

Not the drink you gave up when you met her.

Not the son you shared.

Nothing.

So, what Tessa and I had worked for me. I gave her what I could, and she gave me all of her and never held back. Maybe it wasn't the perfect balance, but it was us. She was open and honest, most of the time. And I wanted to be that way with her. So when she asked me if I ever saw myself getting married and having a family someday, I was fucking honest.

No. I didn't.

Shit, before I met Tessa, I had a different girl practically every night. It was fucking easy to get laid in this town, and not a lot of work ever went in to taking someone home. I could just sit back and let them come to me. But doing that for nine years had taken its toll. No one excited me, or my cock. No one until her.

I had known Ben had a sister, but the thought of meeting her had never crossed my mind. We'd gone through the academy together and he mentioned her occasionally, but I'd never thought twice about her. Until I actually saw her. Then she became all I thought about.

It was at one of our fundraising events at Todd Lakes. Ben didn't tell me that his sister was coming, so when I'd seen him get out of his truck with the hottest chick I'd ever seen, I'd been jealous and really fucking pissed. My best friend had landed himself a girl that my dick wanted to be introduced to. And when they both came walking over to me, I'd wanted to get the hell out of there. I knew I wouldn't be able to stop myself from looking at her, and how fucked up would that be?

Even from a distance she was stunning. She was a tiny thing, coming up to Ben's shoulders, with reddish hair and a tight little body that I could easily throw around a little, which I desperately wanted to do. She had these crazy green eyes that grew more intense the closer she got to me. And they'd been glued to mine, daring me to break the contact I'd been holding. I'd never been looked at like that. Like she knew I wasn't going to be able to stop. Like she was getting off on my struggle. She'd fucking commanded attention, and I'd given it to her.

And I'd been way the hell turned on.

Then, by some fucking miracle, she'd turned out to be Ben's sister. I'd almost lunged at her right then. I'd almost pulled her into my arms and crashed my mouth against hers, needing to taste the sweetness I knew was there, but also the bite, because she fucking had it. Instead, I'd held my hand out for her to take and she'd looked down at it, smirked, and walked away with a smile that had made my dick harden.

That, right there, had pulled me in.

She wasn't like every other girl. She wasn't going to let me sit back and wait for her to make that first move. She was going to make me work for it. And I'd *never* worked for it. I knew she'd fight me. Hell, I'd *wanted* a fucking challenge. I'd given Ben a look, a look I didn't need to explain, and he'd laughed, and given me two words: "Good luck." He'd known what I was going up against. I'd had no idea how difficult it was going to be. But fuck, I'd never wanted anything more than her.

Tessa Kelly. If I'd have known the shit she was going to put me through, I wouldn't have bothered. At least, that's what I'm telling myself.

She'd ended it. She'd been dishonest with me. She'd fucked up everything we had. And now I was on my way to a co-ed baby shower where I wouldn't be able to avoid her. Where I knew for a fact that I'd once again be caught up in her and nothing else.

Who the fuck throws a co-ed baby shower? Isn't that usually just for chicks?

I pull up to Ben's parents' house and park around back. I try to ignore the throbbing anxiety that is coursing through me as I get out of my truck and walk toward the pool. There are balloons everywhere, all blue and green, and Nolan is running around like a mad man with his sword slicing the air.

"Uncle Wuke!" He wraps his arms around my legs and squeezes me with all his might. "Look at all dees balloons!"

I reach down and rustle his hair after he lets me out of his death grip. "You should try to pop them with your sword."

He smiles wide and runs over to a bunch of them that are tied to the food table, and then he begins to stab at them with great enthusiasm.

I love that kid.

I nod a greeting at Ben's dad, who is standing with a few other men next to a table of food, before my eyes begin scanning the crowd.

I find Tessa immediately, like I'm fucking drawn to her or something, and I allow myself a glance. And that glance turns into a stare. Her back is to me as she arranges the presents on a table near the lawn chairs. I look down at the gift bag I'm carrying, full of shit that I randomly picked off Mia's baby registry. And before I realize the direction I'm headed, or the fact that I haven't stopped walking, I'm by Tessa's side at the table.

I take note of her organization, which makes absolutely no sense to me, and I'm suddenly annoyed.

"You should put the taller gifts in the back. That way they don't obstruct the view of the smaller gifts."

She turns to me with wide eyes, sucks in a sharp breath, and then tenses all over as a scowl settles on her lips. I know she's about to hit me with some smartass remark, but my dick is too busy appreciating the sight of her to prepare myself for it.

Those eyes that could will me to do just about anything. Her full, wet mouth and the way I know it looks formed around my cock. And that fucking body that is barely covered up in a bikini top and shorts.

A pool party baby shower? Thanks a lot for intensifying my struggles, Ben.

She leans in, narrowing her eyes and causing me to snap out of my fanatical gazing. I blink rapidly before she speaks.

"Oh, I'm sorry. I hadn't realized the gift police were here." She reaches out and snatches the bag out of my hand. "I'll arrange the gifts how I *want* to arrange them. The bigger gifts will be easier for Mia to reach in her chair, and I'll hand her everything else." She motions with her free hand toward the decorated patio chair that is reserved for Mia. Dropping my gift onto the table, she continues moving the packages around. "Why the hell am I explaining myself to you? Go away."

"Do you always have to be such a bitch? I'm just offering my opinion." *And I'd prefer it if you didn't make my dick hard right now.*

She puts her hand on her hip and tilts her head, her lips curling into a forced smile. "What can I say, Luke? You bring out the inner bitch in me. It must be the giant ass-hat ego you have that sets me off."

Just as I'm about to respond, the sliding glass door opens and Mia walks out with Ben following closely behind her. They both register the irritation on my and Tessa's faces, and come walking over to us.

Mia wraps her arms around me, barely making it with her huge pregnant belly getting in the way. "Hey. I'm so glad you could make it." She lets go and Ben slaps me on the shoulder after I release his wife.

"Yeah, of course. Wouldn't miss it."

Tessa snorts and puts her back to the table, crossing her arms over her chest.

"Hey, buddy. Don't poke at the balloons like that. You're

going to pop them," Ben directs across the pool at Nolan. I turn my head and keep my smile hidden.

"Oh, he's okay, babe. I got all of them for him anyway,"

Ben turns and leans down so that his forehead is resting against Mia's. "Have I told you how beautiful you are today? Or how fucking perfect you are?"

Tessa throws her head back with an exhaustive sigh just as Mia tilts her head up to kiss Ben.

Tessa clears her throat. "Mia, did I mention I have a date with an insanely hot guy next weekend? The one I had that ah-mazing texting session with?"

Fuck. Is she really going to try and make me jealous right now? Why the hell didn't I bring some random girl to this shit?

Mia looks from Ben back to Tessa, her brows pinched together. "Um, yeah. We just talked about it, like twenty minutes ago." Tessa exaggerates her stare and Mia's mouth spreads into a knowing smile. "Oh, umm, no. You didn't. Tell us all about it."

Tessa grins and glances briefly over at me to make sure I'm listening. And I am, unfortunately. I want to walk away from this but I can't.

"Well, his name is Tyler, and he's a gorgeous bartender from White Hall. I figured I'd bring him to the bonfire on Saturday night and then—" Her eyes flick toward mine and she holds my stare, "—who knows? He might just get lucky."

My hands curl into fists at my side. I wasn't planning on going to the bonfire next weekend, but I'm fucking going now.

Ben laughs and turns to me. "You want a beer?"

I relax, grabbing my gift bag and putting it near the back of the table, where it fucking belongs. Tessa scowls before rearranging it.

I nod toward Ben. "Yeah, sure. I'll tell you all about the

girl I fucked last night." I watch as an obvious distaste for what I've just made up spreads across Tessa's face before I turn away from her and follow Ben inside the house.

"Jesus, man. After a year, I thought the hostility between you two would've died down a little," Ben says over his shoulder. He walks into the kitchen where Mrs. Kelly is chopping up vegetables with Reed. I can't help but laugh.

"Where's your apron, Reed?" I ask.

He looks up at me, pausing with a knife in his hand. "Shut up."

"How are you, Luke?" Mrs. Kelly greets me with a smile.

"I'm here," I reply, a bit colder than I mean. I soften the sting of my response with a shrug, and she nods.

Tessa resembles her mother, but only in appearance. The friendly demeanor Mrs. Kelly always has skipped right over her daughter.

She rounds the counter with a tray of food in her hand and kisses me on the cheek. "It's good to see you. Why don't you boys help Reed with those vegetables?"

Ben hands me a beer as I take in a noticeably annoyed-looking Reed. "Oh, I don't know. He seems to be handling the kitchen duties better than we could," I answer, smiling when Reed flips me off.

"Yeah, Mom. I think he's got it under control. Look at the cute little arrangement he's making," Ben adds with a grin.

Once Mrs. Kelly walks outside, Reed places the knife down and throws the chopped up peppers onto a tray. "You're both assholes. If Tessa wouldn't cut my balls off, I'd bail on this shit." He looks up at Ben. "Once again, really happy for you, but the next time you have an estrogen party, leave me out of it."

Ben laughs behind his beer, leaning on his elbow against

the counter. "So, who was this chick last night?" he directs at me.

Chick? What chick? It takes me a minute to realize why he's asking me that question. I'd completely forgotten about the lie I had dropped a few minutes ago. I look out the sliding glass door, narrowing in on Tessa right away as she continues working on her bullshit gift arrangement. "No chick. I just had to say something to shut your sister up."

Reed laughs. "She tell you about this guy she met online?"

I whip my head around, glaring at him. "Online? She's going out with some creep she met online? What the fuck is wrong with her?"

Ben frowns. "What's the problem?"

I take a massive chug of my beer, needing the alcohol to calm my nerves that are now on edge. I look between Ben and Reed, settling on Ben who, for some strange reason, doesn't mind his sister picking up men on the Internet. "*What's the problem*? This guy could be a psycho. She's not seriously going out with him, is she?"

Ben shrugs. "I don't know. Ask Mia. Or Tessa, if you're that concerned."

"Well, what the fuck? Why the hell aren't *you* concerned? She's your sister." I look over at Reed. "Or you? Aren't you two best friends?"

"Hey, I told her to make sure she meets him somewhere public, and she is. I'll be at the bonfire to eye up this guy," Reed states as he picks up his knife and cuts into a cucumber. "People meet online all the time. It's not that big of a deal."

The sliding glass door opens and gains my attention. Nolan walks through and tugs at his T-shirt, trying to pull it over his head. "Daddy, can I go swinnin' now?"

"I'll take you, Nolan," I say, leaving my half empty beer

can on the counter. "I need to go outside anyway."

"She's going to flip out on you if you say something to her," Reed warns me.

I help Nolan with his T-shirt and pull off my own, throwing them both onto the couch. "Let her flip out. She's crazy if she thinks I'm going to let her go out with some punk she met in some chat room." I grab Nolan's hand and lead him back the way he came.

"Why can't you two just do your own thing and not worry about what the other person is doing. Or who they're doing?" Ben asks.

I ignore his question and slide the door open. Why do I worry? I don't know. But after a fucking year of trying not to care what Tessa does, I've given up on fighting it.

It's a losing battle.

"THE GIRL I fucked last night. What a dipshit."

"What?" Mia asks, returning to my side after grabbing a plate of food. She snaps into a carrot as I continue to busy myself with the gift arrangement. Not that it needs it. I just need to keep my hands active right now because if I don't, I might punch someone.

Luke, to be specific.

She nudges me. "He probably only said that to piss you off. How did you think he was going to react to you insinuating in front of him that you're going to have sex with some guy next weekend? With a high-five and a 'go get 'em'?"

I open my mouth to answer her when the sliding glass door opens, and then every single word out of my vocabulary is stolen from me at the sight of who walks through it.

Shirtless.

Tanned.

Tattooed.

FUCK.

"Nolan, hold up a second," Luke says before walking directly toward me. I grab a gift and quickly hold it in front of me, needing a barrier in between that body and me. He stops a few inches away, glancing down briefly at the gift. "You're meeting up with some guy you met online? What the hell is wrong with you?"

"Nolan, wait for Uncle Luke," Mia says behind him.

Luke whips around, grabbing Nolan who is inches away from the edge of the pool, and hauls him up on his shoulder. He returns to his spot in front of me, leaning closer with expectant eyes.

As if I actually owe him an answer.

As if he hasn't done worse.

I place the gift back onto the table, no longer needing a barrier. His mouth just wiped out every tempting thought that was circling in my head and I'd actually like the use of my hands right now. Or a finger.

I straighten, glaring up at him. "Spare me the holier-than-thou attitude you have going on right now, Luke. I don't really see the difference between hooking up with some guy I meet online, and grabbing the nearest willing slut at a wedding."

He steps closer. "What I've done is not your concern."

"And who I do is not yours. Last time I checked, we aren't together. In fact, I don't think we ever were." I see the reaction to what I've just said spread across his face. Shock and then bitterness.

He masks it quickly with a steely look, shifting Nolan's squirming body in his arms. "You're right," he says, leaning down so his face is inches from mine. I swiftly glance at the day-old stubble along his jaw I used to run my finger across before he continues. "We weren't. Do whatever you want, Tessa. See if I give a shit."

You wouldn't. Because giving a shit would require actually caring about someone.

He turns, walking to the side of the pool with the stairs. Nolan slides down his front and they both descend into the water, Luke holding on to him even though my nephew is a good swimmer.

I know Luke cares for Nolan, but seeing him act like a damn parent bothers me. Every time I saw him with Nolan last summer, he acted the same way. Loving. Protective. But back then when I was around it, it sparked a whole new set of feelings inside me. Feelings I've never felt for a guy. It gave me this delusional family image in my head. One starring a man who I now know wants nothing to do with that fantasy. So, when I see him playing with Nolan in the pool, smiling and laughing as if he's actually enjoying himself, it infuriates me. Because it's just another one of his lies.

The door opens and Reed comes out carrying a tray of food, Ben walking out behind him. I walk over to them, wanting to talk to Reed, when my brother grabs my elbow and pulls me to the side.

"Ow. What?" I ask, jerking my arm out of his grip.

He gives me his typical sibling look, one that's full of concern and judgment. "What's the last name of this guy you're talking to online?"

Oh, hell no. First Luke and now Officer Kelly? I'm done with the interrogation.

"Why? So you can look him up in your database?"

"That's exactly why."

There's one thing I know for sure about my brother. He's relentless. If I don't give him a last name, he'll just keep bugging me for it, or he might even go so far as to hack into my online profile and get it himself. I wouldn't put that past him. But this is nobody's business but my own. I'm perfectly capable of taking care of myself. And even though I've only chatted with Tyler briefly, and sexually, he seems like a decent guy. I've seen some of the profiles on Ignite that scream sociopath, and his isn't one of them.

I've never heard of a murderer who also cares deeply for the environment.

I glance around the patio, looking for inspiration. Nolan squeals when Luke tosses him into the deep end, and it hits me.

"Knight. Tyler Knight. Okay?" I keep my voice steady as he studies me. Ben, and everyone else needs to stay the hell out of this. If he wants to look somebody up in his database, he can look up this guy.

He nods, buying my lie. "All right. Just don't do anything stupid with this guy, like go home with him or something."

I tilt my head, motioning toward my very pregnant best friend who is chatting up Reed. "Really? You did not just say that to me."

He laughs and puts his arm over my shoulder as we walk to the food table. "Just be careful, okay? I won't be there to size up this guy, so I'm relying on Reed and Luke to do it for me."

I pull away from him, looking from the pool back to Ben. "What? Luke isn't going to be there. He never goes to the summer bonfires."

Never. I couldn't pay him to go to one last year.

"He'll be at this one."

My anxiety level spikes in my blood. Not that I wouldn't mind making Luke jealous at this thing, but knowing him, he would probably just ruin my chances of getting laid.

Payback for the wedding.

Turning around, I glare down at Luke as he comes up from out of the water, running his hands through his hair and then over his face. My eyes narrow in on his chest, my favorite body part of his, and the *T* he got tattooed last summer after we'd only been together for a month. He'd played it off at the time, pointing to all the other tattoos that covered his body, and telling me that he was the king of rash decisions—getting my initial wasn't really a big deal. But it had to be. I'd never get someone's initial tattooed on me unless I knew, without a doubt, that they were my forever.

I remember being completely transfixed by it, running my fingers over the outline while listening to his seemingly practiced explanation. And when he tried to lessen the magnitude of the gesture, I swore I saw something in his eyes. A hidden declaration, concealed by fear or uncertainty.

You can be permanent too, if you want to be.

Jesus. How fucking stupid was I back then? I should've taken his words to heart instead of interpreting them in a way he obviously didn't mean. Like that tattoo, I was just another rash decision. Not a big deal. Something he could easily black out if he wanted to.

I lift my eyes and see his trained on mine, which I'm not at all prepared for. Luke doesn't just look at you. He gets inside your head and roots himself there, overtaking every thought and making everything around you that isn't him seem insignificant. Those crazy eyes of his are enthralling. Amber, like the color of a sunrise. I've never seen anything like it. Men shouldn't have such beautiful eyes. They shouldn't have beautiful anything. But Luke . . .

"Hey, loser." Reed's voice snaps me back into reality and tears my gaze from the guy I shouldn't have been staring at in the first place. But he was staring at me too. *Wasn't he?* I glance once more at the pool but Luke's back is to me as he plays with Nolan. "I'm gonna head out."

I turn my attention back to Reed. "What? No, you're not. Mia hasn't even opened her gifts yet."

"And?" he asks, pulling out his phone and messing with it. "Your mom thinks I'm some chick, apparently. I'd rather get the hell out of here before she has me on dish duty."

I step into him, and jab my finger against his chest. "You're not going anywhere. Not until Mia opens her gifts." I turn my head, seeing Mia and Ben talking with a few of my cousins. Reed tries to move past me but I slam my hand against his chest and halt him mid-step.

"Hey, Mia! Let's open your gifts now and then we'll play some games."

She acknowledges me with a smile and hands her plate off to Ben before beginning to walk over.

Reed drops his head so that his face is in my hair. "I'm not playing any fucking baby games," he firmly whispers.

I glare up at him. "You're playing all of them. Or did you forget two weeks ago when I pretended to be your wife to get that chick away from you at McGill's?" The memory returns to him and he drops his head in defeat, uttering a muffled curse.

Reed is notorious for picking up girls at bars around Ruxton. He never seems to have any difficulty either. But two weeks ago, he met a major clinger at McGill's who started talking about how she believed in love at first sight. Or more specifically, *love at first sight with Reed*. He'd texted me to bail him out when she wouldn't pick up on the uninterested vibe he was throwing her way. So I'd swooped in, begging him to not give up on our marriage, and put on a good show for everyone watching.

He didn't get laid that night, but he also didn't wind up with a Grade A-stalker.

I tap him on his shoulder and he lifts his head. "Yeah, you owe me. I'm still disinfecting my mouth out from that kiss."

"You liked it," he states, the smile he reserves only for women, returning. I'm sure that works on the general population of Alabama, but it'll never work on me. Reed is permanently in the friend zone, where he belongs. I adore him, but strictly in the "I have no desire to see you naked" sort of way.

I push him toward the house. "You wish. Go grab me a notepad from inside."

He walks away laughing as Mia joins my side. "Ready?" she asks, her smile contorting as she holds on to her belly. I tense, looking over at Ben and then back at her. She shakes her head and blows out a breath forcefully. "Indigestion. I've been getting it a lot lately."

I relax my shoulders, grabbing her hand and walking to the gift table. "Please wait until after the shower to have the baby. My mom will lose her shit if you don't get to eat the cake she slaved over all morning."

She sits in the lawn chair I've decorated with streamers and balloons, her maternity dress stretching across her belly. "Oh, I'm definitely eating that cake, even if I have to take it with me to the hospital."

I grab the gift that was delivered a few days ago. "Do you want to open your aunt's gift first?"

She takes the gift from me, and places it in her lap, sighing. "I really wish she could've been here for this. I love that all your family is here, but . . . I don't know. It would just be nice if she was here too." Her eyes lose focus as she clutches the gift.

Mia's aunt works weekends and didn't have enough vacation time to take off for this, and the actual delivery. I know it kills her to not have the one connection to her mother here, but she's always kept her sadness hidden for the most part. Until now.

I bend down, resting my hand on hers and bringing my face to her level. "I'm sorry she couldn't be here. But she's definitely coming when you have the baby. There's no way she's going to miss that." Mia smiles, nodding. "Are you ready to start?"

She looks over my shoulder. "Nolan. Do you want to help me open my presents?"

"Oh, yeah!" he yells behind me.

I straighten as Reed comes over with a notepad and pen, holding it out to me. "This first gift is from Mia's aunt," I tell him, ignoring the task he's trying to pass off.

He frowns, looking down at the notepad and then back at me. "Seriously? You're making me do this?"

"Aww, thanks, Reed. That's so sweet of you," Mia says with a huge deliberate grin.

He moves to stand next to me, mumbling some response under his breath and he flips the notepad open.

"Here, buddy. Let me dry you off a little." Ben wraps Nolan up in a towel, rubbing it over his wild hair. I see Luke emerge out of the water in my peripheral vision, but my eyes decide they want more than just a glimpse. My head turns to fully engage him when movement over his shoulder grabs my attention. My cousin Leah, who was firmly planted in a lawn chair on the other side of the pool moments ago, is now standing by a small table, covered in beach towels, readying one for Luke.

"No fucking way." I'm moving before I even realize it, marching directly at my slutty cousin and beating Luke to the table. We don't see much of each other. She's only in town for the week, and we've always been friendly, but I will drop kick her in those fake tits if she thinks she has a chance here.

I snatch the towel out of her hands and take in her startled reaction. "What are you doing?"

She looks past me, seemingly in Luke's direction, and then returns her gaze to me. "I'm being hospitable. Give me that."

"Hospitable? Give me a break. You just want to towel him off."

She licks the corner of her mouth, resituating her tube top so more of her silicon-enhanced cleavage is on display. "Who wouldn't? And what do you care, anyway? You said you two broke up."

I step closer, backing her up against the table. "You don't make a play for somebody's ex unless they give you the go ahead first, Leah. What the fuck is wrong with you? Go after Reed. He's single."

She leans back against me, pushing me off a bit. "I've been down that road, remember? Two summers ago, when I visited with my dad? Reed's wild, and I would definitely be up for another round with him, but he made it perfectly clear then that he doesn't double dip." She grabs another towel. "Now, if you don't mind . . ."

"I do mind," I interject, sidestepping so she can't walk past me. Leah towers over my five-foot, three-inch frame, but I will go buck on her ass right in front of everyone here if she goes against the number one rule of girl code.

She lifts her gaze from my face, and immediately paints on her most engaging smile as she connects with someone behind me. And by the look of her, I don't need to turn around to know who it is.

"Oh, hi, Luke. I'm Leah. Here you go."

She holds the towel out and I grab it before he does and shove both of the ones I'm now holding against his dripping chest. "Here," I snarl up at him. "Do us all a favor and put a shirt on after you dry off."

"Or don't," Leah adds behind my back.

Luke grabs the towel, brushing his wet hand against mine, and lingers on my face before he looks past me at Leah. And then either because he's interested, which I wouldn't put past him—she's decent looking, and he's into anything with a mouth—or because I'm standing here and he wants to get to me, he smiles his overplayed and highly alluring playboy smile and steps closer to her, boxing me out.

"What did you say your name was again?"

"Leah. I'm Ben's cousin."

And apparently not mine. Nor is she a friend, for pulling this shit.

She holds out her hand for him to shake, and I'm suddenly glued to the pavement, unable to move or speak as the two of them obnoxiously flirt with each other. I think I hear Mia and Reed calling my name, but I can't be sure. Because right now, all of my energy is focused on the fucked up situation unfolding in front of me.

"So, you'll still be here next Saturday? You should come to the bonfire. I'll be there." Luke turns and briefly glances at me, making sure I've heard what he's just said.

Yeah. I fucking heard it.

"Oh, awesome! I'll definitely be there." Leah digs into her clutch and pulls out a pen. "Let me give you my number and maybe we can hang out before then."

I don't think, I just move. Grabbing onto Luke's elbow, I pull him away from my desperate cousin and the pen she's offering, dragging him toward the house. I hold my hand up to Mia, silently telling her to give me a moment, and she answers me with a sympathetic smile. Luke goes willingly with me, through my parents' house and down the hallway to the bedrooms. I open the door to my old room and shove him inside, slamming the door shut behind me.

"What the fuck is wrong with you?" I ask, as he straightens up and glares at me. I step closer, bringing us only a foot apart. "Are you seriously going to make a play for my cousin? That's screwed up on so many levels."

He tosses the towels onto the bed before coming forward. I instinctively step back but he moves with me, stepping closer until my back is against the door. He flattens his hands on the wood beside my head, closing in on me.

He's so intimidating. Everything about Luke screams predator, from his size to his tattoos, but he's never scared me. Even though he's towering over me, keeping me right where he wants me, and taking away any and all personal space I have, I don't feel threatened.

I feel something I've been trying to block out for twelve months.

He drops his head, bringing us to eye level. "I'll make a play for whoever the fuck I want. Your cousin's hot, and clearly into me, so why the hell shouldn't I have some fun with her?"

"Because she's my cousin, asshole. You don't see me lurking around your family tree."

"No. You're too busy looking for dick on the Internet, like a dumbass," he snarls, brushing his nose against mine.

He's so close to me, his damp, taut body, skimming against the front of mine, teasing me with the slightest bit of contact. I have to grip the bottom of my shorts to keep myself from grabbing him. From pulling him completely against me. From touching his . . . *holy shit.*

"Luke," I pant, letting my eyes take in the hard-on that's pressing against the front of his bathing suit. *Why is he hard right now? Is it the fact that he's practically on top of me? Is it because I'm half-naked myself? Or is it . . . fucking piece of shit.*

I palm his crotch and he grits his teeth, hissing into a moan. Twisting my wrist, I get a better hold before I squeeze. Hard.

"Is this for her?" I challenge, glancing up and meeting his feral stare.

Say yes, and I'm walking out of here with this.

He swallows, dropping one hand, but not the unnerving look he's giving me. He tugs at the drawstring of my shorts. "Did you see me watching you when I was in the pool? When you were staring at me?"

"Yes," I answer, hearing the sudden thickness in my throat distort my voice.

"Then don't ask me stupid questions." He flattens his palm against my stomach before sliding it down the front of my shorts and into my bikini bottoms.

Oh, fuck, yes.

I moan against his touch, blocking out the familiarity of it, and purely focusing on the thickness of his fingers. *Shit, I'm soaked.* Practically dripping. And I know it's for him. There's no other explanation for it. Pissed off, hungry Luke Evans can work my body into a frenzy, without even touching me.

But he is touching me.

When two fingers enter me and his thumb finds my clit, I drop my head back against the wood and my legs shake beneath me.

"Oh my God," I whimper.

"Do I need to tell you what to do with that?" he asks, his voice laced with arrogance as he glances down at my hand that remains stagnant against his cock.

"God, I fucking hate you." I pull his cock free and wrap my hand around it, feeling him thicken in my palm. He grabs the back of my neck, tilting my head up to look at him as I stroke up his length.

"Yeah, I hate you too, babe," he grits out, our faces a breath away from each other.

I ignore the sentiment and narrow in on my task, spreading the pre-cum around with my thumb as my entire body starts to burn up.

"Harder," he growls. "Squeeze me, Tessa. You know what I like."

I do. I know exactly what he likes. And I hate that I know it.

I grip him harder, pumping him faster, as he finger-fucks me against the door. I can't look at him. He's too close. His mouth is right there, and I know it'll kill me if I taste him.

God, please don't kiss me right now.

Clamping my eyes shut, I feel my skin flush as his thumb pulses against my clit. I'm so close to coming and I know he's right there with me. He's throbbing in my hand, moaning against my ear, and I could let this play out how we both want it to. Just a few more strokes, another slide of his fingers, and it'll be over.

This will be over.

And I'll regret every second of it.

"Stop," I faintly plead. I sound weak. Pathetic. Crippled under his power over me. "Luke, stop."

He doesn't. He twists his wrist and curls his fingers inside me, and I know I need to act fast before it's too late. Before I let him use me again. Because that's all he ever did.

Lies. All of it. Every touch. Every word out of his mouth. This will mean nothing to him, and I'll be the stupid girl that hoped for more.

I let his cock fall out of my hand and push against his chest, backing him off me.

"I said, stop!"

He stumbles back, gripping the base of his cock with the same hand that just worked me like some cheap whore. I tie my shorts and turn around, flinging the door open and stepping out into the hallway before he has a chance to say anything.

"God, you're so sad, Tessa." I run my hands up and around my neck, tightening my grip and mimicking the hold he just had on me as I move through the house. I dig my nails into my skin until it becomes unbearable, but at least it gives me another pain to focus on.

Shaking my hands out, and making sure I'm not giving away any indication as to what I just allowed to happen, I step back outside and spot everyone gathered around Mia as she opens her gifts. She's through most of them, and now I feel even worse than I did seconds ago.

You're such a shit. A weak, pathetic shit.

She smiles up at me as I step up to the table, and I know she sees it. She always sees my discomfort, even when I think I'm doing a damn good job at masking it.

"Where the hell have you been?" Reed asks me but I wave him off, focusing on Mia.

The door opens and Luke walks through, T-shirt on and keys in his hand.

"You leaving?" Ben asks.

He nods. "Yeah. I'll see you Monday." His eyes find mine, and I see every emotion I'm feeling in his face.

Anger. Hurt. Resentment. Regret.

I break the contact, watching as my best friend holds up a few bibs for everyone to see. I try to smile, but I can't. I should be happy right now, celebrating the upcoming birth of my nephew, but I'm not. And I should be familiar with the ache I feel burning inside my chest. The overwhelming pain that has me biting back my tears.

But it feels raw.

Luke Evans has opened up another wound inside me.

And, right now, I just want to bleed out and die.

WHAT THE FUCK is wrong with me?

Twelve months of trying to forget about someone and all that hard work got shot to shit when I allow her to drag me into a bedroom. A closed off, secluded spot, where I damn well knew my struggles would be amplified. I could've protested. I could've pulled away from her and continued blatantly flirting with . . . Lucy? Lena? No. Fuck, whatever her name was. But I didn't, because I knew what was coming. I knew I was pushing Tessa to her breaking point, and I fucking wanted to see that snap.

Because there is one thing that can make my dick go from six to midnight in a matter of seconds.

Tessa's mouth.

And as soon as she opens it, and those filthy words come flying at me with enough force to knock a weaker man off balance, that's it. I can challenge her all day, getting in her face and pretending that shit doesn't get to me, but my cock says otherwise.

I'm prepared for it. I fucking know I'll get hard the minute she lashes out, but what I'm not prepared for is her reaction to it.

I'd say she has bigger balls than me if I didn't know every fucking detail of what she has between her legs.

She didn't palm my dick and ask whom I was hard for.

She *demanded* I tell her. And the combination of the ultimatum that had flashed in her eyes the moment that question slipped from her lips, and the feel of her hand against me was too much. She'd grabbed my cock like she fucking owned it, silently daring me to say she didn't, and suddenly, I'd been the one at my breaking point.

It's possible to hate someone, to look at them and wish you weren't aware of their every move, and to want them more than you've ever wanted anything in your life.

I hadn't cared that we were in her parents' house.

I hadn't cared that I was about to fuck up any and all progress I'd made on getting this chick out of my system.

Her hand had been on my dick, and there was no way in hell I wasn't touching her.

And fuck, the feel of her coating my fingers as I slid through the hottest pussy I've ever had, has me close to coming from a fucking hand-job in a matter of seconds. That, and the fact that no one has squeezed my dick like that since Tessa. No one. I've had mouths on me that don't come anywhere close to her grip.

That's a problem. And it's making getting off on the feel of anyone else near impossible.

But in that moment, with my fingers deep inside her, I didn't care about anyone else. She was right there, pulsing against me, so fucking close I could feel her heartbeat between her legs. She told me to stop but I didn't listen. I couldn't. I hated her but I needed this.

Just give me this; the part of you I never doubted.

But she didn't.

And then it was *my* hand around my cock as she left me on the edge with remorse and hurt in her eyes.

At me.

At herself.

I started choking on my own emotions as the situation sank in. As I realized how completely pathetic I was for letting this chick get to me. Again. And I'd needed to get the hell out of there. Away from her. Putting distance between us is the only thing that ever helps. And it doesn't even help that much.

Because even though I've gone mostly all twelve months we've been apart without seeing her, I still think about her constantly.

Like right now.

It's been four days since the baby shower—enough time to get most chicks out of my system, but not this one. I've been staring at the same spot on the floor as Ben and CJ, another cop in our precinct, talk about an arrest Ben and I made yesterday. I could contribute. I was there, for fuck's sake, but I'm too busy picturing the look on Tessa's face when she shoved me away from her on Saturday.

As if my touch repulsed her.

As if her own actions disgusted her.

"Luke."

I look up, seeing two pairs of eyes on me as I run my thumb over the coin in my hand. I focus on CJ, whose voice broke me out of my head. "Yeah?"

He stands from his perch on the edge of the desk, reaching around and pulling out his wallet. "You want anything from Chap's?"

"No, man. I'm good."

He acknowledges me with a nod, thumbing through the cash in his wallet. "Spot me a twenty, Kelly. I'm good for it."

Ben laughs from the chair behind his desk. "You're good for shit. You still owe me from the poker game three weeks ago."

CJ's eyes lose focus as he tucks his wallet away. "Fuck. I forgot about that."

"That's funny. I've only been reminding you every other day," Ben says, the sarcasm coating his words. He leans back, smiling. "Just have it for me by Friday morning. I'm taking off early to get on the road with Mia."

"Yeah, all right. I'll see you guys."

"Later," Ben responds, before his keyboard clicks with his typing. I've zoned out again, but this time it doesn't go unnoticed. "You all right over there?"

I turn the coin over a few more times before glancing up at him. I slip it into my front pocket and tuck my hands behind my head, leaning back in my chair. "How's Mia feeling about the trip this weekend?"

I see his reaction to the question I've dodged, but he doesn't pry. He scratches the back of his head, keeping his other hand on the keyboard. "She's anxious, I can tell. But she really wants to spend the anniversary of her mom's death in Fulton. She's got all this stuff she wants to do with Nolan that the two of them used to do. I just . . ." He blinks heavily, bringing both hands to his lap as he leans back. "I don't want this to be too hard on her. With the baby coming soon, she doesn't need to be upset or stressed out. And I hate seeing her sad. It fucking kills me."

I see the depth of his feelings for Mia every time he talks about her. Or looks at her. It's been like that since last summer, when she showed up and completely knocked him on his ass. No other girl has done that to Ben. Not since I've known him, anyway. I know if something happened to her, to Nolan, it would kill him. He wouldn't come back from it.

"Mia's tough," I say, seeing Ben lift his eyes to me. "She's probably a lot tougher than you give her credit for."

"Yeah, you're right." He scratches his head before leaning forward and typing on his keyboard again. "Does it get easier?"

"No," I quickly reply, not needing to think about it. After twelve years it hasn't gotten easier, and I've stopped believing that it will.

He looks over at me, frowning, and I suddenly feel like a complete shit for not filtering my outburst.

I lean forward, elbows resting on my knees as I crack my knuckles. "It'll get easier for Mia. She has you, Nolan, and the baby. It won't always be this difficult for her. It's still raw right now, but every year, it'll ease up a bit." I put so much conviction in my voice that I almost start to believe it. But the reality of my situation quickly crushes any false hope that could seep into my head and poison what I know to be certain. It doesn't matter anyway. I didn't say it for my reassurance. I said it for his.

"Thanks, man." His look tells me he thinks it'll get easier for me too, and I nod as if I agree. He turns back to his computer screen, leaning closer. "Well, this guy my sister is going out with is either a fucking ghost, or he's never done so much as run a stop sign. I can't find him in here."

"What's his name?" I ask, hitting a few keys and pulling up our search system.

He looks over at me. "I just looked. He's not in there."

"And you spell for shit. What's his name?"

He laughs, standing and grabbing his coffee mug before rounding his desk. "Tyler Knight. Real complicated spelling."

I ignore his teasing tone as he walks away and type in this creep's name. The hourglass spins as it searches before the three words I was hoping I wouldn't see pop up on my screen.

Search not found.

Fuck. If I had more than just his name, I could search

for him in our other system and pull up his license. Then I'd have an idea what this guy looks like, where he lives, if he's a fucking organ donor.

The phone on my desk rings and I close out the search engine and answer it.

"Evans."

"Hey, Luke. Come in to my office for a second, will ya?"

The captain's voice has me on my feet. "Yes, Sir. I'll be right there."

I hang up and walk around my desk, passing Ben. "Where are you going?" he asks.

"Captain wants to see me."

I walk across the room and knock on the door at the end of the hallway.

"Yeah?" the voice behind it calls out.

Pulling the door open, I step into the office and see Captain Meyers behind his desk, flipping through a stack of paperwork. The smell of old wood and cigars fills the air, and I spot a snuffed out stub hanging on the edge of the ashtray on his desk. Captain looks up and motions toward an empty chair across from him. "Have a seat, son."

Son. He always calls me that. He's the only person who has called me that in twelve years.

I close the door behind me and take a seat, nervously picking at the wood on the arm of my chair. I'm not called in this office much, the last time being when this asshole I arrested claimed I was too rough with him. I hadn't been, and Ben had vouched for me, but the captain still reamed me out for it.

Not that the guy didn't deserve to get his ass beat by me. But I'd never do anything to risk my job. Out of uniform, though, I would've knocked him around a little. Or a lot.

The larger than life man across the desk, who always

reminds me of John Goodman, picks up a file that's laid off to the side and opens it in front of him. He clears his throat, running a hand over his goatee. "I got a call today from Captain Kennedy over in Port Deposit. Seems he has a spot open for detective in his unit and requested you by name." He licks his thumb and proceeds to flip through the papers in the file. Pulling out one, he hands it to me from across the desk. "You still interested in making detective?"

"Yeah," I answer, a bit of shock in my voice as I take the paper and read the print across the top. It's the form we have to fill out when we request to be transferred. The form I've never bothered reading until now.

"If you're interested, I think you'd do really well over there. I know you and Ben have talked about becoming detectives for years. You'd be damn good at it."

I look up. "What about Ben? There's only one spot open?"

He nods, closing the file and leaning back in his chair. "Ben wouldn't move right now; not with the baby coming in a few weeks. And he has roots here." He gives me an empathetic look, one I'm used to seeing, before continuing. "How's your dad doing?"

I shrug, because that's all I can give him. I don't talk about my dad. He's practically dead to me.

His phone rings loudly and he puts his hand on the receiver, not picking it up. "The spot's yours if you want it. Kennedy will want an answer from you soon."

I stand, folding the paper up and putting it into my pocket. "Thanks, Captain."

He nods before bringing the receiver to his ear. "Meyers."

I slip out of his office, pulling the door closed behind me. I've always thought about making detective in Ruxton, not transferring somewhere to do it. But who knows when a spot here will open up. It could be years before I'm given an opportunity like this again, if it even happens. And, like Captain said, Ben has roots here. I don't. There's nothing keeping me here.

There never has been.

"What was that about?" Ben asks as I return to my desk.

I slide my chair out and sit down, reaching up and scratching the back of my neck. "There's a detective position open in Port Deposit. Captain offered it to me."

Ben's eyes widen as he sips his coffee. "Really? Shit, that's awesome. Are you going to take it?"

I pull the transfer paperwork out of my pocket and stick it in the top drawer of my desk. "Yeah, I think so. I've wanted this for a long time. It'll be weird, though. Having a different partner." I look over at him. "I'm used to your dumb ass."

He laughs. "You'll have to give me your new partner's number so I can warn him about all the annoying shit you do." He pauses, placing his mug on his desk. "Are you going to tell Tessa?"

"Why would I tell Tessa?" I ask, annoyance in my voice, and suddenly pissed off at the hidden implication that I *should* be telling her. "What the fuck does it matter to her what I do? She dumped me—remember? She kept something from me I deserved to know about. And according to her, we were never even together." I take in a calming breath, trying to swallow down the rage that's burning the back of my throat. "She's a deceitful bitch."

"Hey," he warns me with a raised voice, bringing my attention back to his face. "I get how pissed off you probably feel about what happened between you two, but don't talk about her in front of me like that. I've stayed out of it, but I won't if you call her that again."

I grind my teeth, holding in my rebuttal as I lean back in my chair. "Sorry. I shouldn't have said that. But no, I'm not going to tell her. She gave up the right to know shit about me when she ended it."

He laughs quietly before he replies. "Yeah, because when you two were together, you were an open fucking book."

I scowl at the insinuation in his voice, shaking my head, and busying myself with arrest logs I need to fill out. "Whatever, man. I just need to get out of here. You have shit here worth staying for. I don't."

I keep my head down as I fill out my form, not wanting to glance over and see the concerned stare I know he's giving me. He doesn't respond in any other way, which I'm grateful for. I don't need to hear how this move may or may not affect his sister. I don't care. Maybe moving to the other side of the state will be the distance I need to finally forget about her. Because staying in the same town and not seeing her isn't doing shit.

BEN DOESN'T BRING up his sister for the rest of the day, but that doesn't keep me from thinking about her. I look up every version of Tyler Knight's name in our system, hoping to find something, anything on this guy. I don't want to go to this bonfire unprepared. Hell, I don't want to go at all. But there's no fucking way I'm going to trust Reed to make a judgment call on this pervert. I know him. He'll be so deep in some random chick's pussy, he won't care who Tessa shows up with, or if she's even there. So I'm going, but only to eye up this guy. No one else.

I take a shower as soon as I get home, letting the scalding water beat down on my skin for as long as I can stand it. After securing a towel around my waist, I step out and rub my hand across the fogged up glass. My eyes immediately go to the tattoo on my chest, the only spur-of-the-moment tattoo I have. The only one I regret getting. My arms are covered with ink, some on my back, my hip, and even the side of my ribcage, but all of those tattoos I thought long and hard about before I got them. I'm not a quick decision kind of guy. I never have been, especially with shit that's permanent. But for some reason, I wanted something on my body that represented her, and I thought it over for a whole five seconds before I went and got it done. It's not huge, but it's fucking there. The only tattoo I have on my chest. It's dark, heavily outlined, because I wanted it as deep as I could get it.

Break my skin, and embed her inside me.

I'm an asshole, and I need to get this shit removed. Every time I look at it, it reminds me of everything I'm trying to forget. I picture her fingers tracing over the letter. I feel her lips pressing against it, and the slide of her tongue as she tastes the skin. I see her face; the only one I've seen for the past fifteen months. The one I never want to see again.

I want to shatter my mirror, and every mirror, so I never have to see this reflection.

I want to go back to that fucking fundraiser, but this time, be the one who walks away.

I want to take a knife and carve out not only the mistake I branded myself with, but also every memory I have of her.

I'll probably die from that wound.

But in death, maybe I'll finally find release.

SOME DAYS, I wish I had chosen a different career path. This is my fourth time rewinding Dr. Willis' dictation because I can't understand a word he's saying. I get these from him occasionally, when he decides to record his post-op notes during his lunch hour. Between the sound of chip bags rustling, and his obnoxiously loud chewing, I'm picking up every third word.

"The anterior chamber *crunch* same incision with *crunch* diamond blade to *rustle, crunch, crunch.*"

"Ugh." I hit the pause button for the hundredth time and slip my headphones off, tossing them on my desk.

I need a break from this. Nothing is more annoying than the sound of that man's chewing and if I listen to it anymore, I might just throw a few choice words into my report.

"The patient was brought to the fucking operating room, placed into a supine fucking position on the operating room table. A general fucking anesthetic was administered."

Really fucking professional, Tessa.

Pushing away from my desk with a heavy sigh, I round the couch and sit down, grabbing the TV remote. I know for a fact that the only thing on right now is daytime soaps, but that's better than nothing.

I'm halfway through the episode, completely captivated by these fictional people and the drama-filled lives they have, when my phone rings from where I left it on the desk. I round the couch, picking it up and seeing Tyler's name flashing on my screen.

Shit. He wants to actually talk to me. Not text. Verbally communicate.

I stare at my phone, the weight of it getting heavier in my hand as I hesitantly hover over the *accept phone call* button.

What if his voice sucks? I've imagined what it sounds like—low and rumbly, like a sexy storm in the distance, but I could be way off here. He could sound like some pervy version of Dr. Willis, or worse, a chick.

I take a chance and go for it, swiping across the screen and putting the phone up to my ear. "Hello?"

"Tessa, hey, it's Tyler."

I nearly fall over when the smooth cadence of his voice comes through the phone. "Oh, thank God."

"Thank God?" The sound of his soft laughter fills my ear. "Are you that happy I called?"

"No. I mean, yeah, I just . . . you have a really good voice. I was worried you wouldn't."

"Yeah, so do you. I really didn't want to get hard at work, but that might be unavoidable."

Blushing, I chew on my bottom lip and lean against my desk. "So, what's up? Are you calling to bail on me?"

"What? Fuck no. Are you kidding? I just realized I haven't heard your voice yet. It's been bugging me all day."

"And now you're going to be serving beers to men while you sport wood. I hope you're working at a gay bar."

He laughs again, fuller this time. One of those laughs that makes you throw your head back and clutch your stomach. "Jesus, you're something else, you know that? Why do I feel like I've met my match with you?"

I smile. "Maybe you have. Not a lot of men can keep up with me though."

"Maybe I'll be the first."

You won't be.

I swallow, shaking the unwanted thought out of my head. "Yeah . . . yeah, maybe. So, we are still on for tomorrow night, right?"

"Are you trying to rush me off the phone?"

"What? No, I just assumed . . . Sorry, I just—I figured you wanted to confirm plans and get back to work. I didn't think you were calling to just talk to me."

"Do guys never call you just to talk to you?"

"Not in a really long time."

"Well, I just did. I'm on my break, and I don't want to talk to anyone else. Is that okay with you?"

"That's okay with me." I pull out my desk chair and sit down, bringing my knees against my chest. "What do you want to talk about?"

"You."

I blush again. "Okay . . . What about me?"

"I don't know. Everything?"

I laugh, picking at the chipped off nail polish on my big toe. "Everything, huh? How long is your lunch break?"

"I can stretch it a few minutes."

"Hmm."

"Hmm?"

"Yes, hmm."

"Your *hmm* is very cute."

I drop my head against my knee, sighing. "Oh, man."

"Is there a problem?"

"No, I love this part. The flirty beginning stage, when everything is new and perfect."

"Hmm."

"Don't *hmm* me. That's my line."

"You own the word?"

"Yes. I've been told I'm very cute when I do it. So I call dibs."

"Well, I think the man who complimented you should have some ownership over that word. He made you smile, didn't he?"

"Yes," I answer, reaching up and pressing a finger into my one lonely dimple that sinks in my left cheek.

"Then it'll be our word. We can both say it, but only to each other. Deal?"

"Hmm."

He laughs. "I've been staring at that picture you sent me a lot. I really like your lips."

I drop my hand into my lap. "Wow. I could go so dirty with that right now."

"Yeah? So could I, but I'm at work and no longer alone in the break room."

"Not a fan of public masturbation? It's all the rage."

"You know this from personal experience?"

I shrug. "Nah, I'm more of a 'get off on a complete stranger's text messages' kind of girl."

"Lucky me."

My smile spreads, along with the heat that's burning up my cheeks. "I've been staring at your picture, too. You have really great hair."

"It needs to be cut."

"No. Don't cut it."

"No?"

I shake my head. "No. I like it hanging in your face like that. You look like . . ."

"The guy from that TV show with the motorcycle club?"

"Uh, yeah, exactly. Are you told that a lot?"

"All the time. I'll keep my hair long, but I'm not getting my back tattooed like him. I hope you're okay with that."

"Yeah, I'm . . . I'm not really a fan of tattoos." Or at least, I don't want to be.

"So I'm assuming I won't be finding any on your body tomorrow? No cheesy song lyric or book quote, or some other girlie shit?"

"Nope. My skin is very virginal." I pause, listening to the sound of his heavy breathing. Closing my eyes and leaning back in my chair, I allow myself to be brutally honest with my next admission. "I'm a little nervous about tomorrow."

"Why?"

"Because I like talking to you, and if it doesn't work out, I won't be able to talk to you anymore."

"You sound so optimistic."

I laugh first, and then he joins me.

"Have you ever been out on a blind date before?" he asks.

"No, all my dates have been pretty standard."

"So, go out on one tonight."

I frown. "Uh, what? With who?"

"With one of the hundred guys that have probably messaged you on Ignite. Have you logged on lately?"

I move my mouse around, waking up my computer screen. "Not since when you messaged me the first time." After pulling up Internet Explorer, I type in the URL address and enter my log in information. "Why am I doing this again?"

"Humor me. How many messages do you have?"

I hover over my flashing folder, gasping at the number that pops up. "Holy fuck. Thirty-seven." I'm suddenly sitting up straighter, feeling like I've just been given the best compliment.

Thirty-seven? "That's insane."

He laughs. "Yeah, I thought so. Pick a guy that's not as good looking as me, go out with him tonight, and get all your nervous blind-date shit out of the way. Tomorrow when you meet me, it'll be old news."

I begin filtering through the messages, scanning the faces of some very eligible bachelors. "Hmm. This could backfire on you."

"How's that?"

"Well, I could really hit it off with . . ." Leaning in, I click on a guy's information and scan it quickly before continuing. ". . . Steve from Bridgeport. And then I won't be meeting you at all tomorrow. He likes going to the beach, and listening to country music. I like those things."

I hear the sound of a chair scraping against a surface. "I'm not worried."

"No? Maybe you should be. I'm quite a catch, and you've now made me aware of the thirty-seven other men interested in me."

"Yeah, but they're not me. You can go out with all thirty-seven of those guys and I'll still be seeing you tomorrow. You and I both know that."

His cockiness has me suddenly thinking of someone else and I go silent, no longer focusing on the faces in front of me. Arrogance works for Luke, but with any other guy, it just feels forced.

"You there? I gotta get back to work."

I force a smile, trying to find the elated mood, which seems to have escaped me. "Yeah, sorry. I'll see you tomorrow."

"Hold on." I hear muffled chatter, followed by, "I'll be right there." A door closes before he continues. "You're going to want to party at this thing tomorrow, right?"

His question throws me off, but I suppose it's justified. I didn't really give him any specifics about what goes on at the summer bonfires.

"Oh yeah, definitely. There's always a ton of booze and stuff there. Last year . . ."

"Great. I'll see you then."

The dial tone rings in my ear and I pull my phone away, staring at the screen, slightly irritated.

Well, that conversation had taken a weird turn.

Besides the sudden abruptness to get me off the line, what guy tells a girl he's obviously interested in to go out with someone else? Even if it is to alleviate the nervousness I have coursing through my system. I could definitely hit it off with some guy tonight, and I suddenly want to. If only to prove Tyler wrong. He made it seem as if he were giving me permission to do it, and because this guy wouldn't be *him*, there wouldn't be a chance of it becoming anything.

What the fuck, dude?

I don't need your permission to date. I've never even met you. Yes, you've already made me come, but that would've happened with or without your texts egging me on. You have zero ownership over me, so don't fucking act like you do.

I'm more motivated now to meet up with a complete stranger tonight than I was when I signed up for this stupid dating site. And SteveMD looks very promising.

I click on his profile, open up the message box, and begin typing with a newfound purpose.

> *TK12: Hi, SteveMD. I saw you wanted to connect with me. I didn't know if you were free to meet up tonight, but I am.*

I so fucking am.

I press send and grab a water bottle and some grapes

out of the fridge. A *ding* comes from the direction of my computer and I scurry back over, sitting down and placing my snack on the desk.

SteveMD: Hi, Tessa. I'm really glad to hear from you. I was afraid you had already met someone, since you haven't logged on in over a week.

Yeah, well, Tyler might be a complete dud.

TK12: I've just been really busy.

SteveMD: I get that. I'd love to meet up tonight. I saw you're in Ruxton. That's only thirty minutes from me. Where do you want to meet?

Somewhere with a lot of people, just in case the MD stands for Murderous Dickhead.

TK12: Do you mind driving here? There's this really good sports bar that just opened up in town. Joe's Pub.

SteveMD: Not at all. That sounds great. I just need to line up a sitter for my kids and then I can get on the road.

Oh, sweet. A family man. SteveMD just got hotter.

TK12: Aww, you have kids? How many?

SteveMD: Two. They're my entire life. I can probably leave my house around seven thirty. Is that too late for you?

TK12: Nope. I'll meet you around eight.

SteveMD: Can't wait. I'll see you tonight.

Yes, you certainly will.

I PURPOSELY SHOW up early to dinner, parking near the entrance so I'll be able to eye up Steve when he arrives. Considering the fact that we didn't do the whole "send me a selfie" confirmation, I need to make sure this guy somewhat resembles his profile picture before I waste a perfectly good outfit on him. I pull my visor down and check my hair and makeup for the tenth time in the past five minutes, when a car's headlights grab my attention.

Flipping the visor up, I watch as the SUV pulls into a parking spot and cuts off his lights. A man steps out, straightening his tie, and lifts his head the slightest bit, allowing me to see his face. He runs a hand through his thick, dark hair and closes his door before walking toward the entrance. It's definitely him, thank God, and I'm kinda loving the fact that he dressed up for this. After he disappears inside the restaurant, I grab my clutch and exit my car, ready for my first official online date.

I picked Joe's Pub because I knew it would be packed on a Friday night. I want a crowd; something to blend into in case this guy disinterests me completely. And to have some witnesses, in case he turns out to be a psychopath. Some baseball game is playing on all the giant TV screens, and a group of men are congregating in front of the one hanging above the bar, drinking and exchanging alcohol-induced conversations. Almost every high-top table is occupied as I scan the room, finally landing on Steve who is smiling at me from his stool.

He stands when I reach the table. "Hi, wow, you look great." Unexpectedly, he leans down and presses his lips against my cheek.

"Oh, um, thank you." I flatten my hand against his dress shirt, closing my eyes and inhaling his cologne. These are the first lips that have been on me in twelve months, but my body is responding as if it's been twelve years. My breath catches somewhere between my chest and my throat, lodging itself there. When he ends the kiss, I drop my head to hide my flush, then pull my stool out and take a seat as he does the same.

He slides a menu across the table, smiling. "So, I need to be upfront with you about something."

"Okay," I reply with apprehension as I open my menu. If this guy drops the married bomb in my lap, I will not be held responsible for my actions.

"I'm not twenty-eight like my profile says. I'm thirty-three."

"Why would you lie about that?" I hear the slight tinge of anger in my voice and see him react to it. *Strike one.*

He swallows, dropping his gaze to the table. "I had my actual age on there for a while and didn't get one date. So I did a little experiment and dropped a few years, then all of a sudden, my inbox is flooded with requests." He looks up at me. "I hope age isn't a deal breaker for you."

"No, but lying doesn't really work for me."

He frowns, nervously tugging at the knot in his tie. "I'm sorry. I should've told you earlier when you messaged me. I didn't lie about anything else on there."

I drop my eyes to the menu, scanning the choices of wing flavors I no longer want to consume. *Is every guy a complete tool?* His hand covers mine, prompting me to lift my gaze. "What?"

"I'm really sorry. If you don't want to go out with me again, I get that. At least let me show you a good time tonight. I swear, I'm not an asshole. I'm just lonely."

Yeah, I know what that's like. And it's not as if he lied about something major, like his gender, which would have prompted me to punch him in his or her baby-maker. So, I'll give him a pass on this.

I nod, forcing a smile, and he removes his hand. A young waitress comes up to our table and places a coaster in front of each of us.

"Hi, my name's Erin, and I'll be taking care of you two tonight. Can I start you off with something to drink?"

Steve stares at me, waiting for my response with a look of reluctance. As if he's expecting me to walk out of here instead of placing my order.

I ease his mind and glance up at the waitress. "I'll have a water with lemon, please."

She looks over at him, lifting her eyes from the notepad she just scribbled on.

"I'll take a Coke."

The waitress walks away as Steve opens his menu, his shoulders relaxing as he settles more on his stool. "So, I have to ask the obvious question. How in the hell is a woman that looks like you not married? Or needing to find dates online?"

"I could say the same for you. You're not lacking in the looks department."

He smiles as the waitress places our drinks in front of us. "Need another minute?"

"Please," I reply, taking a sip of my water. I place my glass down and lick my lips. "Have you ever been married?"

He nods, running his finger along the rim of his glass. "Once. We met in high school and married when we were nineteen. I was young and stupid and thought that everything was always going to be perfect. It wasn't, and instead of talking to me about why she wasn't happy, she slept with my brother."

My mouth drops open and I let go of my menu. "Jesus. That's terrible. Is she who you have the kids with?"

"Yeah, but I always cared about them more than she did.

When we divorced, she wanted nothing to do with them."

Shock sets into my features as I take in what he's just said. "Seriously? What kind of a person washes their hands of their own kids?"

"Someone who didn't want them in the first place." He reaches his hand behind him, his lips curling up into a smile. "Want to see a picture?"

I lean forward anxiously, resting on my elbows. "Absolutely."

He opens his wallet, picks out a small photo, and flips it around for me to see.

What in the motherfucking fuck?

My eyes flick from the picture to his face, back to the picture. There's no way in hell I'm drinking water. I must be drinking straight vodka right now for my eyes to betray me like this. In fact, no, there's no way. I must be delusional.

"They're adorable, aren't they?"

I lean closer, blinking several times before I re-focus.

Nope. I'm not imagining things.

I look up at him, taking several deep, calming breaths through my nose before I speak. "Is this some sort of a joke?"

He looks insulted. "Is what some sort of joke?"

I snatch the picture out of his hands, turning it so he can see it. "This! You refer to your fucking gerbils as kids? Who does that?"

He grabs it back, pointing at it aggressively with his finger. "Gerbils? These are Abyssinian guinea pigs. Don't insult them."

"Wow. You wanna know what's a deal breaker for me? Guys named Steve." I stand, grabbing my clutch with one hand and my glass of water with the other. I walk up beside this complete waste of my time, hold my glass over his lap, and turn my hand over.

"What the fuck?" he yells, standing as the water soaks into his khakis. "Why did you just do that?"

All commotion seems to come to a halt around us, the noise level dying down, allowing the sound of the baseball game to become more prominent. I tuck my clutch under my arm, cover my mouth with both hands, and blow him a kiss before holding up both middle fingers as I back away from the table.

"Deuces, loser."

I turn, pushing my way through the packed bar and out to the exit. I can't get to my car quick enough and after turning it on, I watch out my front window as a very irritated-looking gerbil lover walks to his vehicle, ripping the tie off from around his neck. I can't believe I actually thought it was sweet he dressed up for this. That's all Luke's fault. The only time he . . .

I stop mid-thought, dropping my head onto the steering wheel and hissing a curse.

My emotions go haywire in an instant. I feel manic, overwhelmed and incapable of surviving much more of this. I clamp my eyes shut, grit my teeth, and scream as loud as I can. God, why can't I stop thinking about him? Why? What the fuck is it? I just want to go one day without his name poisoning my thoughts. Or one hour. I need one hour.

"Please," I beg, reaching up and wiping the tear that has dropped to my cheek.

The worst part is, I don't think he ever thought about me like this. Constant. Unprovoked. Not even when we were together. But for me? This is how it's always been. Time didn't soften his voice in my head. The pain I feel at the very thought of him doesn't prevent memories from resurfacing. The hate I have for him doesn't touch the part of me that loved him.

And I'm afraid it never will.

THE SOUND OF my cell phone ringing startles me out of my sleep. I'm grateful for the disturbance, even though I'm immediately annoyed. I was in the middle of a dream I shouldn't have been having anyway. The same recurring Tessa dream that has me waking up with my hand fisting my cock. But luckily this time, I was interrupted before I slid my tongue between her tits.

Rubbing my eyes with the heels of my hands, I blink to focus on the red numbers on my alarm clock. 1:13 a.m.

Fucking perfect.

After turning on the lamp, I grab my phone, seeing the familiar number flashing on my screen. Even though I don't have the number programmed, I know exactly who's calling me. It's the only number that calls me in the middle of the night, besides when Tessa would call me last year, whispering to me through the phone about how badly she wanted to ride my . . .

Stop thinking about her.

"Yeah?" I answer, clearing that unwanted image from my head and swinging my legs out of bed. *So much for not waking up with a hard-on.* I grab the shorts I discarded hours ago and step into them, palming my cock through my boxers to calm it the fuck down.

"Hey, Luke, it's Ray. I'm sorry to call you this late, man,

but I got your dad here."

"You serve him?" I ask, pulling my shorts up and slipping my T-shirt over my head. I step into my tennis shoes and grab my keys, making my way out of my bedroom.

"No, man, of course not. My bartenders know not to give him anything. But you know how he is. Shit's getting out of hand really fast. He's already threatened to punch a couple of people, and if he does that, or starts wrecking my bar, I'm going to have to actually call the cops."

I should fucking arrest him myself, but going to jail again wouldn't do shit. That's as useless as rehab. My dad isn't the kind of guy who learns from his mistakes, or who wants help. Maybe he used to be, but he's definitely not anymore. And the two stints he's had in the county lock-up haven't taught him shit.

I step outside, locking the door behind me. "Yeah, I'm on my way."

I PARK IN front of Lucky's Tavern and make my way inside the dimly lit bar. I don't hear the commotion I'm expecting, only the typical Friday night crowd noise that's blending in with the sound of the music blaring overhead. Scanning the room, I spot Ray behind the bar, and he motions me over, empathetic frown in place.

"What the fuck? Where is he?" I ask when I reach the wooden countertop.

"Sorry, man. I tried to keep him here but once he heard you were coming, he bolted."

Of course. This is the shit I need right now.

I exhale roughly through my nose, shaking my head. "God fucking damn it. Do you have any idea where he went? Did he say anything?"

He proceeds to wipe the counter in front of him with a rag. "I'd try the liquor store a few blocks from here. It's the closest place for him to get booze." He looks up at me, his hand stilling on the counter. "Have you tried talking to him about maybe checking into rehab? I know a few recovering alcoholics I could set you up with. I'm sure they'd be interested in helping you get him set up somewhere."

I glare at him. "You're a fucking bartender, Ray, not a therapist. Don't try to give me advice on shit I don't care about."

"Whatever, man," he says in a clipped tone, flipping the rag onto his shoulder and straightening up. "He could get help. That's all I'm saying."

I don't give him a response because I'm not in the mood to hash it out with Ray right now. And if I continue talking to him, I might knock his ass out, which would piss me off further because I really like the guy. So I leave, pushing my way back through the crowd and out into the muggy air.

I get in my truck and proceed down Taylor Avenue to the liquor store close by. But I don't make it there, because slumped on a curb a block away, with a bottle in his hand, is the reason I've been dragged out of bed in the middle of the night.

I'd rather be dragged out of bed to rub my cock over those perfect . . .

God, I'm fucking pathetic.

I pull over and put my truck in park beneath the light post that's illuminating the dark street. As soon as I slam my door, he startles. His body jolts violently, causing the bottle to slip in his hand. He recaptures it before it hits the ground, and slowly lifts his eyes to me.

"Get outta here, kid. I'm not going anywhere." He tips the already half-empty bottle back, gulping four times before lowering it and wiping the back of his mouth with his hand. He looks dirty, as if he's been on a week-long drinking bender and living with the homeless who rotate through the abandoned buildings in town. His long, blond hair is matted and hanging in his face that he keeps turned down, avoiding my judgmental stare.

I step up behind him, grabbing underneath one bicep and hauling him to his feet. "Get up. I'm taking you home."

He rips his arm out of my grip, pushing his hair back to glare at me over his shoulder. "Off! What'd I say?"

I step into him and he stumbles, staggering forward and bracing himself with a hand on the sidewalk. Some of his liquor spills and he curses before righting himself and his precious bottle. "See what you did? What you always do! Get the hell outta here."

My patience just ran out. I knock the bottle out of his hand, sending it crashing to the pavement. Glass and amber liquid stain the cement, and I grab him by his shirt with both my hands, bringing his face an inch away from mine.

"You think she'd be proud of you right now? Of the man you turned out to be?"

"Don't talk to me about her," he snarls as he tries to evade my grip. If he weren't piss drunk, he wouldn't have a problem. Not with the twenty pounds of muscle he has on me. My dad's a big guy; he always has been. But the only time I see him now is when he's fucked up like this, incapable of standing too long without falling over, and no longer a match for me. For the past twelve years, this is the only version of my father I've known.

"Why? 'Cause you know she'd be ashamed of you? Because I am. I'm *fucking done* with this shit." I drag him to the truck, shoving him in the passenger seat with more force than necessary since he's not fighting me. But I don't care.

He deserves worse.

"You don't know . . . You'll never know what this feels like," he says, head hanging down as I pull away from the curb. His body tremors as the sound of his sobs fills the car.

The only thing I hate worse than a drunk is a sad drunk.

I grip the wheel so hard the muscles in my forearm begin to burn. "You really believe that, don't you? You think you're the only one who lost her. Why the fuck would her dying affect me? Right?"

"She was my wife."

"She was *my* mother!" I yell, so loud he leans away from me and slouches against the window. "And I didn't just fucking lose *her* that day! Did I? Fuck you! It should've been you!" My body throbs with blinding rage as I try and focus on the road. I've never said that out loud before. I've thought it, hundreds of times, but I've never spoken those words to anybody. Not even myself.

His soft cries settle me down and I look over as he bends practically in half to put his head into his hands. "I loved her. Oh, God, I miss her so much."

I drive faster, turning up the radio to drown him out. I don't want to listen to this; his excuse for the way he's been the past twelve years. It isn't worth dick to me. Not when he acted like I died right along with her. I was only fifteen years old and I stopped existing to him. My father became a stranger; no longer resembling the man I looked up to, and becoming the version of himself he worked so hard to get away from. He wasn't the only one who lost her, but I sure as hell felt alone while he drank enough to forget both of us.

And now he wants my sympathy? Fuck that. If I had any compassion to give, I sure as hell wouldn't offer it to him.

I loop his arm around my neck, grabbing his wrist with

one hand and holding onto his waist with the other as I maneuver him into his house. He grumbles incoherently as I deposit him on the bed, his voice muffled by the pillow before his body goes lax.

I'm never in this house except for nights like this; when darkness and dead silence surround me. It might as well be vacant it's so eerily quiet. We moved here when I was five years old, and after my mom died, I thought my dad would sell it and we'd go somewhere else. Just him and me. But he couldn't leave her. He couldn't leave the house she fell in love with and all the memories of her it held. And I think that makes him worse, because every time he looks around, he sees her. Standing at the stove cooking a meal, or sitting in her favorite chair and working on the blanket she had been trying to finish for years. He never changes anything about this place, either. It still looks exactly how it did when she was alive, down to the smallest detail. Even the bedroom they shared remains the same. Her clothes are still hanging in the closest, her favorite book is still on the nightstand, and I know seeing that shit every day drives him to drink. He's weak; he can't even handle the memory of my mom without letting it pull him under.

My dad hasn't been living here. He's been slowly dying here.

I open the door to my old bedroom and step inside, flipping on the light. I took most of my stuff with me when I moved out nine years ago, except for the twin bed I was too tall for and a few things I didn't want. I grab the guitar case that's leaning against the wall in one of the corners and set it on the bed. Turning around, I open the bottom drawer of my old dresser and take out the Mason jar full of guitar picks I've always kept in there. I rattle it around a bit, seeing some of the old ones my dad gave me from when he used to play, before tucking the jar under my arm and picking up the guitar case. After leaving with the only two items left in the house that mean something to me, I lock up and head home.

I DROP THE case on my bed and stick the Mason jar on my nightstand with my phone and keys. The case is covered in Pearl Jam stickers, some faded to the point of being almost unrecognizable, while others are peeling and frayed at the ends. I was obsessed with them when I started playing, learning almost all of their songs and idolizing Eddie Vedder. I could play them pretty good, but I always sang for shit. That used to be my dad's role.

A familiar nudge against the back of my leg nearly knocks me over as I'm pulling my shirt off.

I turn and reach down, brushing my hand through the fur. "Where you been, huh? You fall asleep in the bathroom again?"

Max, my Golden Retriever, sits and lifts one paw, thudding it against me and scratching down my leg with it.

I knock his paw away, rubbing my knee. "Stop, that shit hurts. You need to go out or something?"

He runs out of the room, answering my question with his abrupt exit. I walk down the hallway, descend the stairs, and open the back door, letting him dart outside into the yard. After smelling every goddamned blade of grass out there, he finishes up and runs back in, brushing past me.

I walk back into my bedroom and find him sniffing my guitar case.

"Watch out, Max." I pop the four locks and open it up, dropping the lid back and causing him to startle. He moves to the edge of the bed and lies down, the hair on his back standing straight up. I can't help but laugh. "Christ, is there anything that doesn't scare you?" I rub his head, as his big eyes stay glued to the case.

I doubt there is anything he isn't afraid of. I ended up with the biggest chicken shit of a dog when I rescued him four years ago. He's scared of everything—lawnmowers, garbage trucks, basically any noise. Thunder sends him running for the bathroom and hiding in my tub until the storm passes. If someone ever had the balls to break in here, he'd be no help. I'd put money on him hiding under my bed until I handled things. Which I would. If anyone makes that mistake, it'll be the last thing they ever do.

I stare down at the guitar, a gift from my parents on my fifteenth birthday. The last thing either one of them ever gave me. I lived and breathed this thing, playing it every day for seven months until my fingertips calloused over to the point of being numb. My dad taught me how to play on his old Gibson several months before I was gifted this. We'd spend hours in the basement together, going over chords and listening to music that inspired him. He'd tell me stories about playing on the road with his band and some of the crazy shit they'd get into. It was always a hobby for him, but he talked about it like he was born to do it. And his passion for it fascinated me. He told me about the time my mom came to watch him play and he saw her in the crowd, and how he'd been staring at her ever since. He treated that guitar like it was a part of his soul, and I wanted that. And when I finally got mine, it absorbed me completely, quickly becoming my entire world.

Then it was always us playing together, no longer just me watching him in complete awe. He taught me things I didn't know, and I showed him a few things I picked up on my own. For those seven months, we were closer than we ever were. He wasn't just my dad. He was my best friend.

I haven't touched this thing in twelve years. I couldn't even look at it right after she died. It stayed locked up, hidden in my closest or under my bed. A couple of months later, I got it out and asked my dad if he wanted to play like we always used to. I was suffering just as much as he was, and I needed him. I needed a fucking parent to help me deal, and he always told me music could heal a person. I thought we could get through it together. So I stood there, shaking—I was so fucking nervous to hear his voice. The voice that hadn't said one word to me since before the funeral. And he looked up at me like I was the guy who shot my mom, and not the son he shared with her. Like I was the reason for his sadness. It was the first time he had acknowledged my existence in two months, and the first time I wished it were me who died instead of her. There was nothing but hatred in his stare, pure revulsion directed solely at me before he grabbed his old Gibson from where it was perched against the chair, swung it behind him, and smashed it against the wall.

That was the last time I asked my dad for anything, and the last time I held this guitar.

I had no desire to play it again after that day. I don't really know if I'll ever play it again, but if I'm leaving Ruxton, I want to take it with me. Because once I'm gone, I'm fucking gone. I'm not coming back here. I know what coming back here will do to me. Being in the same town as Tessa Kelly is slowly killing me, and I won't be my father. I won't let the memory of someone consume me.

At least not any more than it already has.

"NO. NO. NO. Oh, God. What in the hell is this?"

I hold up the strange-looking top I must've purchased drunk off my ass. That's the only reasonable explanation for owning such a hideous looking piece of fabric. It's suede, with a very unfortunate amount of beading work. *Who the fuck buys suede?* Tossing it behind me, I continue rummaging through my closet for the hottest bonfire-appropriate outfit I can put together.

I need to look slamming tonight, rendering Tyler and every other man at this thing speechless. Because let's be real; if he turns out to be a gerbil-loving freak like SteveMD, I'm dropping all standards, grabbing the nearest willing male, and fucking out my frustrations. Especially since I'm going to have to endure the Luke and Leah show, which has me on serious edge right now. My stomach is twisted in knots, and I know my nervousness will only amplify the closer it gets to 6:00 p.m. I *really* want to like this guy, and I'm praying his weird phone behavior yesterday was just some testosterone-driven *I have a penis, so therefore, I'm a dumbass* moment.

I swear. Men can be such idiots sometimes. If they weren't so stellar in the pussy-loving department, I'd take up celibacy and worship something else besides cock.

Other than his desire to push me toward other men, there's really no reason why I shouldn't like him. We have great phone chemistry, he seems to know exactly how to make me come, and he's got everything going for him in the looks department. So, I'm trying to be optimistic about tonight, even though I'm one strike away from deleting my Ignite account.

First *show me your titties* guy, then gerbil lover. Seriously? There should be a disclaimer on that website.

My phone alerts me of a text as I hold a floral tank top against my body. I lay it on the bed next to the jean skirt I picked out and grab my phone from my nightstand, rolling my eyes at the name of the sender.

Tyler: How was the date last night?

I sit down on the edge of the bed and type my snarky response.

Me: Fan-fucking-tastic. We're moving in together and I'm already picking out wedding venues. Thanks for suggesting I date other men.

My phone immediately starts ringing, which I half expected. I wait until it almost goes to voicemail before I answer.

"Yeah?" I ask, lying back on my bed and trying to sound as uninterested as possible.

He laughs. "You're mad at me."

"Why would I be mad? You tell me to go out with another guy, as if I need your permission, when I'm clearly interested in you. It was fucking weird."

"The date? Or the fact that I suggested it to help ease your anxiety over meeting up with a stranger you met online?"

"Both."

He exhales heavily in my ear. "All right. I'll admit I was a little nervous suggesting you go out on a blind date. I knew there was no way in hell he wouldn't like you, so believe me when I say I paced my fucking apartment last night."

I lick my lips as I picture him, worried and unable to sit still while I endured one of the worst dates in history. I twirl my hair around my finger. "You did?"

"Of course I did," he affirms. "I don't like to share, so yeah, I was fucking worried. But I want you to be relaxed with me tonight, and I thought getting last night out of your system would help. Did it?"

"Not really."

He laughs again. "Well that plan was a complete waste of time. How are you feeling about tonight?"

My smile cracks through the mask of aggravation I'm wearing and I turn my head, eyeing up the tank top next to me. "I'm excited, and nervous. But more excited than anything."

"I'm dying to kiss you. Would it be weird if I did it as soon as I get there? 'Cause I might not be able to stop myself."

"Are you trying to get decked?" I ask, playful smirk in place.

"Hmm, I like it pretty rough so, maybe I am."

"How rough?" My voice teeters on the line between seductive and pure curiosity. His breathing grows louder in my ear before a beep alerts me of an incoming call. "Um, can you hold on a second? I'm getting another call."

"If you wanna know how rough I like it, don't keep me waiting."

I bite my lip, holding my phone above me and seeing Mia's name flashing on my screen. I accept the call.

"You better be calling to tell me you're in labor. Tyler was just about to give me explicit details on how he likes to fuck, and I have a feeling he isn't going to be shy about it."

Her soft chuckle is tense, edgy even, and the reason behind it hits me when I remember what day it is.

"Shit. Hold on one second, okay?" She responds with a soft "Hmm mmm" before I click over to my other call. "Hey, I'm sorry, I gotta go. My friend needs me."

"Yeah? Well, get that outta your system now. I'm coming to this thing tonight to see you, not to tag along with your friends."

I swallow down the smartass rebuttal that stings the tip of my tongue, and decide against taking his words as anything other than playful. He's probably just geared up from the turn our conversation just took. I know I am.

"I'll see you tonight," I reply with genuine optimism.

"Can't fucking wait."

I click back over to Mia. "Hey, I'm really sorry about that. I completely forgot what today is. How is everything there?"

"It's . . . a lot." She sighs heavily. "I don't know why it feels so different being here now. I wasn't this sad when Ben and I came here to get the rest of my stuff eight months ago. But yesterday, when we pulled up in front of my old house so Nolan could see it, I broke down sobbing, and that completely freaked Ben out. He wanted to call my doctor, and take me to the hospital to make sure I wasn't crying too much for the baby."

I stifle my laugh with tightly pursed lips. *Typical Ben.* "Well, it is the anniversary of her death, and you're also very pregnant. It could be the hormones making you so emotional."

"Yeah, I guess. I just really didn't want to spend this whole weekend crying. I wanted this to be a great memory for Nolan, and I feel like I'm ruining it for everyone."

I sit up, leaning against the headboard and stretching my legs out in front of me. "Mia, you're not ruining anything. I'm sure Nolan is having a great time. What's he doing right now?"

"Trying to climb on one of the fighter jets at the air base."

She giggles softly and I smile. "He may have a new obsession. Don't be surprised if dragons take a backseat to airplanes when we get home."

"It's about damn time. That kid has had the same fixation since before he could walk."

"Well, honestly, I hope he doesn't give them up completely. I like the whole knight thing, and I already bought Chase a dragon Halloween costume so Nolan can pretend to slay him."

"How morbid of you," I say through a laugh, hearing her join me.

"Crap, hold on. Nolan, be careful! Ben, can you grab him?" she yells, her voice muted. "Hey, he's running all over the place, so I'm gonna have to go. But you better text me later and let me know how tonight goes."

"Explicit details coming your way," I say as I scoot off the bed.

"Oh, God. I'm going to regret saying that, aren't I?"

I shrug. "All I know is I'm getting laid by somebody. And, if necessary, I'll start batting for Team Reed."

She laughs hysterically, the kind of Mia laugh that I know has her tearing up. "Please, God, let that happen."

"Yikes. I'll talk to ya later. Love you."

"Love you too."

I hang up the call, tossing my phone onto the bed before I stare down at my outfit selection, hands on my hips. If my short skirt doesn't get me some attention at this thing, my curve-hugging top definitely will. There's no reason why tonight shouldn't end my year-long dry spell. I'm more than ready for this. I need to move on, and hopefully after tonight, I'll forget all about Luke Evans.

I PARK AMONGST the other cars in the grassy terrain at the edge of Sandy Point Beach. These things are always a huge turnout, bringing in people from nearby towns to pay ten dollars to drink as much as they want. The music is already pumping through the air as I walk between the cars, stepping onto the sand and making my way toward the crowd. Mike Weston, one of the guys who throws these parties several times a year, is standing by the kegs, collecting money. I walk up to him and he looks down at me, giving me his usual smile after his typical once-over of my outfit.

"There's the girl who refuses to go out with me," he teases, tucking the roll of cash he's holding into his pocket. His blue eyes regard me kindly. "What's up, Tessa?"

I hand him my money with a shrug. "Not much. Is Reed here yet?"

He nods, taking my ten-dollar bill and handing me a red Solo cup filled with beer. "Yeah, I just saw him over by the pit. You here with anyone?"

I smile, knowing exactly what he's implying. Mike has been asking me out for years, but he's definitely not my type, and although I like to do my fair share of flirting, I've never led him on to think we're anything more than friends. I turn, holding up my beer over my shoulder. "I'll see ya around, Mike."

He laughs behind me as I take a sip of my beer, walking toward the giant bonfire in the middle of the beach. There are people dancing around it while others are sitting on logs, talking with other partiers. Or if they're Reed, not bothering with conversation, because they're too busy shoving their hand up some random chick's skirt.

I tap him on the shoulder, breaking up his fingering session with a girl I don't recognize. But that's not surprising at all. The girl shoots her eyes open, panting heavily through ragged breaths, as his hand slides out from between her legs. She glares up at me as she tugs her skirt back down to mid-vagina.

"Can you go grab me another beer?" he asks, causing her to soften the nasty look she's giving me for interrupting her special time with a guy who will want nothing to do with her come tomorrow. It's how Reed operates, and every girl he shows an interest in is made aware of that before he does more than talk to them. Although, I'm not sure it needs to be said. His reputation for only wanting one night with a girl has crossed state lines.

"Sure." She stands, yelping when he smacks her on the ass before she walks away.

He looks up at me, sitting forward and resting his forearms on his knees. "Did Mike hit on you already?" he asks with a mocking smile.

I grimace. "I don't know why he even bothers. There are at least fifty chicks here that he can try and get with. He's wasting his time with me." I keep my eyes on the crowd as I take quick sips of my beer, scanning for two faces and only really wanting to see one. Squinting, I try and focus on the group of people through the tall flames across the pit, but I can't make them out as well as I'd like. I move to the other side of Reed to see better, dropping my gaze to the sand when I don't see who I'm looking for.

"When is that guy supposed to get here?" he asks, prompting me to look over at him.

"Six o'clock. What time is it?"

He pulls out his phone and lights up the screen. "Six thirteen."

I run a hand through my hair, letting out an exhaustive grunt. "I hate lateness. This guy better have a damn good reason for making me wait. And, by that, I mean nothing less than a carjacking. His ass better be walking here."

Reed looks over my shoulder, eyes widening with curiosity. Before I can turn around to see who's grabbed his attention, strong hands grip my hips and a body presses against my back. I'm turned before I can protest and soft, full lips move against mine as one hand wraps around my waist, pinning me against the hard body.

"I had trouble finding the place. Your directions sucked," he says against my mouth, keeping his firm grip on me as he tilts his head and deepens the kiss.

And I let him. I forget all about my threat to knock his ass out if he kissed me as soon as he got here. Because this guy, *fucking right*, this guy knows exactly how to use his tongue, and I'd be a very stupid woman to interrupt something this amazing.

My body goes limp against him as my eyes flutter close and my beer falls to the sand. He tastes like watermelon, and I fully surrender myself to a man I haven't even gotten a good look at yet. But with a mouth like this, I'm willing to wait a few more seconds to make that observation.

I moan as he pulls away, a suggestive smirk playing across his mouth. He runs his thumb along my bottom lip, smearing the wetness along my skin. "Hmm."

I smile before giving him my own, "Hmm." And then I really focus on him, all of him, confirming his identity and loving every detail of it. His blond hair is down, tucked behind his ear and stopping just below his jawline. He's rocking the perfect amount of facial hair, which I now know feels soft against my easily irritated skin. And he's firm. Very firm.

"You must be Tyler," Reed says, standing to his feet. He moves next to me and holds his hand out in front of him. "I'm Reed, Tessa's friend. It's good to meet you."

Tyler stares at him for several awkward seconds before letting go of my waist, and firmly shaking Reed's hand. "Friends, huh? You ever been more than that?"

Reed laughs, as do I, but Tyler remains completely serious. His hand slides along my back, grips my hip, and pulls me closer.

"Here you go, baby," a meek voice says from behind us. Reed's flavor of the day walks up and holds out his beer, glancing over at me briefly before beaming back at him.

Reed smiles, taking the cup and putting his arm around her shoulder. "Thanks. This is Tessa and Tyler," he says, motioning toward us with his drink. "Guys, this is Alice."

"Alicia," she corrects him with a glare.

Tyler laughs next to me, but Reed merely frowns and shrugs it off. "Yeah, that's what I said. Alicia." He looks up at us. "We're gonna go take a walk. I'll catch up with you guys later."

"See ya," I reply, watching as the two of them disappear into the crowd. I look up at Tyler, catching his eyes on me. "Do you wanna get a drink?"

He shakes his head as he shamelessly drops his gaze to my mouth.

"Do you want to sit down and talk?" I ask.

He shakes his head again, never meeting my eyes. "I wanna get outta here."

I shift my footing so we're standing chest to chest, his hand flattening against my lower back. At this closeness, and without the distraction of his mouth on me, I focus on his scent. Like fresh rain water and something else I can't quite put my finger on. Honey, maybe?

Oh, God, yes. That's what it is. Honey.

He steps back with a smile, grabs my hand, and pulls me

in the direction I just came from only minutes ago.

"I thought you wanted to party?" I question as I move with him through the crowd of people. I wave at a few girls I graduated from high school with before glancing over at him.

He grins down at me. "I do, with you. I don't give a shit about anybody else here."

"Hmm," I reply, hearing his soft chuckle next to me. I look ahead of us and stop dead in my tracks, causing Tyler to stumble forward when I refuse to move. I knew this was a possibility. Not even that—I knew it was a damn near certainty I'd see him, but it still shakes me, as if I'm completely unprepared for it.

Luke shifts his attention from my whore of a cousin, who just so happens to be hanging all over him, to me, and then to Tyler. He stands, leaving Leah on the log, and walks straight to us.

"What's going on?" Tyler asks, unaware of the man who is quickly approaching us from behind him.

Before I can respond, Tyler turns around and comes face to face with him, keeping a tight hold on my hand. He looks back at me. "You know this guy?"

I look at both men, unsure if I should use straight honesty with this situation or not. I choose to stick with the vague truth.

"Yeah," I answer after one of the longest pauses of my life. I swallow uncomfortably, wishing I still had my beer to help ease down the lump that's formed in my throat. I keep my eyes on Tyler before continuing. "He's my brother's best friend."

"Jesus Christ. Are you going to introduce me to your parents next?" He tugs me toward him. "Come on. I wanna get outta here."

Luke steps in front of him, raising an eyebrow. "What's the rush? The party is just getting started."

"Luke," I warn, gaining his attention fleetingly. "Mind your own business."

"Like you mind yours?" he asks, already having returned his attention to Tyler. They're both similar in size, but the intimidation Luke has radiating off him right now is enough to make a bigger man recoil. Tyler doesn't falter as Luke steps closer, and I'm not sure if that's a good thing, or a bad thing.

"No priors. No traffic citations. Not even a fucking parking ticket. I'm gonna be honest, that shit doesn't sit well with me."

"What the fuck are you talking about?" Tyler asks.

I suddenly feel dizzy as I realize why Luke knows that information. Either Ben told him after he searched for the bogus name I gave him, or Luke did some research of his own. And this interrogation could easily ruin my chances with Tyler, especially if he finds out he has two cops investigating him.

So I act fast, stepping in between the two of them with my back to Luke. "Can you just give me a minute with him?" I ask Tyler, trying to sound irritated instead of panicked.

A deep crease sets in his forehead as he frowns before stepping back. "Whatever. Make it fast."

I turn and grab Luke by the arm, pulling him several feet away until Tyler is out of earshot. I spot Leah, fixated on us from her log, and that aggravates me further. He's concerned about me, but only after he locks down a pussy for the evening. Good to know his priorities are in check.

"You need to back off. I am leaving with this guy and there's nothing you can do about it."

He looks down at me, arrogant smirk in place. "There's a lot I can do about it."

I take several deep breaths through my nose as I try and keep myself from losing it completely. But I'm right there. I'm always right there with Luke; on the edge of an emotion I don't want to feel.

"What I'm about to do, and who I do it with, is none of your business. I don't need to explain myself to you, my brother, Reed—nobody! So go back to my desperate looking cousin, and stop acting like you actually care."

Tyler catches our attention as he comes up to my side, grabbing my hand and pulling me in the direction of the cars. "Time's up. We're going."

Luke grabs my elbow and puts himself between Tyler and me, getting up in the other man's face. "You're going. She stays with me."

I see red, tearing myself free of both of them and shoving my hands against Luke's chest. I push against him as hard as I can, meeting his resistance. "Stop it! God, just leave me alone!"

He drops his head until I feel his breath against my face. "Don't do something stupid right now."

"Why not? I'm so good at doing shit I end up regretting." I motion at him with a sweeping hand. "Case in point."

"You're a fucking brat."

"And you're ruining my life!" My voice breaks at the end of my response as I step closer to that familiar edge, fighting back my tears. I drop my head, concealing how he affects me. *Please, don't lose it right now.*

"Yeah?" he questions, prompting me to lift my gaze. "Well, now you know what it feels like." He steps back, keeping his eyes on me. "Ruin your own life, Tessa. Do whatever you want. I don't give a shit, and soon, I won't even have to watch." He turns then, not giving either one of us another look before he walks away toward the parking area.

The air leaves my lungs in a loud rush.

"What a fucking loser. And what was with the parking ticket stuff?" Tyler asks next to me.

I decide against giving him any information on that and dismiss his questioning with a shrug.

He grabs my hand again. "Let's go, before you introduce me to anyone else."

I watch Luke fade in between the vehicles ahead of us as we walk away from the crowd, following his direction. *You're ruining my life.* That's funny. I wanted to say, "You've ruined my life", but I think deep down I know there isn't an end to this torture in sight. Not when he acts like that around me.

Protective.

Caring.

Like I actually mean something to him.

"Where are you parked?"

I glance up at Tyler, not having realized we'd reached the parking area. I force a smile and point down the row of cars. "Right over there. I'm the silver RAV4." I drop my hand and look up at him. "Where do you wanna go?"

"Your place," he states, his voice clear. "That's what we both want, right?"

Yes.

The word is right there, tickling my lips, but I'm suddenly having difficulty affirming the one goal I had for the evening. He senses my apprehension and tilts his head with a soft grin as he cradles my face in his hands.

His gaze lowers. "I am dying to be alone with you. Don't make me wait anymore."

All my hesitation evaporates as I blush, nodding before finding my voice. "No more waiting."

"NICE PLACE," HE observes, looking around my apartment as I lock the door behind us. I watch him get comfortable on my couch, slumping down on one end. I toss my keys onto the table and head into the kitchen.

"Thanks. Do you want something to drink?"

"A beer, if you got it."

I grab two beers out of the fridge, and kick my flip-flops off before joining him. As I place the beers on the coffee table in front of me, he reaches into his back pocket and pulls out a small plastic bag that's rolled up tightly.

"What is that?" I ask, leaning forward and watching him hold it over the coffee table.

Two of his fingers grasp the top of the bag, allowing it to unravel and reveal the contents.

I put a hand on his arm as my breath catches in my chest. "Um, those are just regular cigarettes, right?"

He muffles his laugh through tight lips, opening the top of the bag and reaching inside. "They better not be." He pulls out a blunt and tosses the bag in front of him before reaching into the front pocket of his polo and removing a lighter. I watch with what I'm sure is my most alarmed expression as he lights up and takes a hit, holding it in for several seconds before he exhales and offers it to me.

I shake my head, scooting back on the couch.

He moves closer. "Come on. Get high with me."

"I have beer. I'm good."

His brow pinches together before he takes another hit, grabs the back of my neck, and blows the smoke against my mouth.

"What the hell!" I push against him, hearing his amused laugh as I cough into my fist. "I've never done that stuff. Are you crazy?"

He takes another hit and nods. "You're twenty-four and

you've never tried pot? I just did you a favor."

Suddenly annoyed and borderline murderous, I move to stand when he grabs my wrist and pulls me back down next to him.

"I just wanna go to the bathroom really quick."

He releases me, blowing the smoke out above him. "Hurry up."

I ignore the warning in his voice and walk down the hallway, stepping into the bathroom and closing the door behind me. I rinse my hands under the cool water as I stare at myself in the mirror.

My eyes appear glassy and dilated.

Shit. Can you get high off one hit of weed? Is that a thing?

I turn the water off, roughly drying my hands on a towel before balling it up and tossing it against the wall. I could easily walk back out there and follow through with my original plans for the evening, but I'm suddenly no longer wanting to do anything with this guy besides kick his ass out of my apartment. And after forcing me to try drugs, I seriously doubt he's going to take my sudden disinterest in him very well. But right now, I don't give a shit what this guy wants. Nobody makes me uncomfortable.

I exit the bathroom and walk down the hallway, coming up behind the couch and seeing him bent over the coffee table. "Look, I don't think . . ."

I'm cut off by a loud sniffing sound and walk around the side of the couch to investigate it. As he lifts his head, my eyes narrow in on the three white lines of powder on my glass top, and I feel my stomach drop out to the floor.

"What the fuck? What are you doing?"

He wipes underneath his nose and leans back, smiling. "Getting high. You said you wanted to party, remember?"

"Are you crazy? My brother is a cop!" I move quickly, and

without thought, come up beside him and brush the powder off the table and onto my carpet.

I just want it gone.

I want him gone.

"Hey!" he yells, grabbing me and throwing me to the ground.

I land on my hip, wincing in pain before looking at him over my shoulder and taking in his desperate state.

He runs his hands over the carpet, trying to salvage any of his precious drug, and looking like a strung-out junkie in the process. His eyes flash with rage as he turns them on me, balling his fists against the floor.

"You stupid bitch! Do you have any idea how much that cost me?" Before I can answer, he reaches for my ankle and pulls me toward him. "You're gonna fucking pay for that."

I flail against him, bending the leg he doesn't have in his grasp and kicking out, connecting with his jaw. "Get off me!" He lets out a loud groan, grabbing my other leg and pinning me to the ground. I squirm as much as I can, screaming at the top of my lungs, but he quickly silences me with one hand to my mouth and another to my throat. My hands claw at his face, his neck, anything to weaken him.

My eyes go wide with panic when he tightens his grip.

"Yeah, I fucking love that. Look how scared you look right now." He bends down, running his nose against my cheek. "Are you ready to see how rough I like it?"

I close my eyes as I try to pry his fingers from around my neck, but he keeps his hold. And as the tears slip out and my breathing becomes constricted, there's only one word remaining in my vocabulary. One word that I chant over and over again in my head.

Luke.

"RUIN YOUR OWN life, Tessa. Do whatever you want. I don't give a shit, and soon, I won't even have to watch."

I turn and walk away, needing to get the hell out of here before I resort to begging. I refuse to let her see my desperation right now. I don't want this to bother me, I shouldn't care what she does anymore, but it does, and I do.

I fucking care.

"Where are you going?"

I ignore whatever-the-hell-her-name-is as I pass her, walking straight for my truck. I don't know why she's still trying. I barely said two words to her after she sat down next to me, and I was too distracted to act interested in her, or the way she shamelessly brushed against my cock, which didn't react to her either.

Not even a twitch.

That didn't surprise me. Unless I'm imagining Tessa's hands or mouth, it never reacts.

After slamming my door, I start the truck up and sit there, hand on the clutch, ready to shift it into drive, but I don't move. I can't. I let out my breath and slump back against the headrest, looking between the cars in front of me at the bodies in the distance.

I shouldn't even be here. Nobody else seems to give a shit

about what she does, so why the fuck do I? Why can't I turn it off? I don't want to feel anything anymore, except hate. But even that's a dangerous emotion when it comes to Tessa. My hate for her consumes me, ripping me apart, like everything else I've ever felt for her.

It triggers my obsession. Fueling it.

But I know if I don't hate her, I'll leave myself open to feel something else, something I never want to feel again.

It's fucking pathetic how much effort it takes to hate someone. It doesn't come without struggle, but allowing yourself to be vulnerable for them? That's easy, and it's exactly what I did. I held my arms out and watched as she wedged herself deep inside me, only to claw her way out and take shredded pieces of me with her.

Never again. I'll hate Tessa until it fucking kills me, but that's the only thing I'll allow myself to feel.

Movement through the window of the truck a row ahead of me catches my attention, and I focus on it as the figure moves around the front of the hood and to the car next to it. The one directly in front of me.

My back goes rigid in my seat. "Motherfucker."

I lean up, watching as the dipshit I should've laid out the moment I saw him opens the door of his Camero and gets inside. My eyes immediately dart to the license plate as it becomes illuminated, and I commit it to memory just before he drives away, following closely behind Tessa's vehicle.

2A8347J

"Gotcha, asshole."

I GET TO the precinct within fifteen minutes, only bothering to put my truck in park before I run inside, repeating the license plate number over and over again in my head.

2A8347J

2A8347J

I brush past someone, not registering them until I hear their voice behind me.

"Hey, man. What are you doing here?"

I turn my head, briefly connecting with CJ, but continuing in the direction of my desk. "I gotta look something up." *2A8347J*

"Is everything all right?"

2A834 . . . FUCK.

"Stop fucking talking to me!" I yell, halting in front of my desk and running my hands down my face. *God, I'm losing it.*

"All right, Jesus."

I close my eyes, picturing the license plate in my head and focusing on all seven numbers. *2A8347J*

After I have it, I turn my head to apologize, but see I'm too late when my gaze locks onto the empty entryway.

Nice. You're an asshole, Evans.

I sit down at my desk, booting up my computer and staring impatiently at the screen as it takes it times to load. I hit a few buttons to try and speed up the process, and when that doesn't work, I resort to smacking the side of the monitor.

"Come *fucking* on already."

The welcome screen appears and I click on the search engine, hovering my mouse over where I know the blank box is going to load. It does, and I type frantically into the license plate field.

2A8347J

I press enter, watching the hourglass turn twice before the screen displays my results. A license appears and I scan the information, narrowing in on the name.

Tyler Tripp

"Motherfucking shit."

Tessa either gave Ben the wrong name, or this asshole lied to her. Both scenarios are believable right now, and the fact that I didn't go with my gut and investigate this before tonight has me squeezing my mouse so hard it makes a cracking sound in my hand.

"Shit."

I loosen my grip, scrolling down the screen, not caring anymore about what this asshole weighs and needing to get to the information I know is there. There's no way this guy hasn't at least gotten a speeding ticket. Nobody buys a Camero with the intent to obey the speed limit.

Charges

My heartbeat fills my ears, causing tremors in my vision, as I try and make out the words I'm almost afraid to focus on. I rub my eyes, digging my thumb into one and two fingers into the other, before blinking several times and letting the words slowly form in front of me.

Domestic Disturbance   Charges Dropped

Domestic Violence   Charges Dropped

"Tessa."

I'm out the door before I even realize I'm moving, running faster than I ever have. I slide on the gravel, grabbing the door handle and nearly ripping the damn thing off when I swing it open. As soon as I get in my truck, I grab my phone out of my cup holder and with frantic fingers, light up the screen. It fades to black immediately, dying on me and causing me to panic further.

"Fucking shit!"

I toss it to the floor with enough force to break it, and pull out of the parking lot, barreling down Cheseco Avenue in the direction of Tessa's apartment building. I have to believe she's there with him. I didn't think to write down that fucker's address, or even glance at it, and there's no way in hell I'm turning around to do that. She has to be there. I can't think of a scenario that involves her not at her apartment and somewhere else.

Somewhere I might not be able to get to in time.

Eight grueling minutes later, my headlights illuminate the parking lot out in front of her building and I see her car parked in its usual spot. I'm relieved, but only momentarily, as the red Camero parked next to her comes into my line of sight.

My tires screech as I barely make it to a spot before I'm jumping out of my truck and taking the stairs to her level. I'm running, fast, faster, until I reach her door and jar the locked handle.

"Tessa! Tessa, open the door!"

I bang repeatedly, each time with more force than the previous. My hand begins to throb, then burn with a fire that shoots down my arm to my elbow.

No answer. Not a single noise. She's here. I know she is, and she isn't answering me.

Or she can't.

"TESSA!"

I bang one last time before stepping back, turning sideways, and ramming my shoulder into the wood. It cracks against me, driving me into it again and again. My shoulder screams for me to stop, but I don't. I can't. I can barely breathe. My lungs are heaving and trying to pull in as much air as possible while my head fills with images of Tessa, unable to respond to me.

"FUCK! Come on!"

One last drive and the door splits at the frame, swinging

open and allowing me to come crashing into the room.

The scene in front of me has me struggling to stay upright.

To take a step.

To do fucking anything besides stand motionless.

I see his hands around her neck, squeezing, as she tries to remove them. The body on top of her, pinning her to the floor as her legs twitch, struggling to kick off his weight.

Then her eyes grab me.

They're tear streaked, straining to stay open, and paralyze me with a pleading look that has bile rising in the back of my throat.

Tessa.

"Somebody wants to watch? Fuck, I'm down for that."

I hear his voice and it snaps me out of my trance, sending me flying at him. He's knocked to the ground, freeing Tessa, and I get in a few punches before I turn my head at the sound of her desperate attempts to take in a breath.

"Go . . ."

Thwack.

I fall to my side with a blow to my jaw, pulling this piece of shit with me.

"Luke!"

Tessa's voice is hoarse, but still urgent as I slip out of each grip this fucker tries to put on me. I block several blows to my ribcage, a strike to my head, and one to my gut. This guy knows where to hit, but I know better, and I also know he's going to tire soon. He becomes frustrated, slipping up and allowing me to gain the upper hand when his controlled movements become frantic.

I grab his neck, pinning his head in place while I flip him so he's on his stomach. I pull his arm behind his back, twisting his wrist until he cries out.

"Arrghhhffuucckkkk!"

"Sorry. What was that?" I twist it more, feeling his entire body strain against the pressure as his screams fill the apartment. I drop my head next to his ear. "I should fucking kill you right now."

"Yeah?" He laughs, turning his head so his one eye is trained on me. "Fucking do it then, pussy."

He tries to buck underneath me, but I dig my knee into his back and keep him pinned. I look up at Tessa, narrowing in on the purple and red marks coating her neck, the rapid rise and fall of her chest, and the look on her face I never want to see again.

I try to convince myself that my next actions are based purely on my duty to protect Ben's sister. That there's no underlying motivation here. No emotions driving this.

But I'm lying.

Our eyes meet, and I hold her gaze as I twist his wrist until I push past the resistance, waiting for that snap.

I get two of them.

"ARGHH! FUUUUCK! FUCK, FUCK, FUCK!" He flails underneath me like a fish out of water, his hand limp in mine, no longer connected to the bones in his arm. "YOU BROKE MY WRIST! ARRGHH SHIIIT!"

Tessa drops her stare to the man beneath me, eyes wide and wild as she reaches up with a trembling hand and rubs the skin on her neck.

"Where's your phone?" I ask her.

She doesn't acknowledge me. Not even with a flinch. The body I'm holding down goes slack and I shift my grip on him, putting more of my weight onto the middle of his back.

"Tessa."

Her head snaps up, and I see the same stark panic in her

eyes as I did when I first broke in, but it's mixed with something else. Apprehension; maybe some guilt. I'm familiar with this look. It's the same look people have when they're about to confess to something, when they have no fucking clue how it's going to be received.

And now I'm starting to feel uneasy.

She sits up on her knees, straightening her posture. "He brought drugs here. I didn't know he had them with him. I swear. I thought it was just pot, but then he was snorting lines of coke when I came out from the bathroom, and I . . ."

I twist the fucker's other wrist and he squeals, cutting Tessa off. "Are you fucking high right now?" I ask her over his whines.

She shakes her head with rapid movements. "No, I didn't . . . I don't think I am." She squeezes her eyes shut, whispering with a shaky voice, *"Fuck, I don't know."* Her eyes shoot open again, pleading for understanding. "He blew a hit in my face before I knew he was doing it. I've never done it before. I swear, Luke, but I don't know if I'm feeling it. I don't really feel anything right now."

I drop my head, shutting my eyes with such force that it causes my head to throb.

This is just what I fucking need.

"Luke?"

"Where is your phone?" I grunt out through a clenched jaw, my eyes meeting hers.

She quickly reaches onto the table behind her, holding her phone out to me with a trembling hand. "I brushed the coke off the table. I don't know if he has more on him, but it's all in my carpet. Should I vacuum it up?"

I ignore her question and slide my grip to his elbow, securing him better, and letting his limp arm fall to his side.

I'm not worried he'll use that one anymore. I reach into the front pocket of his shorts.

"If I get stabbed with a fucking needle, or anything else, I'm breaking your other wrist."

He whimpers beneath me as I clear his right pocket, moving onto his left. I enclose my hand around something small, feeling the sharp edge of the plastic dig into my palm before I slide it out. Opening my hand, I reveal the baggie, staring at it briefly because I don't need to analyze it. I know exactly what it is.

I put it on the carpet next to my leg and grab the phone from her. "Go start chugging water and get your ass in the shower."

She stands, looking down at me with confusion. "I'm not thirsty, and why am I taking a shower?"

I unlock the screen and pull up her keypad before connecting with her eyes. "Would you just do what I say for once without giving me shit first?" She blinks rapidly, stepping toward the kitchen. "Go, and don't come out until I tell you to."

I begin dialing the number, her footsteps trailing off behind me. The asshole under me decides to laugh and I yank his arm back, stealing his breath from him.

"Don't fucking push me, man."

The call connects in my ear. "Tully."

I loosen my hold, softening his protest so I can hear more clearly. "Hey, it's Luke. Are you patrolling right now?"

"Yeah, why?"

"I need you to come to Cherry Point apartments. Tessa was attacked."

"What? Shit! Is she okay?"

"She's shaken up a little, but she's not hurt. I got here before anything happened. That's why I was in such a rush earlier and couldn't talk. I was trying to look up this fucker's license plate number to get information on him."

"Does he have priors?"

"Two domestic charges that were dropped. Look, man, he's got drugs on him, and I may have broken his wrist, but I don't think we need to rush getting a paramedic over here."

He laughs into the phone. "I hear ya. What apartment number is she?"

"211. Is Jacobs with you?"

"Yeah."

Fuck. He couldn't be patrolling by himself tonight? I don't need that shithead getting on my case.

"You need a new partner."

"Yeah," he repeats, zero humor in his voice.

We didn't all get lucky when it came to partners, and CJ has the worst one in the unit.

"We'll be there soon."

I toss the phone onto the couch after he hangs up, shifting my weight in the process, and causing the prick under me to moan in discomfort.

"You can do better than that," I say, pinning his snapped wrist between my knee and the floor.

He sucks in a breath before bellowing, "ARRGHHH STOP! STOP! SHIT!"

I ease up, feeling the sadistic smile creep onto my face before water rushes on in the distance. And then, simply because I don't want to think about her taking a shower, I make him scream.

Drowning out my obsession.

HURRIED FOOTSTEPS ALERT me of company and seconds

later, CJ fills the doorway of Tessa's apartment. I look past him, locking onto the unimpressed smirk that's permanently fixated on Jacobs' face as he looks at me from over his partner's shoulder.

Dick.

"Jesus, man. Is he dead?" CJ asks, stepping inside and dropping the hand he has on his gun as he surveys the body I'm crushing into the carpet.

I stand, hauling the barely conscious prick to his feet. He'd probably be more alert if I hadn't spent the last fifteen minutes trying to re-break his wrist, but something had to distract me from Tessa in the shower.

"Where's the girl?" Jacobs asks, pulling out his cuffs as CJ takes the guy out of my hands.

I look over my shoulder in the direction of the hallway that leads to the bathroom. "Shower. She said she'll be in there a while." I turn back around, catching the slow shake of his head. "Something you wanna say to me?"

He smiles cunningly. "We need to question her. Tell her to get out."

"We don't *need* to question her right now," CJ corrects him. "I'm sure Luke can relay what he saw. She's probably too shaken up to talk to us." Once the handcuffs are secure, he grabs Tyler by the shoulders and moves him against the wall, pushing with a firm hand to his chest. "Don't fucking move."

"How'd he break his wrist, Evans?"

I leer at Jacobs, and the self-important tone in his voice. "How the fuck do you think he broke his wrist? There was a struggle, asshole. He was trying to choke Tessa out when I got here, and I fucking acted. She's Ben's sister; or did you forget that tiny detail?"

He smiles, showing the teeth I'd love to knock out more than anything right now, as he steps closer to me. "She also dumped your ass last summer, didn't she?"

"Shut up, Jacobs," CJ says, stepping in between us and preventing me from moving any closer, which I unknowingly had been doing. He motions with his head toward the floor. "Is that what he had on him?"

I follow his eyes and bend down, grabbing the small plastic baggie. "Yeah. He had pot, too. Tessa said he snorted a bunch of coke before he attacked her, so I'm sure you'll find it when you run his panels."

"Did she take any?" Jacobs asks, looking over my shoulder in the direction of the hallway.

My jaw ticks just below my ear. "No, she didn't."

"Maybe I should verify that myself."

"Go ahead. I'll let Ben know you're testing his sister for drugs when I call him. I'm sure he'll be really understanding about that."

"All right," CJ says, pressing a hand against my chest and backing me off. He looks over his shoulder and nods toward Tyler, who is barely standing up. "Get him out of here. I'll be down in a minute."

After staring me down for several seconds, Jacobs moves and grabs Tyler, pulling him off the wall. "Let's go."

When he steps out, I sit on the arm of the couch and grab my shoulder, wincing as I move it around.

"You need to go get checked out," CJ says, looking up at me as he picks up the bag containing one marijuana cigarette that was left on the coffee table. He seals it up and puts it in his pocket, scanning the area one last time before he moves across from me.

"I'm fine. I'm just beat."

"You sure she's okay?" he asks, glancing behind me.

I nod, standing. "Yeah, she's tough. You know Tessa. Shit

rolls right off her back."

In fact, I'm sure her recovery time from this will be a hell of a lot shorter than mine. She's practically immune to anything that would normally trigger an emotional breakdown in people.

He laughs, smiling in agreement. "All right, man. Take it easy."

I shove the door closed behind him, hearing it crackle as it latches into the splinted doorframe, and drop my head against the wood. My body feels heavy, as if my bones have been hollowed out and filled with cement. The corner of my mouth tastes metallic, the dried blood re-liquefying with the wetness of my tongue. My shoulder burns, and my right hand doesn't seem to flex as well as it should, but these injuries are nothing compared to the discomfort throbbing where the weakest part of me lies.

Seriously? My heart couldn't stay out of this shit?

STRIKE THREE.

I run my fingers over the sensitive skin of my neck while the water beats down on my head. The slightest bit of pressure has me sucking in a breath, but I do it anyway, probing until I'm on the brink of crying out. Then I ease off a bit, wait a few seconds, and press down again.

At this point, I deserve to feel the pain.

I ignored the signs, and there were several, flashing in blinding neon lights with warnings about that asshole's odd behavior. But did I listen? Did I even hesitate in the slightest when it came time to meet up with a complete stranger, and then proceed to bring him back to my place? Alone?

No, I didn't.

My pussy was running the show, and she's the dumbest bitch I've ever met.

I was so fucking dead-set on getting laid and making last summer a distant memory, I blocked out the tiny, cautionary voice in my head and nearly got myself killed. My own apprehension didn't stop me; Luke couldn't stop me. Hell, if anything, I was more driven to leave with Tyler after Luke voiced his opinion of the situation.

Don't do something stupid right now.

His words fill my head as I let it hang between my shoulders, digging harder into the tender spot on my neck until a muted whimper escapes my lips. I drop my hand when I can't take it anymore, when my legs nearly give out and my entire body begins to tremble from the sting.

But even then, I still feel it. The pain I've felt during the past year remains a constant, like a fever that won't break.

I stay in the shower for what feels like hours, only finally stepping out once all the hot water has been used. I wrap a towel around me, lifting my gaze to the mirror above my sink, and stare at my reflection.

Skin flushed, eyes tired and swollen, a shake in my hand as I raise it to wipe the water drops off my forehead. I turn away when I don't want to look anymore, when I no longer feel any sympathy for the girl staring back at me. I open the bathroom door and peer down the hallway toward the living room, greeted only by silence.

"Luke?"

I investigate further and find an empty apartment. A tidied up empty apartment. The vacuum is out, propped against the wall, and the coffee table has been moved slightly. But other than that, everything is in order. No signs of a struggle. Nothing giving away that anything out of the ordinary happened tonight.

Except for me. I give it away.

I half expected to find Luke waiting for me so he could rip me a new one, or rub in the fact that I should've listened to him, but he's gone. As is the asshole that brought him here. Maybe he's said enough to me tonight. He's done enough, that's for sure. I don't want to think about what could've happened if he hadn't shown up.

I've never been scared like that. I've never felt anything even close to that kind of panic. And it had worsened with the sound of Luke screaming my name, trying to get to me.

He won't make it, I'd thought. *The fear in his voice is the last sound I'll hear.*

But it wasn't.

I thought I was scared when I didn't think he'd get to me in time, but that was nothing compared to what I felt when he came through the door and his eyes found mine.

That look would've stolen my breath, if it weren't already being taken from me.

Luke Evans doesn't usually show emotion like the rest of us. But in that moment, I wasn't sure who was more terrified. Him or me.

I walk back to my bedroom and toss the damp towel onto my bed, grabbing an oversized T-shirt and a pair of panties out of my dresser. After slipping them on, I discard the towel in my hamper and start combing out my hair.

A cracking sound comes from the hallway, followed by another one—louder this time, and given the events of tonight, I go to the worse possible explanation for the noise and let it cripple me with panic.

The comb hits the floor, along with my stomach, as the noise echoes out one final time before the only sound I hear is my heavy breathing.

"Luke?" I barely choke out, moving closer to my partially opened bedroom door. "Luke, are you there?"

I hear something, the softest sound, in the distance. A jingle of keys, maybe? It gets louder as I stare at the two-inch crack in my door and find myself once again flushed with terror. I move closer, reaching for the handle as the incessant noise grows louder.

"Luke?" I whisper, seconds before the door nudges open and the reason for the noise comes barreling at me.

I break, dropping to my knees as my anxiety dissipates

into the air above me. Max sniffs all over my head, rubbing his cold nose in my hair and on my face as I grab onto his neck.

"Jesus, Max. You scared the shit outta me." I grab onto his collar, the two ID plates clinging against each other and causing the sound I was unsure of moments ago. I tilt my head as I rub the top of his, smiling when he leans into my hand. "Yeah, I missed you too."

I stand and walk out of my room, watching as Max pushes past me and goes into my bathroom where he lays over one of my air vents. That dog has the weirdest fascination with bathrooms. Continuing down the hallway, I stop when I come up behind the couch.

Luke drops a duffle bag on the floor by the vacuum, shoves the front door closed, and locks it. He lifts his head, his eyes heavy with judgment as they fall on me.

I glance at the duffle. "What's going on? Why is Max here?"

He runs a hand over his buzzed hair to the back of his neck where he grips it. "Your door isn't secure. I can get it changed out tomorrow but right now, locking it doesn't really do shit."

"So, you're going to spend the night?"

Good God. Can I even handle a sleepover with Luke, knowing that he's in my apartment, and being very aware of what he isn't wearing to bed?

He grabs his shoulder and begins massaging it, keeping his head down. "Your brother would be on my ass if he knew I let you stay here by yourself when someone could easily walk in. And you're not staying at my house." His hand falls to his side with a heavy sigh as his eyes lose focus.

I mask the strange hurt I feel at that reasoning, and also decide against bringing up the obvious solution to this problem—staying at my parents' house. For some reason, going against Luke's genius uncomfortable sleepover plan seems like an argument I should probably avoid.

"You didn't have to do that." I motion toward the vacuum. "I would've cleaned up after I . . ."

"It's done," he interjects bitterly, removing his gaze so quickly after he speaks, it's as if he can't stand to look at me another second.

I bite back my typical response to his asshole tendencies, knowing I owe him a lot right now, and settle for what he deserves to hear from me.

"Thank you. Not just for that. For everything tonight."

He ignores me, popping out the chamber from the vacuum and walking past me with it into the kitchen. He holds it above the trashcan and empties the contents, grabbing the bag and tying it off before walking toward the door.

I block him, putting my body between him and his exit. "Did you hear what I said?"

He looks down at me, and his jaw twitches in the corner just below his ear before he speaks. "Yeah, I heard you."

"Well, aren't you going to say anything?"

"No." He steps sideways to move past me, but I move with him. His eyes find mine, flashing a warning. "Leave this alone."

I tilt my head up, getting closer. "Leave *what* alone? What's your problem? I'm trying to thank you for what you did."

He moves into me, dropping the bag and the canister on the floor before backing me up until I'm pushed against the couch. He places a hand on either side of me, gripping the edge, preventing my escape. His head angles down and I suck in a breath, turning my head to prevent his skin from touching mine.

"Go ahead. Do it," he growls, shifting in front of me so I'm forced to look at him. "Get on your knees and fucking thank me."

I feel heat rush to my cheeks. "What?"

"It's what you want, isn't it? What this whole night was about? You were so desperate to get laid, you took home some psycho you met online, and he almost fucking killed you!"

I feign amusement, concealing the sting I feel at that insult. "The only time I was ever desperate to get laid was last summer, when I got bored and settled for you."

His eyes darken. "The way I fucked you was never settling."

"The way you fucked me required these afterward." I hold up two fingers, wiggling them arrogantly.

He grabs my hand, bringing it between us, and leans in, so close that the only thing I can stare at is his mouth.

Oh, God, please back up.

"Luke," I plea breathlessly, digging my back into the couch to try and put some space between us. He's too close—way too fucking close right now.

"The only time those fingers touched that pussy last summer was when I made them, or when you were so fucking desperate for my cock, you'd beg me to make you come over the phone. I'm sure they've gotten a lot of use since me, but don't stand there and act like I didn't *wring you out*. You and I both know what it feels like when you come."

I snatch my hand away from him. "You don't know shit. I faked it."

He grabs my neck, pinning his body against mine. "Do I need to remind you?"

"Remind me of what?"

I glare up at him as I try to ignore my reaction to this conversation, and his, as it presses into me. But that determination quickly vanishes when he slides his hand to the front of my panties and cups me there. I gasp through a moan, hating myself when it goes unnoticed.

"How quickly I can make you beg?" He slides a finger over my clit. "How I can make *this* enough? Go ahead. Tell me again you faked it. Let's see if you can convince me before I make you come all over my hand." One finger becomes two, rubbing up the length of me, pressing the material of my panties into my wetness. "Say it, Tessa."

"No," I answer through a moan.

"No, what? No you never faked it? Or no, this isn't enough?"

My answer comes in the form of me grinding against his hand, needing the friction. Seeking more than just this, because he's right, on both counts. I never faked it with him, and for the past year, this hasn't been enough.

I reach down and palm his length, causing his hand to still. "What?" I ask, finally removing my gaze from his mouth and looking into his eyes. I give him a squeeze and he twitches. "You wanna tell me *you're* faking this?"

His face remains completely serious, cold even, as he grabs my hand and prevents me from stroking him through his shorts. "I'm not interested in a partial hand job."

"Who said anything about a hand job?"

He tilts his head, an arrogant gleam in his eye. "If you're referring to actually finishing me off this time, that's one thing. But if you're talking about me fucking you, then you better think real hard about it."

"But I don't want to think. I want to do."

"Tessa," he warns. "I mean it. I will not have my cock buried deep inside you and have you tell me this isn't what you want."

I grip him harder, and his hold on me tightens. "Maybe

you should just put your dick in my mouth, Luke. That way I can't say anything at all."

He grabs me, spinning me around until he's pinning my front against the couch. His lips brush against my ear while his hands slide around my waist. "Maybe I should. That smartass mouth looks best when it's wrapped around me." Another brush against my clit has me arching into his touch. "You want more than this?"

"Jesus, do I have to spell it out for you? *Yes*. Y. E—"

"I know how to fucking spell it." He interrupts me, keeping one hand between my legs while another cups my breast through my shirt. "Say *please*."

"Are you serious?" I ask, glaring at him over my shoulder. A sharp inhale escapes me when he slides my panties to the side, dipping into me before bringing his mouth so close to mine I can practically taste it. A different hand, a different guy, and I wouldn't be finding myself mouthing the word against his lips.

But it's Luke.

My panties are slid down to my knees, my body bowing over the couch as he shoves my shirt over my head and discards it somewhere. A hand flattens against the small of my back, sliding up my spine, and my body pulses as he grips my shoulder and holds me in place.

I feel the unmistakable nudge of his cock as he rubs it between my cheeks. Bare.

"Wait."

He freezes, his hand on my shoulder tightening. "Are you *fucking* kidding me?"

"Condom." I strain my neck to look at him, seeing the aversion to my request play on his features. Deep frown lines set in as his amber eyes blaze into mine. I ignore the effect that has on everything below my waist and straighten with a glare. "Spare me your views on wrapping that thing up, Luke. If we're doing this, you're wearing one."

His chest heaves with an inhale as he steps back, that sexy-as-hell smirk touching his lips. My eyes take in the bulge of his bicep, the ink running down his arm to his hand as he leisurely strokes his cock.

"If you're going to stare at me like that, get on your knees and do it. You'll like that angle better."

My eyes meet his with a challenge. "I'm not staring."

"Yeah, babe, you are." His eyes drop to my chest. "Watch. This is what it looks like."

I cross my arms blocking his view. "Don't call me that. And stop pretending your hand feels better than me and go get a condom."

His gaze lowers and his tongue grazes over his bottom lip. "If you want me to wear one so bad, go fucking get it yourself."

I push off from the couch. "God, you're such an asshole," I snarl, stalking past him down the hallway and grabbing the unopened box out of my nightstand drawer.

I was planning on getting it, thank you very much. There's no way in hell I'd let Luke be the first to crack open my purchase from twelve months ago. How embarrassing would that be? But he's definitely wearing one. I don't care how much he hates it. After last summer, I'm done taking chances and relying solely on my method of birth control. Not even for this one time. This one moment of desperation. Because that's all this will be.

I walk back into the living room, halting at the sight of him naked, smugly leaning against the couch. He shifts when I enter, gripping the couch behind him and giving me full view of his heavy cock as it hangs between his legs. It's no longer hard, but that doesn't ease the effect it has on me. Not at all.

I force myself to move and stop in front of him. "Here."

He looks down at the condom, then back at me. "What are you waiting for? Put it on."

"What?"

He grabs my hand, gripping the condom between his teeth and tearing the wrapper. "You heard me. You might want to get me hard first, otherwise you're going to have a helluva time."

I tilt my head with a grimace, removing the wrapper and discarding it on the floor. "How would you know? I thought you refused to wear these things?"

"I refused to wear one with *you*, and if you're so fucking adamant about it now, then you're going to do it." He grabs my empty hand, forcing it against his cock, holding me there as we both feel him pulse to life. "Get the fuck on with it, already."

Every pissy response I have in me vanishes at the feel of him throbbing, begging for this, for more of what we both need. The second he's fully hard, I roll the condom down his length with frantic fingers, ignoring the shake in my hand and narrowing in on my task. He spins me around, tilting my body to the angle he needs to drive straight into me. His cock lines up, slides over my pussy, and I'm so ready for this my legs begin to tremble.

I know exactly what this feels like. No matter how bad I wanted to, I never forgot it. But the moment he bottoms out and digs his deft fingers into my skin, I see stars, and the only thing I can remember is how to moan.

"Oh God," I cry out as he begins thrusting into me, causing my body to practically fold in half. His hard chest forms to my back, his arm wrapping around my breasts and pulling me up until I'm staring at our reflection in the mirror on the wall. His eyes are there, holding me, as his thrusts become feverish.

"Fuck, you're so . . ." His words are broken up by a strangled groan that catches in his throat. He dips his head, tasting the skin of my neck up to my ear. "Why? Why does it have to be this good?"

I ignore his words because I don't have an answer. I wish it didn't feel like this, but it always has, and I hate knowing it always will.

Our eyes never break contact as he grinds into me, his one hand massaging my breast as his other splays across my stomach inching lower, lower, until he brushes against my clit and I arch against him.

"Luke," I pant, reaching up and raking over his short hair as his tongue slides across the curve of my neck. His lips brush against my cheek and I tense. "Please don't kiss me."

I can't feel his lips on mine. The slightest brush I felt earlier before I begged for this is all I can take. Sex is usually the most intimate act two people can share, but not with Luke.

The hesitant yet urgent tilt of his head, the way he sucks my tongue while his hands hold me like I'm delicate . . . Everything else this man does is deliberate, calculated, but not kissing. That's where he loses control. Something snaps, breaking his discipline while he steals every memory of any other kiss out of your head. It's honest and real, and fucking beautiful the way he gives you all of him when he's always held back. And seeing him lose all restraint like that, allowing you a glimpse at how vulnerable he can be is something I know I can't survive.

I never have.

He eases back, allowing his breath to heat my skin while his eyes search for understanding in my reflection. He must see it, how helpless I feel in his arms. It's so strikingly obvious to me, as unmistakable as my need to be here. Right fucking here.

He lunges harder, faster, his pace breaking into a wild frenzy as my lips part with a moan and my head hits his shoulder. This is it. The heat, that sweet fire that I'd die from if it meant feeling like this one more time.

With him.

"I'm . . . oh, God, I'm . . ."

He growls against my ear as his hand squeezes my breast. "Faking?"

"Asshole," I choke out through a moan, catching his knowing grin before my eyes roll closed. The pleasure barrels through me in waves, pushing me further into his touch as his grip on me tightens. I drop my hand, stopping the slide of his fingers against my clit when I can't take it anymore. My body falls lax against his as he slows his movements completely before pulling out.

"Turn around."

Our eyes meet in the mirror, and I realize only then that he hasn't climaxed yet. I steady myself before turning to face him, watching as he tugs the condom off and strokes his cock. A firm hand presses against my shoulder, easing me to my knees, and I go willingly, wrapping my lips around him and letting him hit the back of my throat.

"Aw fuck, yeah. There's nothing like your mouth."

I let him drop out with a pop. "Not even my pussy?"

He frowns, rubbing his cock against my lips. "When I can fucking feel it. Now open up."

His face tenses as I take him all the way, feeling his hands fist in my hair as I begin moving. He's on the edge in seconds, his chest heaving as he thrusts into my mouth. He growls through a moan as I run my hands up his body, over his ink, and I watch as his eyes roll closed, head falling forward as the word "fuck" struggles to escape his lips.

I swallow three times, licking the length of him before sitting back on my heels. We stare at each other, him still trying to steady his breathing while I struggle to figure out what my next words should be.

Thanks?

Let's not let that happen again?

Fuck you?

Max comes into the living room and ends all awkward silence with his clanging ID tags. I scramble to my feet, covering myself as Luke grabs his boxers and slips them on.

"That was—"

"I'm going to bed." My words cut his off, and he blinks heavily before he turns away from me, picking up his shorts and stepping into them. "Sorry, what?"

He shakes his head, grabbing his T-shirt and shrugging it on. "Nothing. Come on, Max. Let's go outside."

I watch the two of them stalk toward the door as my brain tries to figure out what I interrupted. *That was . . . fun? A mistake? Both?*

Luke opens the door, snapping his fingers and getting Max's attention. They both walk outside, and I wait, hopeful, for another look from Luke before the door closes, but I don't get one.

I just slept with the guy I've spent the last year trying to forget.

Tessa Kelly, you are an idiot.

"GOD, YOU'RE A fucking idiot."

I run my hands down my face as Max sniffs around the small lawn in front of Tessa's apartment building. A year, twelve fucking months of trying to dull out my obsession and I go and do the worst possible thing I could do right now. The feel of her pulsing around me as I proved exactly what I knew I could do to her body is staying with me like a phantom limb, causing me to sport a semi even after I've had relief.

No, not even relief. A blow-job from Tessa is way the hell more than that. I can give myself relief. What she gives me? There's not a damn word invented yet to sum that experience up.

She faked it? Fuck that. I wasn't about to let her try and deny everything I gave her. If she needed to be reminded of what I could do to her, then I'd suffer the consequences and let her come all over my fingers just to prove a point.

But the moment she said she needed more, I should've stopped. Protested. Fucking ran out of the room and locked myself in another. I knew exactly how this would play out. I knew I'd be completely screwing myself by satisfying the incessant need I've done a shit job at ignoring. But did that stop me? Did the thought of being more strung-out on her prevent me from acting on every impulse I had?

No. My cock saw an opportunity, and he took it.

Even with a condom, she's still perfection, and that's seriously fucking with me right now. Things would be a lot easier if the sex I just had was anything other than phenomenal, but I apparently forgot a few things about Tessa that I was quickly made aware of the moment I slid inside her.

One: Her tight, warm, unfairly flawless pussy will always hug my dick better than any other, and I'm a stupid motherfucker for thinking a condom would change that.

And two: She's vulnerable in my arms, stripped of that rough exterior of hers that drives me completely wild, and that shit wrecks me. The look on her face, the sounds she gives me, the trust in her eyes as I take everything from her, reminding her how fucking good this is—nothing comes close to seeing that. It's honest and raw and fucking real.

This is the side of her I'll never stand a chance against. The side that has me saying shit I don't want her to know. Or almost saying it, until she interrupts me.

"Max, come on."

I follow behind him as he darts up the stairs to her level. He scratches on the door, pushing it open after a few thuds of his paw. I close and lock it the best I can, turning to see him go running down the hallway toward the bedroom.

"Fucking traitor," I scoff under my breath, pulling my T-shirt off and grabbing my phone and charger out of my duffle.

I plug them into the nearest outlet before collapsing on the couch, wincing as the metal frame digs into my back. I punch the pillow under my head three times, trying to make it somewhat useable, but it's uncomfortable as hell. As is the couch. I turn on my side, my back, my other side, trying to find some angle that will allow me at least a few hours of sleep.

I roll onto my stomach, only to find that position completely out of the question. My cock knows what's in the other room, and he also knows exactly what she wears to bed.

And I know just how comfortable that bed is, which is the only reason I'm walking down the hallway right now. Nothing else.

I stop in her doorway and take in the sight of her, illuminated by the hallway light. She's sprawled out like I'm used to seeing, tangled in the covers with her wild hair fanned out around her. I've never seen someone take up as much room as Tessa does in a bed. It doesn't seem possible, not with how tiny she is, but she does it, stretching her body like a damn starfish and looking way too sexy doing it.

She snores. She moves around constantly. She steals the comforter and talks in her sleep. Nothing about sharing a bed with her should be appealing, and if this were any other woman, I'd be waking up with the worst cramp after the shittiest night's sleep on the couch.

But this is Tessa.

Max lifts his head from where he's laying at the foot of the bed, stares at me for a few seconds, and resumes his position once he's done judging me for standing here right now.

Fuck you. You're just as bad.

I shift Tessa's cocooned body over so she's more on one side than both, and slide into bed, lying on my side and facing the window. The mattress shifts behind me, her breathing changes, and I wait for what I know is coming.

Tessa was always a talker in bed, with or without my cock involved.

"Luke?"

I close my eyes. "Yeah?"

"What are you doing?"

"What does it look like I'm doing? Your couch sucks."

She yawns, moaning softly at the end of it. My dick twitches.

"No it doesn't. My couch is very comfortable."

I fold the pillow over to boost my head up. "Then you go sleep on it."

"You can't seriously think sleeping in my bed is a good idea. Especially after what happened tonight."

"Tessa, roll over and go the fuck to sleep."

The mattress shifts again, she sighs heavily, and I feel the covers being pulled off me slowly. I grab them to keep a decent amount, which barely drapes over my hip.

"I need more covers," she says as she struggles to pull them.

My grip tightens. "You have most of them. Jesus fucking Christ. If you're that cold, put a damn hoodie on or something."

"I'm not *cold*. I'm naked."

I squeeze my eyes shut, dropping my hand to my dick to keep it from reacting. "What?" I ask, my voice tense and edgy. Goddamn it. Why does she have to wrap up in her blankets like a damn burrito? Who the fuck sleeps like that? If I had known she was naked in here, I wouldn't have walked in.

Yeah, okay, Luke. Keep telling yourself that.

She laughs, moving around behind me. "Naked. You know, without clothes."

"Why the hell are you naked? You always sleep in those tiny shorts that barely cover your ass and a tank top."

"You were the one who removed my clothes, remember? I was too tired to put anything on, and I wasn't expecting anyone to get in bed with me. If you have a problem with it, there's a couch with your name on it."

I exhale loudly, scooting as far to the edge of the bed as I can. "Seriously, put something on, Tessa."

"Seriously, get the fuck out, Luke. I'm not changing because *you* have a problem with sleeping on my couch."

I grab my tiny bit of covers and yank as hard as I can, hearing her yelp behind me. "If you want more to cover up with, go put clothes on. You're not hogging all the damn covers."

She moves behind me, sighing heavily after she settles. "Fuck you."

"Fuck you."

Silence surrounds us, but only for a few seconds. She grunts, shifts, and grunts again.

"Tessa," I warn.

"What?" she asks with a heated tone.

"Stop moving around and go to sleep."

"My neck hurts. I can't get comfortable."

My eyes flash open as I picture the marks on her neck, the faint bruising I saw when she was on the floor, panicked and shaken up. They aren't strongly visible, but they're definitely there.

I roll over onto my back and stare up at the ceiling. "Do you want some Advil or something? It'll probably help with the pain."

She doesn't respond and I turn my head, catching her wide eyes on me as she lies on her side, the covers pulled up to her neck. I swallow, struggling with the strongest urge I've ever had in me—one that demands I comfort her right now.

Just pull her into your arms and tell her it'll be okay.

"I was so scared," she finally says, her voice soft and guarded. Her gaze lowers to the space between us on the bed as I feel that familiar weight lay heavy on my chest. "What made you come here tonight? I mean, I know you didn't like the guy, but I heard your voice when you were trying to get in. You must've known something."

You. You made me come here.

I avert my gaze to the ceiling again. "I saw his license plate before he left the bonfire. Asshole was parked right in front of me."

"So, what? You used that to look him up?"

I nod. "I had a feeling that piece-of-shit was hiding something. I don't know. It's hard to explain. I just felt it. So when I got his plate number, I used that to search for him in our database. He had domestic charges filed against him, but they were dropped. Usually when that happens, the person who filed them is being threatened or doesn't want to make things worse for themselves. I've never had it be because the charges weren't valid. As soon as I saw his record, I came straight here."

"You saved my life," she states, matter-of-factly. Her lengthy pause has me glancing over at her, which I regret immediately. Even in the darkness, her eyes still hold me with an honesty I can't deal with right now. It's the way Tessa always used to look at me, back before she made me doubt everything we had.

She swallows noisily before licking her lips. "I don't know if I'll ever be able to thank you enough for that. But I promise I'll try. I know shit's complicated between us, but . . ."

I roll back over onto my side, cutting her sentence off. "I need to get some sleep. It's getting late."

What I *need* is to stop talking about this. I don't want her to know how scared I was, how I wouldn't have thought twice about killing that asshole if I had been a few minutes too late. How losing her would've crippled me, even though I've spent the last year wishing I had never met her.

I hear her amused laugh before the mattress shifts. "Luke

Evans. Shutting down when things get serious. Can't say I'm surprised."

I close my eyes. "Go to sleep, Tessa."

"Whatever."

I know I'm getting flipped off right now, and that causes a smile to touch my lips before everything around me fades to black.

I RUB MY eyes with one hand, while my other digs into the counter in front of me. I'm fucking drained after Tessa's sounds, movements, and sheer presence kept me up last night. If that wasn't bad enough, I, like a dumbass, forgot how she likes to wrap herself around me when she sleeps. The feel of her tits up against my back as I strained to keep myself from rolling over and sucking them into my mouth had my dick on high alert most of the night.

Sleep wasn't happening. Not until he calmed the hell down.

I kept thinking I would've been better off staying on that shitty couch, but even with those thoughts filtering into my fantasies about what I wanted to do to her in that bed, I didn't get up and leave. I stayed, enduring every shift of her body against mine, and somehow managing to keep my hand off my dick. If she had fucking clothes on, it wouldn't have been that bad.

Panties. That's all I was asking for. Jesus Fuck. Give me at least some sort of a barrier.

I hold my hand up, silencing the ramblings of the dipshit in front of me. "What do you mean, she has to pay for it? This is an apartment. You take care of maintenance issues, right?"

The manager behind the counter smiles, and flips through the contract in front of him. "Yes, we take care of maintenance issues that aren't the direct result of something brought on by one of our tenants. If she broke her door, she will have to pay for it." He turns the documents on the counter and shoves them across to me. "If you'd like to read the guidelines that every tenant signs as part of their contract, go for it."

I don't bother glancing down. If I read what he's spent the last five minutes explaining to me, I'll rip this shit up in front of him before I drag his ass over the counter.

"Aren't there clauses in that contract? She was attacked last night. It's not like she decided to take an axe to it 'cause of shitty management."

The older man glares at me over the top of his glasses, halting the odd stroking of his mustache that I've had to endure since I walked over here. "Excuse me?"

I lean in, flattening my hands on top of the documents I don't bother reading. "I broke her door. I had to get to her, and that shit was in my way. You can either replace it for her, or face a lawsuit when someone walks in to her very unsecure apartment."

He straightens up, a cunning grin smearing on his bloated face. "It clearly states in the contract she signed that I'm not responsible for anything her or a *guest* destroys. There will be no lawsuit, so don't stand there and threaten me with one." He slips the papers out from underneath my hands and tucks them in a folder. "Maybe you should pay for it, since you're the reason she no longer has a working one."

He turns away from me, sits back down in his chair, and raises the volume on the small TV that's sitting on the counter. I'm tempted to knock it off, to drag him out of here and watch as he replaces that door for her, but I know he's right. He doesn't have to pay for it. Money isn't the issue. It's not why I'm here. I have no problem buying Tessa a new door; I just can't handle her watching me while I install it.

Or me watching her while I install it.

I go to the nearest hardware store in town, hauling ass to get there. I left Tessa still in bed this morning, and I know she likes to sleep in, so I might be able to get this done before she wakes up. That's the only way this shit will work out in my favor. Get in and out before she engages me. I can do that.

My phone starts ringing the minute I step out of my truck. I look down at my screen, cursing at the name that flashes across it.

Goddamn it.

"Yeah?" I answer with zero interest in this phone call as I walk into the store.

"Hey, it's Jolene. Are you home right now?" Her overly flirtatious tone does nothing for me. It never has, but she plays it up anyway because she thinks I'll fuck her again.

I won't. I made that mistake four months ago. She caught me at a desperate moment when I couldn't shake Tessa from my thoughts and I needed a distraction. It was bad timing, really, and all Max's fault. If he hadn't needed to go outside at that exact moment, when the only thing I could think about was getting my dick wet, it wouldn't have happened. Not with her.

Don't fuck your neighbor unless you plan on continually fucking her. Trust me. It's not going to end well for you.

"No, I'm not home, and I won't be for a while. Why?"

She makes a soft pouting sound in my ear as I pay more attention to the door choices in front of me than anything coming out of her mouth. "I was wondering if I could come over and borrow your washing machine for a few hours. Mine is doing that weird thing again where it doesn't want to drain the water out of the drum. And I need to do laundry. Today.

I have, like, zero panties left, Luke. I'm not even wearing any right now."

I'm sure that last line was added for my benefit, but I don't react. I hold the phone between my ear and my shoulder as I work the locks on the door I'm examining, inspecting them for any defects.

"Luke?"

"What?" I twist the bolts again, clicking them into place. Five locks may seem excessive, but not to me. Not after last night, and if Tessa wants to bitch about it, she can go pick out her own door and do this shit herself.

She sighs in my ear. "I asked if I could use your washer. I can get by with just a few loads, so I won't even need to be that long. Can you just call me when you get home so I know when to come over?"

Hell no. Having Jolene in my house only leads to her throwing herself at me, and I'm not in the mood to watch her mope after I reject her again. But I don't want to be a dick about it. She's a nice girl; she's just clingy as fuck and wasting her time on me.

I grab the door and lean it against the wire racks before reaching up and gripping the phone in my hand. "Just go over and do it now. There's a keypad on the side of the garage. Enter the code 1533. It'll let you in the house."

"Oh . . . okay, I guess I can do that. I just thought maybe we could hang out or something while I waited."

I frown at the obvious disappointment in her voice. "Jolene . . ."

"Yeah?" she replies eagerly.

"I don't wanna hang out with you." I flinch at my own bluntness, but I don't know how else to spell this out for her. Forcing her hand off my dick sure as hell doesn't seem to be clear enough.

A soft *tsk* sound comes through the phone before her suddenly irritated voice. "You can be so conceited, you know that? I didn't mean I wanted to hang out naked."

"Really?" I ask, unconvinced.

"Yes, really."

"So the whole I'm-not-wearing-panties comment, what the fuck was that?"

She pauses briefly before responding. "Well, I mean, if we ended up naked, I'd be okay with that."

"Just lock up when you leave. All right?" I'm done with this conversation, and this chick. Thank fuck that detective position will require me to move. I can't deal with this shit much longer.

"God, whatever. Thanks a lot."

I hang up and slip the phone into my pocket before grabbing the door and taking it up to the register.

TESSA'S CAR IS gone when I get back to her apartment. This scenario is actually better than the one I was hoping for. Now I don't even need to worry about waking her up while I do this, and not having her naked down the hallway should help me focus and get this done before too long. I'll just need to meet up with her later to give her the new key, or I can leave it with that prick I talked to this morning.

That seems like the best idea. After what I allowed to happen yesterday, and the way I felt last night as I lay next to her, I need distance.

Lots of fucking distance.

tessa

I STRETCH MY arms above my head as my eyes adjust to the light streaming in through my window. I'm on Luke's side of the bed. No . . . not Luke's side. Jesus. The *other* side of the bed that he just so happened to occupy last night. A thought filters through my mind that has me sucking in a sharp breath.

Oh, God. Did I cling to him like I used to do? Seeking his warmth and the feel of his skin against mine was something I craved, even in sleep. I'd always end up scooting closer, never realizing I did it until I'd wake up with my body practically embedded in his. Wanting that connection to him at all times, even when I didn't do it consciously. But did I do it last night? Naked?

I cover my face with my hands and groan into them as I roll over onto my side.

You did, Tessa. You know you did.

But if I did, what did he do? Did he cuddle me back? Did he even look at me anymore after he abruptly ended our conversation? Luke was never one for PDA, but in bed, he indulged in tiny acts of affection. Even though he was probably only doing it to get comfortable, while I claimed as much of him as I could. Thinking it meant anything more to him was dangerous, comparable to handing over your heart and trusting him with it. The problem was, I'd wanted it to be true. I'd wake up with his arm draped over me, and his head buried in my hair, and I'd think . . . *this is it. This is what it's like to have all of him.*

I don't know if I got that side of him last night. The fact that I'm alone in bed could mean he didn't even stay with me. And although I'm glad he isn't how I'm used to seeing him in the mornings when he would sleep over, because that shit would seriously mess with my head, I need to talk to him. I don't care how much he's gonna hate it, we're talking about last night. All of it.

I PARK IN front of the garage and take the steps up to the landing, knocking on the door as my mind takes me back to the last time I was at this house. How nervous I was coming over here, thinking I was pregnant and not knowing what his reaction would be to that. In typical Luke fashion, my attempts to have an actual serious conversation were distracted with sex until I finally threw the question out between us that changed everything.

It's crazy how you can love a person and hate them at the same time. It shouldn't be possible, but I think the more you love someone, the easier they are to hate. I'm sure a lot of people can flip that switch and go from one extreme to the other, letting themselves forget every perfect moment as if it never happened, and look at the one person they held above everyone else as if they have no right to be on that pedestal. But apparently, I'm not one of those people. I left this house last summer hating the man I loved more than anything. Two emotions that have the capability to destroy me, and for the past year, I've let myself feel both.

The door opens and I tilt my head up expectantly, only to lower it a few inches as a slender blonde fills the doorway. She looks comfortable. Too comfortable, like she's just rolled out of Luke's bed and didn't care what little clothing she grabbed before coming to greet me.

What the fuck? Does Luke have a chick living with him? My stomach rolls and drops out beneath me as I process why she would be answering his door.

A perfectly manicured hand goes to her hip where her fingers begin to strum the material of her camisole. She gives my outfit a scrutinizing once-over, pops the piece of hot-pink gum in her mouth, and gives me *the look*.

You know, the look girls give other girls when they're staking a claim on a guy. That unspoken threat of "I will seriously punch you in your ovaries if you so much as look at my boyfriend again." Yeah, that look, and it's all the confirmation I need as the reasoning behind her presence becomes clear.

That fucking asshole has a girlfriend.

"Who are you?" I ask, concealing all the guilt and hurt I don't want to acknowledge and only letting myself react to the overwhelming jealousy that's coursing through my system. It's a natural reaction I can't ignore, one that has me sounding entitled to the information she's about to give me as I mimic her position with a hand on my hip, but doing it in a classy way. I, unlike her, am at least wearing a bra.

Her plum-colored lips curl up sadistically. "Jolene. Who are you?"

"Tessa."

Her eyes widen with interest. "Really?" She looks me over once more, this time with more curiosity. "So you're the big regret, huh?"

My hand slips from my side as I stare, stunned and wounded from the sucker-punch she just delivered, because that's exactly what it feels like. An unexpected blow from a chick who seems to know exactly who I am.

I struggle to keep my breathing steady, to seem unaffected by this, but I fear I'm failing as the air leaves my lungs in a shuddering rush. This shouldn't upset me. I shouldn't care what he labels me, but this, what I'm feeling right now, this is different, and I can't act like I didn't just hear those words slip past her fake-as-shit lips. I'm used to feeling certain emotions involving Luke, no matter how hard I've tried to push them away, but right now, my chest is pulsing with a new pain, something unlike anything I've ever felt, and I know it's because the man that never once shared any of his feelings with me has apparently confided in this woman. She's staring at me like she knows everything; all the secrets he kept from me, the parts of him I wanted that I thought were off-limits to everyone. Believing that made it easier, acceptable, at the time. But maybe it was just me, standing alone on the other side of the wall he put up.

I was the only one he wanted to keep out.

"Shocked he told me that?" She pops her gum again, looking almost proud of herself for knowing that information. "You know how guys like to open up after sex. Put 'em between your legs and they'll tell you practically anything. And he had a lot to say about you."

I could sulk right now, focus solely on the throbbing discomfort that's causing my heartbeat to slow as if it's struggling as much as I am. But the entitled look on this chick's face, the way she's practically begging me to cut her down to size—*that* I'm more than happy to put all my energy into. I've yet to meet a bitch that can outwit me, and I seriously doubt this gum-smacking bimbo is about to take that title.

"You sound happy about that," I state, before shaking my head. "I'd hate a guy to be balls deep in me while they're talking about another woman. Unless of course that other woman is actually participating." I arch my brow suggestively. "You must be rather boring."

Her sly demeanor fades in front of my eyes as she straightens up in the doorway, the obvious distaste for what I've just said hardening her features. "He only mentioned you after he was satisfied. By me."

Wow. She's not making this difficult for me. I almost feel bad for what I'm about to say.

Almost.

I smile, ready to silence this bitch. "If Luke can remember any name but yours after you've *satisfied* him—" I accompany my sarcasm with a delicious set of air quotes, "—you're doing it wrong. Let me know if you want me to show you how it's done."

"I know what I'm doing. Thanks."

"Clearly." I tap my chin with my finger. "What's your name again? I forgot, and Luke didn't bring you up last night."

Her eyes narrow in on mine as she grips the doorknob, ready to shut me out. "When he comes home, I'll have him call you while I'm riding him. He'll be saying it a lot."

"Your name's Tessa's too?" I ask, obnoxious smile accompanying my fake enthusiasm. "That's crazy! We should totes hang out sometime. I can show you this move I like to do with Luke that drives him completely nuts. Trust me. He'll be screaming my name so fucking loud when you do it to him, the entire state will know who I am."

Her mouth drops open, displaying the hot-pink wad of gum she stopped popping like an idiot once I got my shit together and put her in her place. She tries to regain her snotty self-control, but I don't miss the way her knuckles turn white as her hand grips the doorknob.

"Whore," she finally says after being shocked into silence for a good minute.

I shrug. "I prefer lady of the evening, but I understand if your vocabulary is a bit limited. That high school diploma is a *bitch* to get."

I see the anger in her boil to the surface, flushing her cheeks. "I'll be sure to tell Luke you stopped by, after I'm done fucking him." She backs into the house, slamming the door hard enough that it causes the glass panel to rattle.

My face falls, and I drop the victorious smirk I'm wearing as I step off the landing.

I should feel good right now. I just schooled that bitch and I did it without breaking much of a sweat. But now I have nothing distracting me from the wound that's commanding my attention.

Thunder claps overhead, and I glance up at the sky that's now ten shades darker than the light blue color I noticed stepping out of my apartment. I get into my car just after the first drops of rain hit my shoulder, wetting the thin material of my tank top. Pulling out of the driveway, I head down the street I never want to be on again. The one I should've avoided today.

The rain comes down in buckets, limiting my vision as I try and see the road in front of me. I'm relieved when I'm able to pull off of the busy main street and onto the back road leading to my apartment building. I can barely see anything, and having other cars around me is making that problem dangerous. The thunder startles me every time I hear it, cracking so loud it feels as if I'm submerged in the storm cloud. The only thing visible is the illuminated road in front of my headlights. Nothing else around me stands out as I lean closer to the wheel and look to the sky for an expected lightning strike, signaling the next crash of thunder. The sound of a horn blaring startles me, snapping my focus to the road as a large pick-up truck comes flying at me.

"FUCK!"

I swerve to my left, pulling off into the grass and slamming on my breaks as the maniac driver with no headlights flies by me. My hands grip the wheel, my chest heaving with quick, sharp breaths as I try and relax. I turn and look out my back window, but all I see is darkness.

That fucker didn't even stop? He runs me off the road and he doesn't even check to make sure I'm okay?

Why am I even surprised? I'm sure it was a man driving that thing, and all men in the state of Alabama are complete dickheads. Except the ones I'm related to.

I press on the gas to pull back onto the road but my tires spin. The car jerks forward as I push the pedal to the floor, but nothing happens. I'm stuck.

"You've got to be kidding me."

I swing my door open, letting the rain beat down on me as I lean out and examine my tire. Only half of it is visible, the other half swallowed up by the mud. I slam my door shut and grab my phone, dialing Reed's number. Four rings and his voicemail picks up.

"Hey, leave a . . ."

I disconnect the call and dial my parents, cringing when their answering machine picks up. Both of their cell phones go straight to their voicemails and I'm on the verge of tears as I scroll through my contacts, looking for someone else to call. Ben and Mia won't be back from Georgia until late tonight, so they're off-limits. I need someone with a pick-up truck who could help pull me out, and there's one option, one person besides my brother and Reed who could be useful, but you couldn't pay me to call him right now.

I do an Internet search of the closest tow company and dial them instead.

"Rick's automotive," the man on the other line answers.

Thunder claps again, startling me before I can reply. "Hi, I'm going to need a tow truck to come get me. My car's stuck."

"Where are you, miss?"

I look out my window for any sign of how close I am to the main road. "Umm, I'm on Moravia. I think . . . I don't know, maybe five miles from O'Donnell Street. Could be less."

I hear the sound of a soda can opening. "Pretty backed up today. Lot of people gettin' stuck." The sound of him slurping comes through the phone, followed by his quenched sigh. "Might be able to be there in a couple hours."

I sag in my seat. "A couple hours? I can't sit here that long on this road. You can't see anything and I'm barely pulled off. Someone could hit me."

"It's the best I can give ya. Put your flashers on and we'll be there when we can."

I close my eyes and bite back my tears. "Fine. Do you need my keys? I really don't want to wait here."

"Just leave them under the floor mat. We'll call ya when somebody gets there."

"All right. Thank you,"

"Yup."

I end the call and arch my back, sliding the phone into my jeans pocket. I turn the car off and place the keys under the mat before hanging over my seat, praying for an umbrella to magically appear from somewhere. I know for a fact I've never bothered to put one in here but it would be fucking awesome if God could just throw me a bone right now. But no. Let's make this day suck even more for Tessa, and give her absolutely no protection from the elements.

I turn back around and swing the door open, stepping out into the mother-of-all rainstorms. The muddy river my boots sink into is slow moving and thick, like oatmeal that needs more water. I slam my door closed and struggle to get around the car, grabbing onto the hood for leverage to pull my feet out of the mud. Once I get onto the gravel in front of the hood, I stomp my feet, removing some of the muck as the rain beats down on the back of my head. I turn my head up and let it soak my front, my shirt and jeans clinging to me within seconds. It's a cold rain, and my teeth chatter as I stand there and allow myself to get used to the feel of it. The water pelts against my skin like ice, and suddenly, the air around me seems to drop in temperature. Five miles is going to take forever, but I can't wait in the car for the tow. Not for as long as he says it'll take them. And especially not with assholes like the one who ran me off the road driving out here today. So, I'm walking, freezing or not, 'cause my only other option is calling Luke, and that's not happening.

A few cars pass me as I stay as far to the side of the road as I can without trudging through the mud. No one stops to ask if I need a ride—not that I'd take it. But the decency factor is missing today from everyone making the trek down Moravia.

I don't know how long I've been walking, but given the ache in my feet I'm going to guess at least fifteen minutes. That's usually how long these boots allow before I'm cursing myself for ever buying them. My hands tremble as I cup them in front of my mouth and attempt to breathe life into them, but even the air in my lungs seems frigid now, like the rest of me. Another car drives by me and I ignore it like the others, until the sound of it skidding to a stop prompts me to look over my shoulder. The reverse lights come on before the truck backs up in my direction.

The silver truck I'm way too familiar with.

I walk faster, suddenly not giving a shit about the rain and how slick it's made the pavement. I could slip and knock myself unconscious, but even the threat of that seems better than this chance meeting.

The truck creeps into my peripheral vision but I ignore it, keeping my attention in front of me.

"Tessa?"

I ignore that also as the rain continues pelting down, loud enough to distort the voice I don't want to hear. I push the hair that's plastered to the side of my face back and tuck it behind my ear.

The truck moves with me, staying at my side. "What are you doing? Where's your car?"

"Fuck off!" I yell.

The engine revs again as I quicken my pace.

"What the fuck? Look at you. Get in. You're going to catch pneumonia or some shit."

I turn my head and glare at him through the sheet of rain, straining my neck to see up into his truck. "I'd rather catch pneumonia than be anywhere near you! Go fuck yourself, you piece of shit!"

The back end of the truck whips off the road, backing into the mud and blocking my path. I round the front of it with determination just as a door slams shut.

"Are you fucking crazy?" He grabs my arm and spins me around, keeping his grip on my elbow as the rain soaks the front of him. Water runs down his face, grazing the bump in his nose, and beading up on the stubble along his jawline. His other hand runs down my arm and he frowns. "Jesus, Tessa. You're freezing. We need to get you dry."

"*We* don't need to do anything." I yank my arms out of

his grasp. "Get back in your truck and get the hell outta here. You're just slowing me down." I barely turn away when his hands find my waist, hauling me against his side and moving me in the direction of his truck. I twist my body, trying to elude him. "Luke! Stop it!"

His grip stays firm, forcing me to move. "You're not walking on the side of the road. Nobody can see shit out here and someone could hit you. *I* barely saw you."

I wrench myself from his grasp and push against his soaked chest. My hands slide along the material, and I resort to pounding my fists against him to keep my palms from clinging to his muscles.

Because they would. They like doing that.

I take in a shaky breath before admitting, "I'm so sick of it being *you* who sees me. Stop seeing me! Just stop!"

He drops his head down and grabs my wrists, pulling me closer. Water builds up on his bottom lip, and I struggle to avert my gaze to anywhere but his mouth. If I keep looking, I'll run my thumb across it. My tongue. Trap the drops between his skin and mine and feel them burst against my mouth. I blink heavily before focusing on his eyes, catching the quick shift of his attention off the very thing I was just fantasizing about.

"Do you think I *want* to see you?" he asks, the frustrated anger resonating off his words. "If I could've stopped, I would've fucking done it a year ago. I always see you, Tessa, and I'm not leaving you on the side of the road. So get the fuck over yourself, and get in the truck."

I bite my lip to stop it from trembling before shaking my head. "Just leave, Luke. Please. Please don't do any more for me."

He releases one of my wrists and runs a hand down his face. His eyes pinch closed for a moment as he thinks something over. "You wanna make this difficult? Fine." His hands grab my waist, lifting me off the ground and carrying me around the front of his truck.

I flail as much as I can, pushing against his shoulders and trying to peel my front away from his. He mumbles how challenging I am, how he doesn't need this shit. I open my mouth to protest but my voice cracks like ice being stepped on as he shifts me in his arms to open the door. I'm shoved inside and the door is slammed shut as the rain pelts on the windows.

My entire body trembles as I rock in my seat, seeking warmth, keeping my head in my hands as my knees knock together. I'm going into shock. This has to be what that feels like. My body is shutting down because I can't get warm. I think I hear the door open over the chatter of my teeth and the loud whoosh of air I push into my hands, but I can't be sure.

Not until I feel the slide of his hand along my back.

luke

I SLAM THE passenger door shut as the rain continues to beat down on me.

Of course this has to happen. It has to be Tessa on the side of the road, and not some chick I can ignore. I'd gone all morning without seeing her, installing her door and thinking I was in the fucking clear, and now, this. She's out of her fucking mind if she thinks I'll leave her here. I can't. It's not physically possible. My instincts take over the second I realize it's her, commanding me to stop, to grab her, and to put her defiant ass in the truck myself. I don't know why the fuck she's walking out here, but I do know she isn't walking anymore.

I brace myself for the fight I know we're about to have as I step up into my truck, shutting the door behind me. But it's not her verbal lashing grabbing my attention the moment I get inside. It's her, rocking back and forth in the seat, trembling so badly I fear something worse than pneumonia. Her teeth chatter as she keeps her head down, body almost folded in half. I don't think about what touching her does to me. I can suck that shit up and deal with the ramifications of my actions later, because the only thing that matters right now is getting her warm.

My hand slides along her back, startling her with a jolt that blends into her tremors. We're both drenched, but she's colder than me, frigid even. I swear to Christ my hand drops in temperature ten degrees just from the gentle pressure I'm giving her. I need something to wrap her up with, so I grab the beach towel I keep in here for days I go to Rocky Point.

I drop it next to me and grab the bottom of her shirt with both hands.

"We need to get you out of these clothes. Lift your arms."

She pushes me off and slides closer to the door. "J . . . j . . . just t . . . t . . . take me home, Luke. I'll g . . . g . . . get warm th . . . th . . . there."

I don't have time for this. She doesn't have time for this.

I rip her shirt off, throwing the dripping material on the floor as she fights me every inch of the way. I reach for her boots to remove them but she kicks at me.

"S . . . s . . . stop it! Luke, what . . ."

I grab her ankles, pinning her legs against the seat in between us, and lean closer. "Tessa, you're fucking freezing. Wrapping you up in this towel isn't going to do shit unless you take these clothes off, so stop fucking fighting me and let me do this. I *have* to do this."

She slouches against the window, her body going limp in surrender. "Why?" she asks, so soft I almost miss it.

I look up at her as I pull off her one boot, then the other. My eyes search her face before I finally admit, "Why did I spend my entire morning putting in a door for a girl I'm not supposed to care about? Why do I do everything?" I drop my gaze to her legs. "It's you, Tessa. Nobody else would've made me stop."

My eyes pinch shut for a moment before I toss her socks to the floor.

Smart. Admit you're still hard up on her. Really smart.

"You p . . . put in a new d . . . door for me?"

"Yeah. Your key is with that dickhead manager." I refocus

and unbutton her jeans, sliding them off and discarding them with the rest of her clothing. I'm able to wrap the towel around her twice as I shift closer, pulling her up so she's sitting next to me.

I push her hair out of her face, feeling her lean into my touch, and I suddenly don't want to drop my hand.

Her eyes, full of unshed tears, draw me in, and slide me even closer to her until she's right up against me. I don't fight the commanding need in me that wants to be with her right now. I don't block it out with memories of our past. I let myself indulge in this. In her.

"Hey," I whisper, afraid if I speak any louder, she'll pull away from me. "What is it? Are you still cold?"

"Why her, Luke? Why does she g . . . get you like that?" she asks, blinking and sending the tears down her face as the quiver in her jaw seems to settle.

I stare, confused, shifting my body so I'm looking at her straight on. "What are you talking about? Why does who get me?"

"What all do you give her? Everything? Does she even have to ask for it?"

Maybe she's actually in shock right now, because she sure as hell isn't making any sense.

I lift her chin that's dropped down, meeting her eyes. "Tessa, I don't . . ."

Her hands spring out from underneath the towel and grab the bottom of my shirt, lifting it up to mid-chest. "Does she get this?" Her finger grazes the name on the side of my ribcage. "Does she? Did you tell her who this is?" she asks, her voice breaking as she pushes against me, separating the connection we just had. She takes in a loud breath before yelling, "I wanted this! I had you for three months and I begged you! I fucking begged you, Luke! And she gets it? Why? Why, goddamn it? I gave you everything! I never held back with you and I got nothing." Her movements slow, the force of her hands weakening as her sobs fill the inside of the truck.

I grab her shoulders and push her back so I can see her. "Who? What the fuck are you talking about?"

"Jolene," she cries. "You slept with me last night and you have a girlfriend? And you tell her shit about me? Fuck you! I hate you! I fucking hate you."

She tries to get out of my grip but I hold her in place, pulling her closer as her hands fist my T-shirt. "Goddamn it! Stop fighting me!" She squirms more and I pin her against me, wrapping my arms around her body. "Calm the fuck down a minute. Jesus Christ. She's my neighbor, Tessa. What, did you go over my house or something? Is that where you're coming from?"

She nods.

"She's not . . ." I pause, taking in her guarded expression. Like she's actually afraid of my answer. "Why do you care who she is? You ended us. You're the fucking reason why I hooked up with her in the first place."

"So you *are* sleeping with her. You fucking dick!" she grits out, and the entitled look on her face, like I owe her this information and so much more, causes me to break.

All the anger I've reserved for this woman boils to the surface, and I'm suddenly not concerned with keeping her fucking warm anymore. I don't care that she looks shattered, on the verge of more tears and struggling to keep herself from falling apart completely.

I drop my head, getting as close as I can get to her face without touching her. Her eyes go wide as she stops breathing, and I feel the resistance leave her body as she practically melts against me.

"I'm not sleeping with her. I fucked her. Once. And it was empty. Just like all the other pussy I've had the past year. I don't feel anything when I'm with them. I don't even see them. I see you. *I taste you*. And when they ask me who Tessa is, because that's the only name I'm saying in their ear, you wanna know what I tell them?"

She sniffs loudly and her lip trembles, but she doesn't answer. And I don't wait for her to, either.

I lean closer, brushing my nose against her cheek and up to her temple. "I tell them she's the worst fucking thing that ever happened to me, and I can't let her go."

I lose all control, all reserve, and crash my lips against hers, moaning the second I feel her skin. She whimpers through a gasp, but she doesn't fight it. Her head tilts with the guidance of my hand and she parts her lips with a sigh. I run my tongue along her lip, dipping into her mouth and tasting—no, more than that—fucking devouring her like it's been longer than a year. Like I've never had this. Her hands slip underneath my shirt, teasing my skin as I shift her into my lap.

She breaks away, panting, her lips pink and swollen. "Luke . . ."

"I'm kissing you, Tessa. Don't tell me not to," I say against her mouth before pressing my lips along her jaw.

Her throaty laugh vibrates against me as I taste the skin of her neck.

"We're on the side of the road. Actually, not even on the side. You're kinda blocking half of it."

"Don't care."

"We could get hit."

"Don't care," I repeat, opening up her towel so it falls around her waist. My eyes take in the sight of her, and I'm reminded that this, fuck me, *this* is why I haven't been able to move on. The delicate rise of her chest. Her skin, flushed and unmarked, such a contrast to mine. Not that she wouldn't look damn sexy with some ink. I trail my finger down her cleavage, dropping my head and licking along her collarbone. Her fingers curl around my neck as I lift her up, burying my face in her chest.

I shift us so my back is against the seat and she's straddling my waist. The towel is discarded, along with her bra, and she scratches along my scalp the second my tongue slides over her nipple. She whimpers when I bite down, and I smile against her skin, brushing my nose against her other breast.

"Luke," she says, breathlessly, sliding her hands down to my shoulders and fisting the material of my shirt.

I move, allowing her to pull my shirt over my head. Then her lips are on me, frantic, greedy, and tasting as much of my skin as she can before settling over the tattoo on my chest. I look down, watching as she traces over the letter with her tongue, catching the smirk on the corner of her lips before they press against me.

"Fuck," I groan as she palms my cock.

I fist the material of her panties and pull, her gasp mixing with the loud rip I create.

"Put your weight on your knees," I order as I pop the button on my jeans. She hovers over me, and I slide my pants and boxers down before grabbing her waist with one hand and the base of my cock with the other. I rub the head against her clit, sliding into her wetness.

"Oh my God, yes," she purrs.

She looks down between us, tilting her pelvis, rocking into me. Her lips brush against mine, giving me her moans. "Condom?" she asks, releasing my bottom lip from between her teeth.

I tighten my grip on her waist and hold her still. "Shit. Stop moving."

"Why?"

"Because I'm two seconds away from driving straight into you."

She groans, wiggles forward, and teases me again. "You started it."

"Tessa, I'm fucking serious. I don't have any condoms."

Her head tilts back, lips parting with a moan as she grinds against me, making this more unbearable than satisfying.

What the fuck? Is she trying to kill me?

"Tessa." I warn, gritting my teeth. "I swear to Christ. You can't . . ."

"Do you want to stop?" she asks, her voice husky and teetering on the edge of playful. Like she knows she has me by the balls here, or more accurately, the cock.

Her chest brushes up against mine and I feel my hold on her loosening in position, sliding up her back. Giving in to this torment.

"I don't want to stop, Luke." Her lips press to my ear, and the moment she flattens her chest against mine, I feel the wild beating of her heart. Like she just ran a mile to get to me. "Please," she rasps, kissing the skin of my neck. "I wanna feel you. Just pull out, okay?"

I dig my fingers into her hip, positioning her where I want her, regaining control, 'cause she's done playing and I'm going to take her how I want to take her.

I support all her weight, sliding her down my cock, feeling her body surrender as I draw this out. Reminding her what this feels like. I rock her hips into me, moving her in a slow rhythm. Her eyes close when I run my lips over her breast, full and soft, her nipples hardened, begging for my tongue.

"Mmm, you're so thick," she moans, grabbing my head, holding me against her.

I release her nipple and press my thumb to her lips. "Open. Get it wet."

Her lips wrap around my thumb, sucking me, and when she adds her tongue, the slow burn in my groin begins to spread up my spine. I thrust my hips off the seat, and the second her lips open with cry, I drag my thumb down her body and press it against her clit.

Her head falls back as she softly chants my name, desperately, like she needs me as much as what I'm giving her. I feel her body tense, the familiar pulse of her around me.

"Coming," she whispers.

I ride it out as long as I can before my spine feels as if it's about to snap. I lift her hips, shifting her back on my thighs, and watch as she takes over rubbing her clit, her eyes focused on my cock as I stroke it against her fingers.

"Fuckkkk," I grunt, coming on both our hands, seeing the sated look in her eyes grow hungry as she stares, transfixed, between us. I clean us both off with my T-shirt before she shifts off my lap, falling limp in the seat next to me. Pulling up my jeans, I resituate myself before looking over at her.

Her eyes are on me, wide and unsure.

I reach over and grab the towel, wrapping it around her shoulders, feeling her stare as I cover her up completely.

"I'm sorry I didn't tell you." She waits until I look up at her to elaborate, her face tense with guilt. "Last summer . . . I only thought I was pregnant for a couple of days, but you still had every right to know."

"Yeah, I did," I reply, sounding more resentful than I feel right now.

She nods at my words, dropping her gaze to her lap. "I think about that day a lot. What I would've done different. What I would've said. It's crazy; I couldn't tell you what that asshole was wearing last night, but I remember everything about that day." Her eyes lift to mine, and I break the contact, shifting over in my seat and starting up my truck. "Do you think about it?"

My eyes pinch shut as I grip the back of my neck, debating how honest I want to be right now. I could tell her I think about it all the time, and the longer I go in between seeing her, the more I think about it. I could say I replay every second I had with her that weekend in my head; when I'd fucked her all night and into the morning—how we couldn't get enough of each other, as if we both knew that it would be the last time. How I'd felt having her in my arms, calm and settled for the first time in my life, and how I'd felt the second she pulled away from me. Like I'd repulsed her; like what we'd had was something I'd made up. The tears in her eyes when she'd told me she hated me, and the ones in mine when I'd sat there, alone, wondering what the hell had happened. Feeling like I was just told I'd never be able to take another breath.

What the fuck good would that much honestly do? For either one of us?

I turn to her, one hand on the wheel, the other on my gear shift, and give her the only answer I can.

"I'm thinking about it right now."

She looks at me with understanding before facing forward in her seat.

Christ. Even that admission seems to rattle something loose in me. I shake my head, clearing out the bullshit I don't want to think about, and pull out onto the road, driving in the direction I was headed before I stopped.

"Why were you walking on the side of the road? Where's your car?" I ask, breaking the silence.

She sighs heavily, and I catch the annoyed look on her face before I focus on the road, squinting through the sheets of rain.

"Some asshole ran me off the road up here. I called for a tow but they said it could be a few hours, and I decided walking was safer than sitting in my car."

I shake my head. "That was stupid. You could've gotten hit."

"I could've gotten hit in my car, too. I'm barely pulled off."

Okay, true, but I'm not agreeing to that. I almost took another way home and would've missed her, so her ass should've stayed in her car. She would've at least had something to protect her.

"See," she says, pointing at the window in front of us. "There's my car. Look how much of it is still on the road."

I drive past it, turning up the speed on my windshield wipers when the rain starts to pick up again.

"Um, aren't you going to tow me out?"

"I don't have my rope in here. I took it out this morning when I had to drop Max off at the vet. His dumbass chews on it if it's in the back."

She laughs, soft and perfect. "Of course he does. Anything to annoy you, right?"

I ignore that truthful statement, turning off the side road and onto the main strip. "Call the tow company. Tell them to take your car to my house." I turn my head after she doesn't respond, not with words or some muffled sound of disapproval.

She tucks a strand of hair behind her ear. "Why am I going to your house?"

I look back at the road. "Because that's where I'm taking you."

"Why?"

"Because I am."

"Okay, but why?"

I scratch the side of my face, thinking back to my words when I brought my duffle to her apartment last night. How I didn't want to take her to my house and the reason behind it, which seems obsolete right now.

I open my mouth to give her some vague answer, most likely bullshit, but she interrupts me with a heavy sigh.

"It's fine. Whatever. You have better food anyway." She bends forward and grabs her jeans off the floorboard, tugging out her phone. "Oh crap." She holds in the button on the side, but the screen stays black.

I pull my phone out of my pocket. "Here."

After Tessa calls the tow company, the rest of the drive is made in silence, or as much silence as being in a vehicle with her allows. She hums softly to herself, some song I know I've heard on the radio but can't place, and only stops when I pull into the driveway. I open the garage door and park my truck, grabbing her wet clothes and my T-shirt off the floorboard and depositing everything into the washing machine after I empty her pockets. I remove the battery out of her cell and set everything on top of the dryer.

"Your phone should be fine. Just give it a couple of hours before you put the battery back in."

After starting the load, I see her waiting for me in front of the door that leads into the house.

Her body is wrapped up in the towel, which she opens slightly the moment I step in front of her, granting me access. I slide my hands around her waist to her back, pulling her against me.

She tilts her head up. "Luke?"

"Yeah?"

"If I come in, I might . . . actually, I know . . ." She blinks heavily, struggling to find the words. "I know I'll . . ."

I tilt my head, forming my mouth to hers. "Just come in, Tessa. Don't overthink it. I want you here."

I back her up the steps, opening the door as her tongue slides into my mouth. The towel is dropped somewhere between the living room and kitchen as I wrap her legs around my waist and carry her upstairs.

"God, I love how you kiss," she says against my mouth as we reach my bedroom doorway.

I pin her against the doorframe, swallowing her tiny squeal before taking control of her mouth and fucking owning it. It's how I've always kissed Tessa, only her, and I'd do it for hours right now if the sound of a throat clearing didn't pull me out of it.

I look over in the direction of the noise, as does Tessa, both of us panting, caught up, but still able to focus on the person who interrupted us.

Naked.

In my bed.

Where she's never belonged.

I GLARE AT the skank I should've knocked out hours ago as she lays propped up on her elbow, facing us. She's topless, covers barely draped over her, a twisted smile in place. I'd be angry if this attempt to seduce Luke wasn't the perfect blend of desperate and amusing. No guy wants to come home to a botched boob job waiting for him, one that just so happens to be in a very unflattering position. Especially when he's just spent the last half hour worshipping the fantastic pair that belong to me.

I wiggle in Luke's arms, loosening his hold on me so I can slide down to my feet.

"What the fuck are you doing in here?" he asks, stepping into the room and keeping me behind him.

I try to move next to him, not giving a shit if this chick sees me naked or not, but Luke darts an arm out and pushes me back. I huff loudly, earning myself a warning look over his shoulder. It's brief, but intimidating nonetheless. Of course, that doesn't stop me from standing on my toes and exaggerating my stare, wide-eyed and apparently humorous, given the smile that touches his lips before he turns back around.

"You said you needed to do laundry. I don't remember hearing anything about you wanting to take a fucking nap. Don't you have a bed?"

Her low, obnoxious laugh fills the room. "You know I do,

baby. You've been in it."

Oh, hell no. I was content on staying behind Luke for the time being, mainly because the back of him shirtless is just as insanely attractive as the front, but it looks like this bitch forgot her place, and I have no problem being the one to put her back in it.

I shove Luke's arm out of my way and move next to him, not bothering to cover myself up because I really don't give a shit. Besides, I'm sure she hasn't seen a pair of real tits in years, and while I'm at it, I might as well make this verbal beat-down educational.

See this? It's what a nipple is supposed to look like.

I hold my hand out, palm up, motioning toward the bed. "You know, we just started a load. Now those STD-riddled sheets are going to have to wait at least an hour before they can be disinfected." I sweep my gaze down her body, grimacing. "*Heavy* disinfected. And, honestly, I'm not even sure bleach can handle this situation."

"Do you ever get tired of running your mouth?" she asks.

I flatten my hand to my chest. "Me? No, I never get tired of *anything* involving my mouth." I hitch a thumb toward Luke. "Neither does he."

"Tessa," Luke warns.

I shrug, gathering my hair over one shoulder and twirling pieces of it. "What? You don't."

He gathers the clothes off the floor and tosses them onto the bed. "Get dressed and get the fuck out of my house. And next time your washer goes up, go to the Laundromat, or buy a new one. Don't ask to come over here again."

She sits up, shock setting into her features and tightening the lines of each and every one of her wrinkles. "What? But I thought . . ."

He points his finger at her. "You thought what? That I'd come home, find you in my bed, and actually consider fucking you again? Even if she wasn't here—" He gestures toward me with a nod, "—your ass would've been thrown out. I told you, I'm not interested. The only reason why I even looked at you before was because I needed a distraction. From her." He turns his head, locking eyes with me, and I feel my mouth go dry.

I blink several times; in fact, that's the only thing I can seem to do at the moment. He stares at me for what feels like minutes instead of seconds, keeping himself perfectly still while I feel the hand submerged in my hair begin to tremble.

"I don't want any more distractions," he states, standing up a bit taller.

Whoa.

I try to swallow, to produce any amount of saliva, but my tongue suddenly feels as if it has doubled in size. His forehead creases, just below his hairline, like he's studying my reaction to what he's just said. I'm not sure what he's seeing, but I feel like I probably look completely mental right now. I know I'm not moving, I'm barely breathing, and I'm naked. Very naked. I hear movement in the room, covers shuffling, some low, muffled noises, but I can't peel my eyes off Luke. Not while he's looking at me like that.

"Move."

He shifts over, allowing Jolene to push past him and continue in my direction. She knocks purposely into my shoulder, meaningful scowl in place, before exiting the room with an exaggerated grunt.

I flatten my back against the door as Luke eliminates the space between us with two long strides. "I'll be right back. I just wanna make sure she leaves."

I drop my head into a partial nod. "'Kay."

'Kay? I can't even manage to put an "o" in front of that? Has the ability to pronounce a simple vowel escaped me?

He places a gentle hand on my arm, just above my elbow, squeezes, and slips out of the bedroom, leaving my hopeless vocabulary and me alone.

I shake my hands at my sides, blowing out a quick breath.

Christ. Get your shit together, Tessa. It's not like he dropped the *L* bomb. He simply looked at you with unashamed honesty, and confessed . . . what? That he's doesn't want to get his mind off me anymore? That he's done hooking up with other women? Or did he just mean he doesn't want to have sex with Jolene again?

I let my head fall into my hands with a heavy sigh.

Shit. You're overthinking things. Knock it off.

I walk over to Luke's dresser, grabbing a pair of boxer briefs and one of his worn T-shirts to slip into. As I'm popping my head through the top, I spot a glass container sitting next to his bedside lamp, full of guitar picks. I sit on the bed with it, holding it up and staring at the contents. I don't remember ever seeing this in Luke's room before, but most of the picks in the jar look used. The logos are faded, the designs barely visible, and some of them are even chipped along the edges. As I'm fishing through the jar, letting the picks clink against the glass, something else catches my attention.

A guitar case, black and covered in stickers, is leaning against the wall in the corner. I place the jar down and move across the room, crouching down to examine it. The stickers on the case are peeling off, and I run my finger over the edge of one, pressing it down to try and reattach it. My curiosity becomes too much to ignore, and I lay the case down and pop the snaps, flipping the lid back.

"What are you doing?"

The unexpected sound of Luke's voice sends me falling back onto my ass, striking my upper back against corner of the dresser. "Ow. Son of a bitch."

"You okay?"

I reach back and rub my shoulder, looking up at him just as he takes a bite of something he's holding between his thumb and finger. "Yeah, I'm fine." I push to my feet and glance between the open case and him. "Do you play the guitar?"

He shakes his head, takes a few steps toward me, and kicks the case closed. "No. Here, they dropped your car off."

I take the keys and set them on his nightstand next to the jar of picks. "Why do you have all these, then? Do you like collecting them or something?" I turn my head when he doesn't answer, just in time to see him pop the last bite of a cookie-dough square into his mouth. His attention is on my outfit, with raised brows and a brazen smile twisting across his lips.

"Luke."

"Babe," he replies after swallowing his bite.

I roll my eyes at the title he always used to label me with. In private. "Can you look at me please?"

"I am looking at you. Are you wearing my boxers?" He lifts the hem of the T-shirt I'm wearing, exposing my left hip. "That's fucking hot."

I'm quickly tossed onto the bed, and the moment my head crashes down on the pillow, a cloud of Whores-R-Us perfume surrounds me. I cover my nose and mouth with my hands, rolling to the edge, and wiggling off. "Ugh, gross. Your sheets smell horrible."

Luke bends down and grabs a handful of his sheet, bringing it up to his nose. He gathers them up, mumbling something under his breath, and takes them out of the room, returning moments later with a clean set. "Sorry," he says, meeting my eyes.

I shrug, watching as he makes the bed, leaving the covers turned down before looking over at me for approval. I scramble back onto the bed and lean against the headboard as he reaches for the button on his jeans.

"So, why do you have a guitar here and all those picks if you don't play?"

His eyes go to the floor where the case remains closed but unlatched. "I just do."

"Why?"

"Tessa . . ." His chest heaves with a deep breath as his eyes reach mine. "I just fucking have them, okay? People accumulate all kinds of shit that doesn't mean anything to them. It's just here."

I stare, unconvinced, arms crossing over my chest. "Nobody collects things, like guitar picks, if they don't mean something. Why would you have more than one if you didn't want to?"

He slides his pants and boxers down, stepping out of them. "I don't want to talk about this."

There's a finality to his words. That familiar hidden warning Luke always projects when I touch on a subject that is too personal for him. Twelve months ago I would've backed off, changed the subject, not dug for answers to things I desperately wanted to know about. But I can't be like that anymore. Not when I know how it ends for me.

I hold my hands out, palms facing him as he crawls toward me. "Wait. I want to talk."

"So talk." He grabs my ankle and pulls me 'til I'm flat on the bed. "Nothing's ever stopped you from being vocal before. You know I get off on that." He presses my legs apart, and I flatten my hands against his head, keeping him inches away from where I know he wants to be.

I wait 'til he lifts his eyes to mine before I explain. "That's not the kind of talking I mean, and you know it. You gotta give me something. If you don't want to tell me about the guitar, fine, but I want to know who Sara is."

He presses his lips to my inner thigh, trailing higher on my skin, pushing into my hands. "Stop fighting me."

"Tell me who she is," I repeat, tilting my head to read the name scrolled across his ribcage. I push harder against him, meeting his resistance. "Luke, I'm serious. I . . . oh, God. Don't do that." I keep one hand on his head, reaching between my legs and grabbing a hold of his wrist as his finger slides along the front of the briefs I'm wearing. I close my eyes when I feel his lips press against my hip, and suddenly my hands go limp, falling in surrender to the mattress. "I want to talk. Please talk to me."

"Go ahead and talk, babe. Nothing's stopping you." He blows against my clit, cooling me through the thin material separating us as his hands slide under my ass.

I need to be strong right now. To demand answers. To reach down and grab the briefs he's sliding down my legs. Why does he do this to me? Why can't I block him out and focus on anything but the rough grip of his hands? The sound he makes when he bites my skin, or the urgent slide of his tongue? Practiced. Familiar. But never routine. The only predictable facet regarding the way Luke Evans eats pussy is that he's getting at least one orgasm out of you. Most likely several, and good fucking luck saying anything but his name while he's doing it.

I bunch the sheet I'm lying on in my hands. "Goddamn it. Why can't you just wait a couple minutes before you . . . Oh,

God, just wait . . . That's . . . fuuuck." I take in a shaky breath, then sigh. "I hate you right now."

"Yeah?" he asks, stroking my clit with his tongue. "What do you hate? This?" He tilts my hips up, slides his tongue inside me, and fucks me with it. "You hate this?"

"Yes," I answer through a moan.

"Tell me everything you hate. Make me feel it."

I arch my back when two fingers replace his tongue. "I hate that you know I like that." I scratch along his scalp when he sucks on my clit. "I hate . . . mmm, I really hate when you use your—" I gasp. "Teeth, right there."

"What else?"

I go to open my eyes, to stare down at him 'cause I know he's looking at me, but they just roll farther back into my head the moment he pinches my nipple. "I don't know. I hate a lot of things."

He pushes my knees against my chest and bites my ass. "Don't give me some vague bullshit answer. You don't just hate me because of what I can do to you, and right now, you're gonna get that shit off your chest before you come all over my face." He drops my legs over his shoulders, and our eyes meet. "Because when I swallow that last drop, it'll be my turn, and I'm not holding back. I'm gonna tell you everything I hate about you and you're gonna feel it. So start talking."

I grab his head, arch my back, and cry out the second I feel his tongue between my legs. "I hate that you don't talk to me. I wanna know everything about you, and I . . ." I gasp when his thumb moves over my clit. "I feel like you were just with me because you wanted sex." I bite my lip, digging my nails into the mattress. "I hate that I want this, and that I stop caring about how much you don't give me the second you . . . shiiit, the second you make me feel this way." My breathing becomes heavy as my shirt clings to my skin. "I hate that I'll always want more, and I hate that you won't give it to me. Oh, God, right there." I groan, feeling the pressure build and slowly spread out from my core. My body submits to this, to what he can do to me, and I fill my lungs to capacity one last time just as the wave of pleasure rolls through me.

"I hate that I can't hate you enough to forget you. That for the past year I never stopped thinking about you. Not even for one day."

My legs fall off his shoulders as he shifts his weight, kneeling between my legs. I think he's going to give me a few seconds, stare at me a little, maybe respond to what I've just said, but he digs his fingers into my hips, lifts me off the bed, and drives straight into me.

"Luke," I pant, digging my nails into his shoulders.

He wraps my legs around his waist before bracing himself with a hand on either side of me. Arms flexed, ink covering his skin, lips wet and inches from mine. "My turn," he says through a soft voice. "I hate what you did to us. That what I gave you wasn't enough, and that you fucking kept shit from me that I had every right to know about." He begins thrusting into me, so hard my body slides up the bed and he has to wrap his arm around my waist to keep me still. "I hate you for not telling me why you broke up with me. That shit came out of nowhere, and you just dropped me like I never meant anything to you. I was going fucking crazy, and you ignored me. You wouldn't talk to me. You wouldn't give me *shit.* I deserved a fucking reason, and you treated me like it was nothing. Like *I* was nothing." His lips fall open with a groan, and I reach up and flatten my hand against his chest, right over his tattoo.

My eyes well up with tears as my body begins to heat up. "Luke," I whisper, sliding my hand along his skin to his neck, gripping him to bring us closer. He grabs my hand, flattens it above my head, and locks it there with my other, holding me at my wrists.

His thrusts pick up, become wild and frantic, as our eyes stay on each other, never breaking contact.

"I hate that I felt shit for you I never wanted to feel for anyone," he says, dropping his forehead against mine. "That you made me feel it, and you didn't give me a fucking choice."

I stare into his eyes, the weight of my remorse hitting me like a Mack truck. "Luke, I'm . . ."

"No. You said what you had to say. Now I'm saying mine."

He slams his cock into me over and over, fucking me with raw force while his face remains distant. I'm already struggling from his words, choking on my own emotions, but seeing him like this solidifies everything he's just said to me.

He bares his teeth, laughing through a growl. "Do you feel it, babe? How much I hate you?"

I nod, biting the inside of my cheek to keep myself from falling apart.

"Good, 'cause I'm done. I can't hate you anymore, Tessa. I won't."

He claims my mouth, roughly, his day-old stubble burning my skin while his hands form to my face. He's giving me that helpless side of him I only get to see in moments like this, and it's exactly what I need. It's such a contrast to the Luke everyone knows, the self-possessed man who doesn't look like he'd know the first thing about being gentle. But he does. When he breaks like this, when he loses control and gives me this perfect combination of wild and sweet, I become the defenseless one, willing to hand over my heart, unprotected, for a simple kiss.

But it's anything but simple.

My eyes flash open the second he bites down on my lip, and I'm there, sliding my legs higher up his waist as my climax rolls through me.

"Oh, God, yes. Right there."

"Fuck yeah, babe. Come on my cock." He grabs my hip and grinds himself into me as his lips move to my ear. "I missed this. How you squeeze me like that . . . Fuck, there's nothing like it."

I stare, breathless, as he pushes back onto his knees, bunches my shirt above my breasts, and strokes his cock over my stomach, coming with his head thrown back.

I don't realize my eyes have closed until I feel Luke wiping me clean. Minutes later, the mattress shifts and the covers slide over me, but I'm too tired to open my eyes. My body feels stripped, devoid of the ability to do anything besides cling to sleep right now, so that's what I do. I let myself drift out of consciousness, in the bed I never expected to be in again.

A WEIGHT SHIFTS off my feet before something heavy presses against my stomach. Warm breath tickles my face, and I open my eyes just as Max begins sniffing my head. I grab him, pushing him off a bit before I scratch his neck.

"You weigh a ton. I think you need to get more exercise."

He rolls onto his back to give me access to his belly. I scratch along his fur, sitting up and pushing my hair out of my face with my free hand. I feel well rested, not how I normally feel after taking a nap in the middle of the day. Usually that screws with my system and leaves me more tired, but not to-day. I pat Max's belly and swing my legs off the bed, following behind him as he barrels down the hallway toward the stairs.

I'm halfway down the staircase when the sound of a

guitar stops me. Slowly inching to the bottom, I peer around the corner and see the back of Luke sitting on the couch. He's playing as if he's done it for years, casually and without effort—a soft, sorrowful melody that causes my heart to ache. I find myself inching closer, holding my breath so as not to miss one chord or alert him of my presence. I wonder if he looks as tortured as he sounds right now, and if he does, could I stand seeing him like that, full of shameless emotion? So unlike the Luke I'm familiar with.

A phone ringing freezes me in place and halts his playing. I should move, slowly retreat back up the stairs, but when he stands and turns around, lifting the phone to his ear, our eyes lock and the only thing I can do is give him an apologetic smile. He doesn't give me one in return before he answers the call.

"Yeah?" His eyes pinch shut and he runs a hand down his face. "Where? Yeah, all right. I fucking know, Ray. Just hold him." He ends the call and stuffs the phone into his pocket, locking eyes with me.

"I thought you said you didn't play."

He stays silent, watching me take a step closer.

"It's good. You're really good, Luke. Will you play for me some more?"

His phone rings again, and I think I curse louder than Luke. I want this moment with him. I need this moment.

"What?" he growls into the phone, rounding the couch and heading toward the stairs. "I fucking said I'm coming. Would you give me a minute?"

His voice trails off behind me as I remain still, unsure what to do. I'm only left alone for a minute before he comes back down, keys in hand.

He looks at me, briefly, before dropping his gaze to his shirt I'm still wearing. "I gotta go. You can stay if you want but I don't know how long I'm going to be."

"Where are you going?" He lifts his head, and I see that wall slide up between us, keeping me out. I step closer to him, determined to get answers. "Who was that? Who's Ray?"

He avoids my eyes and moves to slip past me, but I block him.

"Don't. I need to go, and if you don't move, I'll move you."

I step to the side, but grab his arm when he walks past me. "Luke, just tell me where you're going. Why is it so fucking secretive?"

He wrenches his arm out of my grasp, glaring at me over his shoulder. "Stop, Tessa. Jesus Christ. If I want you to know shit, I'll fucking tell you."

The door slams shut behind him, and I suddenly no longer want to be here. In fact, the only thing I don't regret about today is spewing my hatred to Luke—I only wish I had done it without him between my legs.

I quickly slip into my jeans that are now completely dry, tuck my shirt and bra under my arm, grab my keys from upstairs, and walk out to the garage. I stick the battery back in my phone and power it on, grateful when the screen lights up. On the way out to my car, I notice three missed calls on my cell phone. Two from Mia and one from Reed. I don't want to talk to anyone right now. The one person I wanted to talk to still won't give me anything, and I was stupid to think he would after what happened between us today.

But people don't change. They'll always disappoint you, and I can't keep holding out for someone who will never give me what I want. I need to let go of Luke, but that's easier said than done.

luke

I HEAR THE commotion inside the bar before I even get the door open. I should turn around, go back home to be with Tessa and keep this piece of shit out of my life. That's where I want to be—with her. She drives me completely insane, but I fucking live for that. Even sitting a floor below her while she sleeps in my bed settles me somehow. I don't need to be in direct contact with her to feel the effect she has on me. But that shouldn't be a surprise. It's how it's always been with Tessa. The proof of that is in the excruciating year I've had, knowing she was within a fifteen mile radius of me, that at any point in time I could've gone to her and satisfied my need to see her. I'd diverted my thoughts to those of hate, tried to push out everything else I'd never wanted to feel. But now that I've gotten all my animosity toward Tessa out of my system, there's nothing distracting me from that constant throbbing desire I have to be near her.

Nothing except for this bullshit.

Stepping inside, I immediately spot Ray and one of the other bartenders, their arms wrapped around my dad as they strain to keep him in the far corner of the bar, away from the liquor. He's putting up a fight, and I know it's because he's sober. That's the only time he can actually give you any amount of physical resistance. He'll just run his mouth when he's drunk. Put a few drinks in him and he becomes a stumbling, mouthy idiot; the version of him I'd actually prefer to deal with right now. Because when he's completely coherent like this, fully aware of how much of an asshole he's being, this version of him has my right hand curling into a fist.

I push through the crowd that's gathered around the scene, shoving the dickheads back who think this is some kind of a fucking show for them to amuse themselves with. Ray sees me over his shoulder, a look of relief washing over him as I step up in front of the three men.

My dad raises his head and laughs. He fucking laughs.

"If you think I'm leaving here without getting a drink first, you got another thing coming," he says, leaning into the hands holding him against the wall.

He looks put together, for the most part. His typical flannel shirt is tucked into his jeans, and his hair is pulled back, out of his face. Plus he seems to have showered today, unlike the last time I saw him. But even sober, he still looks like a desperate drunk—irrational and half-mad, willing to do anything for that one drink. And I'm too pissed not to see how far he'll go to get it.

I step closer, holding my arms outstretched. "You want a drink? How about this then?" I stab a finger against my chest. "*I'll* fucking buy you one. All you have to do is get past me."

"The hell, man?" Ray asks, wide-eyed. "What are you doing?"

I'm sure he's wondering how I'm gonna match up against a guy who's got at least twenty pounds of muscle on me. I'd be concerned myself, but I'm too geared up right now to give a shit.

My dad smiles, his eyes twinkling with optimism. "Yeah? You think I won't lay you out, boy?"

I step closer, the adrenaline spiking in my blood. "I don't

know. Let's find out."

"Shit, Jack," Ray says, pressing against my dad's chest. "You need help. Serious help, man. Why don't you let Luke take you home?"

"Take me home?" he repeats mockingly. His chin tilts up and he looks at me straight on, grinning like he's just won the fucking lottery. "You heard him. He wants to buy me a drink. I'd be a damn fool to pass that up."

Ray looks back at me. "You better know what you're doing."

"Are we really going to let them go at it?" the other bartender, Pete, finally speaks, struggling to maintain his hold on a man who is now highly motivated to come at me.

Ray steps back, causing Pete to scramble to grab hold of my dad, but Pete's half the size of him, and Dad easily barrels at me. He wraps his arms around my waist and takes me down to the floor, hard, hitting me with all his weight.

My head slams against the hardwood, distorting my vision, as the weight on top of me crushes my lungs like an accordion. I gasp in a breath when I'm able to roll him off, and I try to flip him to his stomach to immobilize him, but for a fifty-year-old man, my dad moves like a Goddamn ninja.

"Where's that police training, huh?" he teases, prying my hand off his shoulder and trying to get a good grab on my arm. "Come on, then."

It's chaos, each of us fighting for power, rolling around on the floor as the bar noise around us seems to fade out completely.

"Luke, if you don't control this, I'm gonna have to call somebody."

I register Ray's warning as I try to put my dad in a couple of holds, but he breaks free every time. He gains control, then me, and then him again. The struggle goes on for what feels like hours and I wait for my dad to grow tired, to give in, to end this bullshit, but he comes at me again and again, gaining the upper hand once more and pinning me on my back.

He's sweating, panting heavily, but his strength hasn't weakened. He wants that fucking drink, and he thinks he's going to get it. His eyes are glazed over, the same color as mine but he looks half-possessed. Strung-out and frenzied. My head is throbbing from getting knocked to the ground, but I can't pay attention to that right now. Not when he raises his hand next to his head and slowly makes a fist.

He's going to punch me. The asshole's really going to do it.

I don't react. I give him the chance to stop himself, to bring his hand down to his side, to realize exactly what he's about to do, and he takes those few seconds and uses them to whiten his knuckles with a tighter fist before striking me against the jaw.

Blood fills my mouth, the metallic tang seeping to the back of my throat as he rears his arm back again. I know he's not going to stop. I can see the manic, uncontrolled fire burning behind his eyes. He's no longer looking at me like I'm familiar to him. I'm just the guy he needs to get through, and that addiction-fueled ignorance causes me to snap.

I move fast, slamming my fist into the side of his face and sending him falling to the floor, removing his weight off me. I scramble to my knees and strike him again, this time connecting with his nose. Blood splatters on the wood, streaks across my knuckles, and he places a hand to his face as he winces in pain.

"Come on! That's all you got? I thought you wanted that drink," I taunt, bringing my arm back to strike him again. A hand grabs my wrist, halts me mid-swing, and I look over my shoulder and connect with Ben seconds before he grabs under my arm and hauls me to my feet.

"What the fuck? What's going on?" he asks, just as Ray comes walking up with a rag.

I watch as my dad takes the rag and puts it to his nose before standing up. He looks at me briefly, dropping his gaze with a disgusted shake of his head before walking through the crowd that has congregated around us.

"Hey." Ben shoves against my chest, prompting me to look over at him. "What the hell's wrong with you? Ray called me and said you offered to buy your dad a drink. Is that true?"

I shake my punching hand out, flexing my fingers as I watch Ray walk my dad outside. "I said I'd buy him a drink if he got past me. He didn't."

He frowns. "So you're just going to start challenging your dad to fights now? You think maybe that'll keep him from drinking? 'Cause that sounds pretty fucking stupid to me."

I walk to the bar, ignoring Ben, and grab a couple of napkins off the counter. I hold them to my lip as he walks up to me.

"Why don't you try talking to him? Like, actually having a conversation with him when he's sober?"

I slowly turn my head, glare at him, and bring the napkin away from my mouth. "Oh, you mean like right now? 'Cause he is fucking sober, and he really seems to be in the mood to have a little chat with his son." I pinch my eyes shut before focusing on the liquor bottles lined up behind the bar. "He doesn't want to talk to me. He's probably on his way now to another bar right now where they'll actually serve him."

"Actually, he's headed to the hospital."

Ray walks behind the bar, stopping on the other side in front of us. He takes a handkerchief out of his pocket and wipes his forehead with it.

"Why is he going to the hospital?" I ask, bunching up the napkins before tossing them into the trashcan behind the bar. "If he told you that, he's lying. He's getting drunk tonight."

Ray folds the handkerchief and runs it around the back of his neck. "Maybe, but I'm pretty sure you broke his nose. I suggested he go get it checked out, and he wasn't all that disagreeable. He looked like shit." His eyes fall to my mouth. "You all right?"

I feel a tinge of guilt, but quickly swallow it down when I remember the look in Dad's eyes before he hit me. I shrug off Ray's question.

Ray shifts his gaze between me and a spot on the bar. "Luke, you know I'm always trying to help you out, keep your dad out of trouble and everything, but I can't have him coming in here anymore. I told him just now if I see him walking in here again, I'm calling the cops, and I don't mean you."

I nod. I knew this was coming. It was only a matter of time before Ray got sick of this bullshit.

"Do what you gotta do, Ray. Let him get arrested. I don't care anymore." I tap the bar and turn away, walking through the crowd and out the door.

"Are you going to the hospital to check on your dad?" Ben asks, joining my side in the parking lot.

I pull my keys out of my pocket. "No. I'm going to go see Tessa."

He chuckles softly behind me as I reach my truck. "Are you sure you wanna start another fight? You might not win that one."

I lean back against the driver's side door, crossing my arms over my chest. "There won't be any fighting. Me and her are good."

He raises a skeptical eyebrow. "Really? We're talking about my sister, right? Tessa Kelly?" He holds his hand out, palm down, at chest height. "About this tall, red hair, wanted nothing to do with your ass before I left the state?"

I flip him off and he laughs, shaking his head in disbelief.

"Jesus. I was gone for two days. What the hell happened?"

"A lot, actually. Some really fucked up shit went down with that guy she met up with at the bonfire." He studies me, waiting for me to expand on that statement. I reach up and scratch the back of my head before continuing. "So, you know I went to that stupid thing, 'cause I fucking had to. I tried to keep your sister from leaving with him, but I'm sure you can imagine how that played out." I grip the back of my neck, squeezing to relieve some of the tension. "I was so fucking pissed. I should've just thrown her ass in my truck, but I just said fuck it, and I went to leave."

A short laugh bubbles in my throat, and I see his forehead crease with confusion. I shake my head. "I couldn't leave, man. I sat there like an asshole, because after a year, I'm still completely strung-out on her. And you know what? It's a good fucking thing I am, because if I would've left, I never would've gotten that asshole's tag number to run in our system."

"He had priors? We looked him up. There was nothing on him."

"That's 'cause we were looking up the wrong guy. Either he gave her a fake last name, or she lied to you about it, 'cause he had domestic charges against him." I drop my head, my eyes losing focus as I hear a faint "motherfucker" coming from Ben. "I went straight to her apartment, out of my mind, fucking praying she was there with him. He was choking her when I got there, and I almost killed him." I look up. Ben's eyes are filled with rage. "I *wanted* to kill him. If Tessa wasn't watching me, I would've done worse than break that fucker's wrist."

Ben inhales deeply through his nose, his chest rising then falling, before he speaks. "She's all right? She's not hurt?"

"Her neck is sore. She has some bruises on it, but she's fine."

"And him? You actually broke his wrist?"

"Yeah."

He drops his head into a sharp nod. "Good. Those assault charges will get plead down in court."

"Yeah, but he had drugs on him too, so he could get a year for possession, maybe eighteen months with the first-degree assault added to it. He's at least looking at some jail time."

Ben runs a hand down his face before pulling his cell phone out of his pocket and looking at the screen. "He's lucky. If he weren't locked up, I'd hunt his ass down and rip him apart. I wouldn't give a shit about my job." He looks up at me, clutching his phone in one hand and placing his other on my shoulder. "Thanks a lot, man. You didn't have to go to that bonfire."

"Yeah, I did," I counter as he drops his hand. I see the smirk twisting across his lips and shove him out of the way so I can open my door. "Fuck off. I'm not as pussy-whipped as you are over Mia. I just did what I had to do."

He steps aside, laughing. "Call it whatever you want. The only difference between me and you is that I wasn't scared to admit how I felt. Not to myself, or anybody else. I didn't give a shit who knew how crazy I was about Mia."

"Tessa knows how I feel."

"Does she?" He looks at me straight on, dropping all humor as I settle into the driver's seat. "I'm sure she knows you care about her, but she doesn't how you feel. She won't, not until you tell her, and don't make her wait for that. I made that mistake with Mia and I almost lost my chance."

I grab the door handle to pull it closed, but he stops it with a hand gripping the edge.

"What are you so scared of, Luke? That all the shit you've been through is too much for her to deal with? Do you think she'd run from that?"

I glare at him, feeling my nostrils flare. "She doesn't need to know about all this. All this shit—it's mine. It's my fucking burden, and I won't make it hers. I let her in as much as I can, and it has to be enough because that's all I can give her."

I see him struggle with his next words, or maybe he's struggling with mine. Either way, it takes him several seconds before he nods his understanding. "Well, for your sake, I hope it's enough for her, because you're a miserable piece of shit without her."

I let out a breathy laugh, and he does the same. "Yeah, well . . . fuck you."

He laughs harder and allows me to close the door.

I can't argue with Ben. He's right; I have been a miserable piece of shit. I read once that addiction is hereditary, a crutch you inherit that's ingrained in your genetic makeup. It would make sense; explain the starving compulsion I've had over the past year. My dad might be dependent on alcohol, but I'm at the mercy of Tessa Kelly, and right now, I'm going to feed my obsession.

TESSA'S CAR ISN'T at my house when I get there, which doesn't completely surprise me. After I let Max outside, I drive over to her apartment and knock on the door. I hear a muffled "hold on," followed by the clicking sound of several locks being turned.

The door opens and I look down at Tessa, her green eyes doubling in size the moment she trains them on me. She's still wearing my T-shirt, but she has on these tight black pants that I know hug her ass in a way that has me reaching down to adjust my slowly hardening cock. One of her hands is clutching a small container of ice cream, and the spoon she has shoved in her mouth nearly falls out as she reacts to my presence, clearly not expecting me.

"Mmm mmm," she says around the spoon with a shake of her head before slamming the door closed. A lock clicks.

"What the hell?" I bang on the door, turning the knob and scowling when it won't budge. "Tessa, what the fuck? Let me in."

"No, no, no, no, NO. You are not coming in here."

"Why the hell not?"

"Because if I let you in, I'll have sex with you."

My brow pinches together. "Why is that a problem?"

I hear her breathy pause. "It just . . . it just fucking is. Okay?"

"No, it's not okay. *'It just fucking is'* isn't a reason, and if you're keeping me out 'cause you're worried I'll have sex with you as soon as I get in there, don't be."

"Oh really?" she asks through a laugh. "You mean to tell me if I open this door right now, you wouldn't try sticking it in, immediately? I call bullshit."

I smile, dropping my head against the door. "Immediately? No, because I can still fucking taste you, Tessa, and I want more of that before I do anything else. When you open this door—not if—the first thing that's going to be sliding into you will be my tongue. Then my fingers. Then my cock. In that order."

I hear a soft, purring sound, followed by a grunt.

"Goddamn it. Why do you have to talk to me like that?"

I palm my now fully hard cock. "'Cause you like it. Now let me in."

"No."

I jar the knob again. "You know I can break down doors. You've seen me do it."

"Then you'll be buying me another one."

I shut my eyes. "Look, I've had a shitty night. A really fucking shitty night, and I just want to be with you. Let me in so I can do that."

"Did this shitty night have anything to do with Ray? Or Sara?" I don't respond and I hear more locks clicking. "You wanna come in?" she asks, her voice dropping the certainty it just had seconds ago.

I nod as if she can see me, feeling my desperation for her coursing through my blood.

"There are five locks on this door, four too many in my opinion, and if you want in, you need to answer all five of my questions."

I stare blankly at the door. "Don't do this right now."

"Question number one," she starts as I run both hands down my face. "Who is Ray?"

Easy. I can answer that.

"He's a bartender I've known for a couple years. He owns Lucky's Tavern."

A lock clicks. "See, that's wasn't so hard, was it?"

"Is that your next question?"

I hear her irritated sigh. "No, it's not, smartass. Who is Sara?"

I crack my knuckles as I begin to pace back and forth in front of the door. "Tessa, I fucking answered one of your questions. That should be enough."

"Don't be pissy with me because you bought a door with five locks. You know the rules of this game."

A game; that's exactly what this is. A fucking game.

I stop in front of the door. "I want to be with you. You fucking settle me, okay, and I need that right now. Stop this shit and just let me in."

Silence lingers between us as I step closer, flattening my hand against the door.

"Tessa." I nearly plead, not giving a shit if she hears how weak I am when it comes to her. She's controlling this, and the helpless feeling that started off as a minor discomfort weighing on my chest has intensified, making it difficult for my lungs to fully expand.

I can hear her breathing through the door as she makes me wait, and it's funny how that doesn't crank up my anxiety. Waiting for Tessa to make her decision doesn't make me uneasy. It's the fear of not seeing her right now that does.

"No, Luke," she finally says, her voice unwavering and sure. "I can't have you keep me out like that. It sucks for me, especially when I get moments with you where I think you're letting me in, but you're not. It's not fucking fair. If you don't want to tell me who Sara is, then leave, because you're not coming in here."

My chest gets tighter, like she's just added another weight by keeping me out. "Fine," I reply through gritted teeth, turning and heading for my truck.

I'm not going to fucking beg to see her, and I don't need this shit right now. Not after the night I just had. She's probably just pissed I left her the way I did earlier and after a day or two, she'll get over it. Tessa can't deny she wants to be with me. What we had last summer was damn near perfect, and we will have that again.

Just as I'm about to pull away from her apartment, my phone rings. *Fuck yes.* I pull it out of the pocket of my shorts just as I cut the engine, but it's not Tessa calling me. It's a number I don't recognize.

"Yeah?" I answer, pissed off that I'm starting up my truck again.

"Hi, I'm trying to reach Luke Evans. This is Dr. Cohen calling from St. Joseph's Hospital."

My tires screech as I quickly peel away from the apartment building and out onto the main road. "What is it? Is he being an asshole or something?"

"Sir, we need you to come down. If not tonight, then first thing in the morning. Your father is being admitted."

My hand wraps tighter around the wheel as I glance at the time on the dash. "Yeah, I'll be there."

I toss my phone onto the empty seat next to me as I drive in the direction of my house. He can wait; whatever it is they need me for, I'm done for tonight.

I'm fucking done.

tessa

A KNOCK ON the door startles me awake, sending the empty Ben & Jerry's and my spoon that was shamelessly still in my grasp crashing to the floor. I sit up as my eyes adjust to the sunlight pouring in through the window, giving them a moment to focus before I reach for the container and tilt it toward me, not surprised in the least that there isn't any trace of *Brownie Batter* remaining. When heartache calls for ice cream, I go at it hard, and last night was no exception. At this point, I'm practically a walking advertisement for the kings of dessert. The number of times I've made late-night trips to the freezer section of the local market over the past year has to be in the hundreds by now. But it's how I cope with this shit. I'm not new to this game, nor am I unfamiliar with the dull ache that settles over me at the very thought of Luke, making even breathing seem somewhat painful.

Another knock has me standing from the couch, placing the evidence of my misery on the coffee table before I step up to the door.

"Who is it?" I ask, holding on to the top lock, not turning it even the slightest until I know for sure it isn't whom I really can't handle right now. It shouldn't be him. It's Monday morning, and he should be at work, but after not letting him in last night, I wouldn't be surprised if he tried for a quickie before he started patrolling, and that shit isn't happening.

Not if he stays out of my apartment anyway. I can't be held responsible for what would happen if I let him in, so I won't.

"It's me."

I turn all the locks at the sound of Mia's voice, and she wraps me up in a hug as soon as I swing the door open.

"God, I want to kill that asshole. They don't send pregnant women to jail, do they?"

"Probably. Which asshole are you referring to?" I ask, stepping aside after ending our hug to allow her to enter.

She looks over at me, flattening a hand over the stretched tank top that covers her belly. "The Internet guy. Who else is being an asshole?" Before I can answer, I watch as she glances around the room, her mouth falling open as she fixates her gaze on the coffee table. She walks over to it and peers down at the empty container. "Uh-oh. Late night binge eating?"

I nod when she looks over at me.

"Yikes. Did something happen after I talked to you last night?"

I slam the door shut. "Yeah, Luke happened." Her eyebrows rise as I walk over to the couch, falling on it with a heavy sigh. I lean my head back onto the cushion to look up at her. "He came over about an hour after I talked to you. But I didn't let him in."

"Really?"

"Yup."

"You didn't let him in?"

I shake my head.

She drops her gaze to my lap. "Well, I'm very proud of you."

"Did you just direct that to my vagina?"

A small smile teases the corner of her mouth before

she points a finger at the subject in question. "Yes, because I know how much *she* loves Luke, and I'm sure that wasn't easy to ignore."

I pull my knees up to my chest, resting my chin on top as I stare blankly in front of me. "No, it wasn't. But I did. I wouldn't let him in unless he answered five of my questions, and he only made it through round one. He still won't tell me who Sara is."

"Is that the other name he has tattooed?"

"It's the *only* name he has tattooed. I have an initial, and I don't care if he doesn't put a lot of thought into what he gets permanently etched onto his skin. She's someone to him, and I want to know who she is." I drop my head so my forehead is now resting on my knees. "I'm tired of only getting pieces of Luke. I want all of him or nothing."

Just hearing that ultimatum out loud makes my stomach twist into a tight coil, because I know exactly how he'll take that challenge. You get what you get with Luke, and if he were willing to give me more, he would've given it to me already.

Mia's footsteps trail away from me, and I lift my head up, turning it as she disappears down the hallway. "Where are you going?" When she doesn't answer, I push off the couch and follow the noise coming from my bedroom.

She's opening the bottom drawer of my dresser, struggling to bend over with the huge bump protruding from her. I watch as she pulls out some workout clothes and tosses them onto the bed.

I step further into the room. "Um, Mia, you know I love you and everything, but our days of swapping clothes are behind us until you pop that thing out."

She lifts her head and grimaces. "Thing? He's your nephew."

"Well, he's preventing you from squeezing into this top, that's for damn sure." I hold up the tank she threw onto the bed, pulling the taut material between my hands. "Not happening, sister."

"It's for you, dumbass." She grabs it out of my hands only to shove it against my chest. "Get changed. You're coming with me to yoga."

"Ha!"

"Why is that so funny?" she asks, pulling the elastic tie off her wrist and securing her long brown hair up into a pony.

I toss the shirt onto the bed. "Because I'm not crashing a pregnant yoga party. Being around a bunch of knocked-up, spouse-happy women is just going to annoy me further."

"There's only, like, two or three pregnant women in the whole class, including me, and trust me—" she pauses, picking up the shirt and tossing it at my face, "—you're gonna thank me for this invite."

"Why?" I ask, as she turns and exits the room with a smile on her face. "Is there going to be hard liquor there? Or maybe a life-sized cut-out of Luke I can throat punch?"

"Shut up and get dressed. You're going!" she yells from somewhere in my apartment.

"Since when did you become so bossy?"

I hear a muffled, mouthful response, followed by a chip bag ruffling as I look down at the tank top in my hand.

What are my options? Stay here, pout, and eventually get some transcribing done, or be with my best friend, twist my body into positions that usually require a man, and hopefully get my mind off all things Luke related. Mia knows how to distract me, and she definitely has my interest piqued with the whole *you're going to be thanking me later* comment. So, I begin stripping, settling on option two, and hoping for at least thirty minutes of relief from the thoughts filling my head.

The fact that the yoga studio just so happens to be at the gym owned by the Ruxton Police Department might make that difficult.

"HIS TRUCK ISN'T here. Relax. Him and Ben are probably patrolling," Mia says as we walk through the gym, her eyes on me while I scan the line of treadmills.

"You couldn't take a yoga class at another gym?"

"Not when I can go here for free."

She opens the door to the small studio and I walk in behind her, looking around the room and counting seven very distinct pregnant bellies.

I gesture in front of me. "Really? Two or three? Am I seriously about to attend a pregnancy yoga class?"

She sets her water bottle and small towel down on the bench along the back wall, kicking her flip-flops off and pushing them underneath. "There's other non-pregnant women here, but yes, things are modified for those of us who are no longer able to see our feet." She points to the far side of the room. "There's two mats available next to each other. Let's grab those."

"Or," I counter, planting my ass on the bench and pulling out the phone tucked into my sports bra, "I could sit here and play Fruit Ninja while you learn exercises to prevent pre-term labor." I'm yanked off the bench and nearly lose my phone in the process. "Jesus! All right."

I tuck my phone away as we reach the two empty mats. Mia begins stretching out her back, twisting from side to side as I stand there, not feeling any sort of activity that involves moving.

"Can I just sit and watch? We can still talk."

"Not in my class you won't be."

I turn my head, connecting with the steel-blue eyes of the man standing to Mia's left. If his accent didn't cause my jaw to nearly hit the mat, the sight of him as he steps in front of us does.

Sweet baby Jesus in a basket.

He's all long, lean muscle, which is on full display thanks to his decision to not wear a shirt. He has tanned skin, and a sweet smile that hits me when I finally pry my eyes off his damn fine body.

"Mason, hi. How are you?"

He looks back to Mia, but gives me one last glance before he answers. "I'm good, Mia. But more importantly, how are you?" He holds a hand out to her belly, inches away. "May I?"

"Of course. Go ahead."

I don't know what to do, so I just stand there, gawking at this sexy-as-fuck Aussie while he rubs his hand across my best friend's belly. He's wearing the cutest expression, a mix between fascination and wonderment, as his blond, wavy hair falls out from where it was tucked behind his ear.

"He's kicking," he says, moving his hand along the side closest to me. "I think he's ready for class."

Mia laughs, hitching her thumb in the direction of me as he straightens up and drops his hand. "Yeah, but this one? Not so much."

"What?" I ask, sounding shocked by her accusation. "I'm so ready for class. I fucking love yoga. Let's do this."

The gorgeous Aussie rubs along his jaw, looking amused, as Mia laughs at my obvious lie.

"Mason, this is my sister in-law, Tessa, and apparently, she fucking loves yoga, all of a sudden."

He steps closer to me and extends his hand. "Hi, Tessa. I'm excited to have you in my class today."

My eyes widen as I realize what he's just said. "Are you teaching? *You?*"

Oh, hell yes.

He smiles, dropping his hand from mine, and that's the only response I get before he walks in between the other mats toward the front of the room.

"Holy shit," I utter under my breath as the room continues to fill, and that's when I notice the alarming number of women filing in. Herds of them, dressed in cleavage-baring tops and pants that leave zero to the imagination in the snatch department. These ladies are in it to win it, and none of them look like they give a damn about yoga.

"What the hell? I've been struggling with getting over Luke for the past year, and you've been hiding this guy from me? How long have you known him?" I whisper, eyeing up my competition as two bimbos claim the mats in front of us and obstruct my view entirely.

"This is only my forth class," Mia replies. "And up until last week, I thought he was gay. I mean, what guy teaches yoga?"

"So he's straight?" I ask, standing on my toes to see above the Barbie in front of me.

"Ex-girlfriend straight."

I turn to her with my mischievous grin, leaning closer as the noise level in the room dies down. "Well in that case, I'd love to show him my Down Under."

She throws her head back and we both crack up, gaining the attention of practically everyone in the room.

Mason steps to the center, smirking at the two of us. "Ladies, are we ready?"

"Oh, yeah," I reply, as Mia struggles to control her

hysterics. "I'm *so* ready."

I watch as his smile twists into a full-blown grin. "Excellent. Let's get started."

"WELL, IT'S OFFICIAL," I say, before taking a swig of Mia's water bottle. I wipe my mouth with the back of my wrist as she studies me, holding her hands out and motioning for me to finish. "I'm a major fan of yoga."

She grabs her bottle out of my hands. "Told you you'd be thanking me for the invite."

I look up to the front of the class where a group of women have surrounded Mason. He lifts his head to me, smiles, and says something to the group before breaking away from them.

"He's coming over here," Mia says, nudging me in my side. "Are you going to give him your number?"

My thoughts immediately go to Luke, and I'm suddenly flooded with uncertainty. Why? This is exactly what I need. I've spent the past hour eye-fucking Mason across the room, letting him help me into positions I didn't really need help getting into, and not once did I feel guilty about what I was doing. But now?

I don't have time to clear my head, or wipe the sweat off myself before he reaches us with his quick strides.

"Did you ladies enjoy the class?" he asks, looking between the two of us but letting his gaze linger on me. He's still shirtless, his muscles now gleaming with a fine sheen of sweat. An hour ago, this would've done something for me. I would've come up with at least ten different scenarios involving me, him, and a yoga mat. But now, I'm finding myself wondering why his skin isn't covered in tattoos.

"It was great, right, Tessa?" Mia looks over at me, tapping

her finger on the arm crossed over her chest as she waits expectantly for my agreement.

I nod, letting a ghost of a smile touch my lips. "It was."

He steps closer to me. "Good. I'm glad to hear that. Does that mean you'll be coming back?"

I swallow, looking over at Mia who's nodding at me like a lunatic. "Umm, I don't . . .

"'Cause if not, I'd really like to get your number," he interrupts, pulling his phone out of his shorts. "You aren't seeing anybody right now, are you?"

"Nope," Mia answers, smiling at the two of us. "She's *very* single."

Mason looks from her to me. "Yeah?"

Come on, Tessa. You need to let go of Luke.

I nod quicker than I intend, maybe to help convince myself that this is the best move for me, and it does ease some of my doubt. When I get my damn head under control, I hold my hand out, accepting his phone. "Yup. Very single." I program my number in and quickly give it back, nearly throwing it at him to keep myself from erasing my information.

He smiles. "Great. I'll call you."

"Okay."

He walks back up to the front of the room where a line seems to be forming for him.

"What happened? You froze up."

I grab Mia's towel off the bench, handing it to her as we file out through the door. "I don't know," I finally respond just as we step out into the parking lot.

"He's really nice, and I think he'd be good for you. You can't keep waiting around for Luke to give you more."

"I know."

"Because you might be waiting forever for that."

"I *know*," I repeat with emphasis, stopping in front of my car. I watch as she walks around to the passenger side. "I was fine. You saw me. My flirt game was on point, and then I just . . ." I pinch my eyes shut, gathering my thoughts before looking over at her. "I think about him, and it fucks with my head. It always does."

She tugs the elastic band out of her hair. "I think it fucks with your heart more, 'cause you love him."

I roll my eyes, but the words "No I don't" can't seem to find their way out of my mouth. Maybe it's because I've just had a weekend with Luke, where I let myself feel things I've tried to forget. Or maybe it's because I'll never be able to dispute it. I sure as hell haven't been able to for the past year.

I know I love him. I feel it every day, even when I don't want to. Even when he keeps me out. Even when he breaks my heart, it's there, and it scares me.

Because when you fall in love with someone exactly the way they are, how do you convince yourself they aren't enough for you?

I BUSY MYSELF with work when I get home, knocking out twenty-seven transcriptions after my shower. I know exactly where my idle mind likes to wander off to, so I don't give it the chance. After devouring my grilled cheese sandwich, and washing up the few dishes I dirtied, I pack up my files and head to the hospital to drop off my work.

Dr. Willis isn't in his office, so I leave the stack of papers on his desk with a note, letting him know that three of his dictations will need to be re-done due to excessive background noise. I stick the note to the box of Cheez-Its next to his computer screen, spelling out my point, and set that on top of the stack of papers before exiting the office.

The mass of people waiting to take the elevators down to the main floor deters me in another direction. I cross over to the east wing of the hospital, waving at a few of the nurses I recognize from Dr. Willis' unit. As I'm walking down the long hallway which leads to the other set of elevators, a familiar voice coming from one of the patient rooms has me slowing down until I'm just outside the open door.

"Were you even listening to the doctor? He didn't say limit yourself to one or two drinks. He said quit drinking. Period."

I peer around the doorframe, and spot Luke standing at the foot of the patient bed in his police uniform. Even at a distance, he looks tired, like he's been here for hours. It's the look people have when they haven't seen daylight in a while. A glint of something metallic turns over in his hand by his side, drawing my attention down.

"I can't just stop drinking. It don't work like that, Son."

Son?

"Don't call me *son*, and how the fuck do you even remember how it works?" Luke asks. "It's been twelve years since you tried giving that shit up. I mean really tried, not those bullshit attempts before where you made it 'til lunch without grabbing a beer. This is different. It's not about me asking you to stop anymore, it's about you killing yourself if you don't."

A hear a soft laugh, followed by three deep coughs before the other man clears his throat. "It's kinda funny, this shit."

"What is? What the fuck is funny about any of this?" Luke crosses his arms over his chest, but continues to flip over the object in his hand.

I try to look further into the room, but the most of the bed I can see is the bottom of the white sheet covering it.

"The one thing, the *only* thing that's ever given me relief from thinking about your mom is slowly leading me right to her. Now, that's fuckin' funny."

My heart drops out to the floor between my feet as my back hits the wall, flattening next to the doorway.

She's dead. Luke's mom is dead. Why would he keep that from me?

I hear his voice, but I can't make out what he's saying. All my focus is on my own heartbeat that's now throbbing at the base of my skull.

Sara. Oh, God. Is that his mom?

The overwhelming urge to run into that room and wrap my arms around Luke is staggering. I can't imagine losing a parent, but I know what it did to Mia. She at least had Ben to comfort her.

Who's been there for Luke?

"What are you doing?"

I snap my head to the right, meeting Luke's wild eyes.

Shit.

I slowly peel my body off the wall and step in front of him, fighting back the urge to touch. His chest heaves, his jaw his clenched tight. He looks . . . pissed. Really fucking pissed, and that look keeps my hands flattened against my thighs.

"I, uh, I was dropping off my transcripts and I heard your voice."

His chest rises with the breath he takes in through his nose. One hand grips the back of his neck, a habit I've noticed of Luke's, while his eyes pinch closed on his exhale.

I step closer, hesitantly placing my hand on his chest. "Is Sara your mom?" I don't wait for him to answer after his eyes flash open. I'm not even sure he'd confirm anything at this point, since he's always kept this information from me. "I'm so sorry. I wouldn't have kept asking you who that was if I would've known. Why didn't you tell me?"

"It's not something I like to talk about." His eyes study my hand, as it stays flattened against his shirt.

"Ray called you the other night because of your dad, right?"

His hand wraps around my wrist, pulling me off. "Stop."

"All those times you had to leave me late at night, when you wouldn't tell me why, it was because of him, wasn't it?"

"Tessa, stop." He releases his grip on me, almost repulsively, as if he can't stand his skin against mine. "This shit is none of your business. I'm not going to talk about it with you."

"Why? Let me help you. I want to be there for you."

"No."

I grab his hand, pressing, molding us together. "You shouldn't have to deal with this by yourself."

"Stop! What the fuck?" He wrenches his hand away. "I just told you I'm not going to talk about it. I can't, okay? I will never talk about this with you."

I flinch at his words as if he's just delivered them with a knife to my chest. As soon as I take a step back, he reaches out for me, his eyes softening with remorse.

"Tessa . . ."

"No! Fuck you, Luke! I'm done. I'm so fucking done with this."

I storm away, not bothering to look back when he calls out for me. The tears stream down my face as I bypass the elevators and enter the stairwell.

He's just confirmed my biggest fear, the one I was almost certain of. He'll never talk about this with me. *Never.*

I'm the one standing on the other side of that door, begging him to let me in.

I force myself to keep moving when I want to collapse onto one of the steps. I want to curl up into a ball, shield myself away from anyone and everything around me. When I finally step out on the bottom floor, my phone rings.

I almost don't look at it. I know it's him, but something has me reaching into my pocket and pulling out my phone. A number I don't recognize flashes on the screen and I step to the side of the main entrance before lifting it to my ear.

"Hello?" I answer, brushing off the tears on my cheeks with the back of my hand.

"Tessa?"

I recognize Mason's voice immediately. "Yeah."

"Are you all right? You sound like you're crying."

I lift my head, looking out into the main lobby of the hospital, letting my eyes follow the crowd of people. "No, I'm okay. What's up?"

"I really wasn't planning on calling you this soon. I was going to at least wait a day, but I can't seem to stop thinking about you."

I let myself smile. "That's not a bad thing."

"Good, 'cause I wanted to see if you'd go out with me sometime this week. What are your plans?"

I open my mouth to respond, but Luke's face breaks through the crowd and finds mine instantly. He's walking toward me with purpose, his face a blank canvas that I can't read.

"Tessa?"

I grip the phone tighter as Luke steps up in front of me.

You're done with him. Let him go.

"I'd love to go out with you," I reply, watching as the mouth in front of me slowly drops open. His eyebrows set into a hard line as he stares at the phone in my hand, but I don't let that stop me. "Actually, one of my best friends is celebrating his birthday tomorrow night at McGill's Pub. Do you know where that is?"

"Yeah, on Calvert Street, right?"

"That's the one. If you want to pick me up, say around seven-ish, you could go with me."

Luke steps closer, and I turn, keeping my phone out of his grasp in case he tries to snatch it.

"All right. Text me your address and I'll pick you up."

"Okay, I'll send it to you later. I gotta go."

"Cheers, babe."

I end the call and turn back around, running straight into Luke. "What?" I step to the side to get to the entrance but he moves with me.

"Did you just invite another guy to Reed's party?"

"Yup."

"What the fuck? I thought we were together?"

Now it's my mouth that's dropping open. I jab my finger into his chest, digging in until my knuckle cracks. "*We* aren't anything. Maybe we were something over the weekend, or ten minutes ago, before you told me you'll never talk to me about the shit you're going through, but not anymore. I can't do this. I will never be okay with what we had last summer again, and if you have a problem with me bringing a date to Reed's party, then I suggest you stay the fuck home."

I turn to walk away but he grabs my arm, spinning me back around. "I still want you."

"You can't have me," I growl up at his face. "Let me go."

"I can't." He pulls me into him, sliding his hand around my neck. "I can't let you go, Tessa. Please, don't ask me to do that."

I shove him off me before I lose it, before I break completely. "I'm not asking you. I'm telling you. Let me go, Luke."

I walk out of the hospital, leaving him and the pleading look he's giving me, because I can't stand to see it anymore.

It's the look I pictured him having last night when I locked him out, causing me to second guess my decision, and it has the same effect on me now as I walk away from him.

The pain is unbelievable, but I ignore it. It has to be this way.

"MAN, THESE CUFFS are too tight. They're diggin' into my skin."

I look up from the plastic bag I'm searching through, leering at the piece of shit who Ben and I just busted for selling a dime bag in front of the local high school.

"Shut the fuck up before I make them tighter."

"I'd listen to him if I were you," Ben says, rounding the front of the car and dropping the hoodie we took off the guy next to the bag. "He's in a shit mood today, and I wouldn't care if he used excessive force on your dumb ass."

The asshole spits in the direction of Ben, but misses him by a long shot. "Fuck you, pig. I know my rights."

"No, man." Ben steps up in front of him, waiting until the guy looks up from where he's perched on the curb. "You're the one who's gonna be getting fucked. Not me, and I got pull down in Jessup. If you spit at me again, I'll make sure they put you in with the big boys."

"There's nothing else in here," I say, balling up the plastic bag and grabbing the sweatshirt off the hood. "Did you find anything in this?"

"Just a wad of cash. It's on the front seat."

"Man, motherfucker, that's my money. You know I'm gonna be gettin' that back." He makes a "tsk" sound while shaking his head. "If I wasn't in these cuffs, shit."

The last spec of tolerance I have left vanishes, and I drop the hoodie before hauling him to his feet. "If you weren't in these cuffs what, motherfucker? What would you do?"

"Luke."

I ignore Ben, keeping one hand on the handcuff chain and pulling down until this asshole squeals.

"Fuuuck! Shit, man! Shit!"

Ben grabs the guy's shoulders and pulls him out of my grasp. "I got him. Grab his stuff."

I pick up the hoodie and ball it up as Ben puts him in the back of the car. He shuts the door, slowly lifting his head, and I ready myself for the fucking lecture I know I'm about to get.

"What the fuck?"

I move to the driver's side door, avoiding his stare. "Like you haven't done the same thing to assholes like that, or worse."

"Yeah, if they're being combative. If they're just running off at the mouth, we ignore it."

I meet his stare over the top of the car. "What do you want me to say?"

He stretches his arms out on the roof, his hands interlocked together. "Maybe it would be a good idea if you skipped Reed's party tonight."

I set the hoodie on the roof, keeping a fist around it. "That's a shit idea. Wherever Tessa is, I'm going."

"She's bringing a date, man, and the way you've been acting today, I don't think it's a good idea for you to see that. I'll be fucking pissed if I have to arrest you, but I will if you start something."

The tension in my body settles at the base of my neck. Reaching back, I rub out the knot that's forming. "You know, there was a time last year when Mia wanted nothing to do with you. But she was yours, and there wasn't a damn thing anyone could do about that." He nods once, leaning back a little. "You think it's any different for me? You think just because I don't make a fucking announcement at Rocky Point that Tessa isn't mine? Maybe I'm not as honest about my feelings as you always were with Mia, but that doesn't change the fact that being around your sister makes it hard for me to fucking breathe." I open the driver's side door and toss the sweatshirt on the seat. "I'm going tonight. I don't give a shit if it's a good idea or not, and you know damn well if this was last summer, and it was something involving Mia, nothing would've stopped you from going." I lift my eyes to him just in time to catch the smirk twist across his mouth. "What?" I ask, one hand gripping the door while the other flattens on the roof.

He laughs before opening his car door. "Now I really don't think you should go."

"Why not?"

"Because I know exactly what I would've done last summer, and it would've been you pulling me off whoever Mia showed up with." A look of understanding passes between us before he seems to realize how pointless this lecture is. He runs a hand down his face. "You know this is your own damn fault, right?" He waits until I look up before he continues. "Either let her in or let her go. This in-between shit isn't fair to her."

He gets into the car while I stare blankly across the roof. The tension that had settled at the base of my neck is now coiling between my shoulder blades, tightening into an unforgiving knot. My muscles begin to feel stressed as I think about how tonight is going to play out. I don't handle jealousy well, and I know my first reaction to seeing Tessa with another guy is going to be me tearing her away from him. Maybe I can try something different; give her some piece of me to distract her from grinding salt into the wound in the center of my chest. Show her how fucking good this is, how good it always used to be before she decided it wasn't enough.

Let her in or let her go.

Neither one of those options work for me. So this has to.

WE DROP THE mouthy prick off at the detention center before heading to the precinct to finish up some paperwork. I drop my ticket book on my desk and catch the blinking light on my phone, indicating a voice message.

"You want some coffee?" Ben asks as I take a seat.

I look up at him after entering the voicemail code. "Yeah, thanks." Leaning back in the chair, I press the receiver to my ear and wait for the message to begin playing.

"Evans, this is Captain Kennedy. I spoke with Meyers the other day and he told me he offered the detective position to you I have available. Just wanted to see where your head is at in all this. I'm hoping to get a decision out of you soon, otherwise I'm going to have to offer it to somebody else. I heard Jacobs is also interested. Call me when you get a minute."

The message ends, and I grip the receiver harder.

Fuck. The job. I forgot all about it. Last week I was ready to leave Ruxton and every memory I have of it without hesitating. I don't want to deal with my father's shit anymore. Who knows if he'll even take the doctor's advice and seek help to sober up? Failing liver or not, he loves his drink, and like he said, it's the only thing that helps take his mind off my mom. I've made it clear to him that I'm not bailing him out anymore, and if he gets arrested for anything, I'm letting it happen. But I know that won't stop the phone calls from coming.

And Tessa, that's a whole other issue. I've let go of all the anger I had last week that made this decision easy. The anger that had me wanting to put more distance in between us, because being in the same town wasn't doing me any good. But now I no longer feel anything besides the one emotion she's always evoked from me, and I don't need to ask myself if I could leave Tessa, because I already know the answer to that.

A beep rings through the phone, leading me to the next message.

"Yeah, it's me." My dad clears his throat, masking the incessant beeping of the machine he's hooked up to. I can't remember the last time he called me, and I don't think he's ever called my direct line at work before. I didn't even know he had that number.

"I just wanted to tell ya I'm thinking of putting the house up for sale. I need the money. This shit isn't cheap, and . . ."

I delete the rest of the message before slamming the phone down.

Un-fucking-believable.

He's out of money. That asshole has already burned through my mom's life insurance policy with his habit. Why else would he need to sell the house? I never knew how much money he got from her death. I never saw any of it, but it seemed to be enough to keep him from working. Not that he'd be able to hold a steady job, being intoxicated twenty-four hours a day. But now that money must be gone. All of it, and he's going to sell the biggest memory I have of her to keep up with his habit.

I guess he's made his decision. Not even a death wish will stop him from drinking.

"What's up?"

I raise my head to Ben's voice before leaning back in my

chair. He places the paper cup down in front of me and walks behind his desk.

"Nothing," I reply after taking a sip, letting my eyes lose focus amongst the papers in front of me. Several minutes of silence pass between us before Ben begins typing on his keyboard. I pull the coin out of my front pocket and begin turning it over in my hand, studying the words on the one side.

The typing stops, then more silence, before he speaks. "How long is he going to be in the hospital for?"

"The doctor told me just a few days. They are waiting for some tests results to come back before they release him." I run my thumb along the triangle in the center of the coin. "Like anything else is going to make a difference."

"What do you mean?"

I nod toward the phone on my desk. "He's made up his mind. He told me yesterday in the hospital that he can't stop drinking, and now he just told me he's going to sell his house 'cause he's out of money. Can you believe that?" I look over at Ben, propping my ankle up on my knee. "That asshole is actually going to sell the house he shared with my mom, just so he can pay for his booze."

"He's not worried he could die if he keeps it up?"

"You kidding? He thinks it's funny."

Ben shakes his head before tipping back his paper cup. He swallows before continuing. "I'm sorry, man. At least if you take that job, you won't have to be around to watch him kill himself."

"I don't know if I'm going to take it." I watch as he sets the cup down on his desk and turns his body completely toward me, leaning forward to rest his elbows on his knees. "What?" I ask at the sudden undivided attention.

He tilts his head. "You wanna know what I think you

should do?"

"I don't know why you're asking me, 'cause you're going to tell me anyway."

His face hardens. "Fuck you. I was going to say I don't think you should go."

The coin goes still in my hand. "What?"

"You heard me. You've got too much shit here, Luke. I know you try and act like you don't care about your dad, but you obviously do. You've always gone to the bar to stop him from drinking, or wherever the hell he is when someone calls you. He's your dad. He may be the worst one on the fucking planet, but he wasn't always like that."

"He's not the reason why I wouldn't take it."

"Yeah, and then there's that," Ben replies, leaning back and grabbing his cup. He looks down at the contents, a loud exhale escaping him before he continues. "You two have a lot of shit you need to work out. I've told you how I felt about it, so I'm not going to sit here and lecture you. But if you left . . ." He seems pained as his eyes slowly lift to mine. "I can handle my sister being sad over you, but I don't want to see what that would do to her."

I feel my hand slowly tighten around the coin.

I don't want to see what that would do to me.

"Plus," he continues, dropping the serious tone and replacing it with the one I'm used to hearing as he looks past me, "I'd prefer to keep my partner. He's an asshole, but at least I'm not stuck with Jacobs."

I swivel my chair to see CJ walking into the precinct, his dickhead partner trailing behind him. CJ looks how you'd expect a person to look if they were stuck in a car all day with Jacobs. Irritated and spent. Ben laughs quietly behind me as CJ nods in our direction, while Jacobs can't seem to decide whom he wants to give a dirtier look to, Ben or myself. I prop my feet up on the corner of my desk and scratch my cheek with my middle finger.

"Dick," Jacobs addresses me as he walks in front of the desks.

I almost forget what smiling feels like until my lips twitch in the corner.

It's a good feeling, and after Tessa leaves with me tonight, I'll be doing more of it.

I'D GOTTEN TO McGill's early, beating everyone and claiming a stool at the bar. I know what it feels like seeing Tessa with another guy, and the effects are already beginning to set in as I pick at the label on the beer I've been nursing for the past half hour. I'm trying to stay somewhat calm, but my eyes are glued to the door and every time it swings open, the air in my lungs gets stolen from me. As another group of women step inside, I pinch my eyes shut and reclaim my breath.

Jesus Christ. Calm the fuck down, Evans.

"You want another beer?"

My eyes flash open and connect with the bartender. I lift my nearly empty bottle and nod. "Yeah, thanks."

He sets another Coors Light down in front of me just as a hand slaps me in between my shoulder blades. I look over as Reed grabs the stool next to me.

"Hey, man. I said seven o'clock, right? How long you been here?"

I look behind him, letting my eyes sweep across the crowd. "Are you by yourself?"

"Yeah." He motions for the bartender. "Why?" He lifts his head and smiles. "Oh, right. Tessa. You know she's bringing some Aussie, right?"

I wait 'til he orders his beer before I answer. "She's leaving with me."

He breathes a laugh before taking a swig of his beer. "Yeah, all right. Chicks love accents, and you don't have one. You'd be better off grabbing yourself another pussy and making her jealous."

"How's he supposed to do that when you've already claimed every snatch in here?"

I look up from my beer as Ben slides two stools over, putting one closer to the corner of the bar that Reed is sitting at and helping Mia up on the other one.

She smiles at him before her lips pull down in disgust. "I hate that word."

"What word?" Reed asks as Ben takes his seat.

"Snatch," she replies, making a distasteful face. "I'd prefer pussy over snatch, and I really don't like that word either."

"You liked that word last night." Ben drops his head and buries his face in her hair.

The blush spreads across her cheeks as she slides a card across the bar, her other hand pushing against Ben's chest, although she doesn't really seem to want him to back off. "Here. Happy Birthday, Reed."

Reed swipes the card off the bar with enthusiasm. "Aw, babe. You shouldn't have." Ben straightens up, snapping his head in the direction of Reed who shifts on his stool. "Kidding. Jesus." He tears open the card and pulls out a folded up piece of construction paper, covered in crayon drawings. One of the stick figures has the words Uncle Weed underneath. "Ben, you can't draw for shit, man."

Mia laughs, covering her mouth with her hand. "It's from Nolan, ass."

"Nah, really? I couldn't tell."

Ben nearly shoves Reed off his stool before Reed tucks the card back into the envelope. "Tell him I said thanks. His pictures get me laid all the time."

"What?" I ask, looking between the envelope on the bar and Ben, who seems as confused as I am.

Reed nods through a swallow, setting his beer down. "Yeah, women love thinking I have a kid. They eat that shit up."

"Give me that." Ben slams his hand down on the card and slides it in front of himself. "My kid isn't getting you laid tonight."

"No matter. I got a picture of him in my wallet I can always use."

I shake my head as a loud laugh grabs my attention across the room. Three girls walk through the door, announcing their arrival with the different octaves of cackles emanating from each of them. The door nearly closes before it's pulled open again, and everything around me fades as red hair fills my line of sight.

I swallow hard as she nervously chews on her bottom lip, sweeping her eyes across the crowd until they finally land on me. Her feet become glued to the floor as she stops in the middle of the bar, but she stumbles forward when someone pushes into her back. I look behind her as a guy drops his head closer to her ear, way too fucking close, and she nods once, her eyes meeting his briefly before moving with him toward Mia's side of the bar.

The blood in my veins feels like jet fuel that's just been lit, burning me up from the inside out. Sweat pools at the base of my neck as I wrap my hand around the chilled beer bottle—I need something to counter the heat surging through me.

I only see Tessa.

There has to be at least fifty people in this bar, including the asshole she's arrived with, but it's just her and me in this room. The dress she has on shows off the flawless skin of her chest, plunging low enough for me to see the top of her cleavage. I know what that spot tastes like, the feel of her hands holding my head as I slide my tongue over her skin, consuming and claiming, which is exactly what I want to be doing right now. Her green eyes appear bigger, the color more pronounced as she moves closer, meeting my gaze every other step. I know she's nervous by the way her bottom lip is being tortured, that and the fact that her hand keeps tucking the same strand of hair behind her ear, even though it hasn't moved. She's putting as much distance between her and me as possible while still joining the group, but it wouldn't matter if she were on the other side of the fucking planet right now. Every part of me is reacting to her, some more than others as I drop a hand to my lap.

Everyone seems to notice her presence at the same time, while I noticed it the second she walked in the room. Mia turns on her stool as the guy behind Tessa steps to the side, standing between her and the bar.

"Hey! There you two are."

Tessa smiles at Mia before moving her gaze down the line of people, stopping at Reed. "Guys, this is Mason." She looks up at him before pointing to each of us. "You know Mia, and that's her husband, Ben, my brother. That's Reed, and that's Luke."

My name drops from her lips so fast, it's as if she can barely form the word. Mason shakes Ben's hand and leans across the bar, offering his hand to Reed, then myself.

"Nice to meet ya, mate," he directs at me.

I look over at Tessa briefly before dropping my head into a nod and accepting his handshake. "Yeah, you too."

The two of them claim the stools on the other side of Mia as I work out what my next move should be. Conversation around me picks up, all background noise I can't focus on as I stare at the hand flattening against Tessa's back.

My hand quickly finds the phone in my pocket and I keep it concealed in my lap as I open up a new text message. I don't know if this is going to work, but it used to. This always used to get her attention, no matter if she were pissed at me for something or not.

It's all I have right now, so I go with it.

Me: You are so fucking beautiful when you come.

The small purse she put on the bar in front of her vibrates, and I watch her hand slip inside.

And the reaction I get is exactly what I was hoping for.

"YOU WANT SOMETHING to drink?"

I hear Mason's question seconds before his hand presses against my lower back. This should feel natural. We are technically on a date, so a little PDA is expected, but the fact that Luke is sitting no more than ten feet away from me has my body slowly arching away from the gesture. I force myself to relax back, to *want* his hand there, as I lift my eyes to meet his.

"That would be great, thanks. Whatever you're having."

Just as he calls over the bartender, my clutch vibrates against the wood. I snatch my phone out to quickly silence it and swipe my thumb across the screen.

Luke: You are so fucking beautiful when you come.

Shit!

I tilt my phone down, knocking the screen against the bar as my thighs pinch together. Luke is looking right at me, gauging my reaction with that sexy-as-hell smirk lifting the corner of his mouth. He's clearly satisfied by what he's just earned, and I hate myself for giving it to him, for needing to look anywhere near his general direction. I break the contact with a heavy blink before it all becomes too much.

It already is too much. Who the hell are you kidding, Tessa?

My free hand flattens on the wood, and slides along the

grain as my palm begins to sweat. A buzzing sound rattles against the bar as the phone begins vibrating again. I slide it into my lap, forcing my eyes to look anywhere but the screen, which doesn't come without a struggle. That annoys me. I'm on a damn date, and I'm more interested in the texts the asshole at the end of the bar has no business sending me than the guy I'm supposed to be paying attention to.

"Lime?"

I wonder what the text says. Is it just as dirty? Is he going to get into specifics about what exactly it is about me that's beautiful when I come? Like, are we talking noises, or actual facial expressions?

Damn it. Now I'm really curious.

"Tessa?"

A voice close to my ear startles me, bringing my attention off my lap. "Huh?" I lock eyes with Mason as he holds a lime wedge between his thumb and finger, his eyebrows set into a curious pinch.

"Oh, yes please."

While he stuffs the lime wedge down the neck of my bottle, I give in to the temptation in my lap. Keeping the phone concealed as best as I can, I tilt the screen up and let my eyes focus on the message.

> *Luke: I've been obsessed with it since the first time I slid my fingers inside you.*

Oh, God.

"Everything all right?"

I look directly at Mason and watch as his eyes shift from one side of my face to the other.

Damn my reaction to Luke. I know exactly what I look like right now. He thinks I'm beautiful when I come, and he's getting me to the point of allowing everyone in this bar to see exactly what that looks like.

Mason reaches out and runs the back of his fingers across my cheek. It's a tender move, one I'm not expecting, and it soothes some of the ache building between my hips. "You look like you've just run a marathon. Do you feel okay?" His eyes drop to the phone in my lap. "Is something wrong?"

"No," I reply with enough conviction to hopefully persuade myself. The hand in my lap clutches the phone, while the other grabs the beer that's been placed in front of me. I take several generous swigs as Mason watches me closely.

"So, how long have you known these guys? Aside from your brother."

I turn my body until my leg touches his, forcing my attention away from everyone else in the bar. His eyes take notice of the contact and he smiles as his fingers drum the bar-top.

I lick the beer off my lips, swallowing hard, as Mia laughs loudly next to me.

My best friend. I can talk about her.

I smile. "I've known Mia since we were kids. She used to live here until she had to move to Georgia. Then last summer, she came to visit and fell in love with my brother, so now she's here permanently. Reed and I have been friends since high school."

"And the other bloke?" He looks down the length of the bar, dropping his head into a nod. "He's been staring at you since we walked in here."

My smile fades. "He's an asshole."

His eyes shift to mine. "Ex-asshole?"

I start to shake my head, to deny him that information, but what's the point?

"Yeah," I confirm, running my hand over the condensation

that has built up on the bar.

"I'm guessing he doesn't want to be an ex-anything."

"I don't care what he wants," I reply, just as the phone in my lap vibrates. I somehow manage to ignore it as movement at my back draws my attention over my shoulder.

"Birthday shots!" Mia yells, her face lit up with excitement. "Here, you have to drink mine. I'm shooting water."

"Party animal," I tease, sliding a shot to Mason and putting my two in front of me.

"Shut up. I need to stay hydrated." Mia winks at me as she holds up her shot glass of H2O, her other hand resting protectively over her belly.

Reed clears his throat, gaining everyone's attention with his glass raised in the air. He looks around, seemingly waiting for something, and then sets his shot back down when he doesn't get it. An irritated frown gets directed at all of us. "Well, what the fuck? Somebody better make a toast."

"You just announced that you like to use my kid to help you get your dick wet. Fuck you and your birthday," Ben says, shooting his drink.

Everyone but Reed lets out a laugh as I pick up one of my shot glasses and bring it to my lips.

"I'll toast to something."

The sound of Luke's voice sends my body completely rigid. I slowly lower my glass and turn my head, waiting.

He looks directly at me. "To Tessa," he states, raising his glass in my direction.

"What?" My word seems to echo off every surface in the bar, amplifying around us.

"That's it?" Reed asks, a frown pinching his forehead. "Nothing about me?"

"That's it," Luke affirms, keeping his eyes on me while

he tilts his head to swallow his shot.

Mia makes an emotional sound next to me, which she quickly covers up with a cough when I shoot daggers at her.

Anger boils in my blood, but it's the kind of anger that can so easily blend into another emotion. The kind of anger that makes your whole body shake as you fight back your tears.

I raise my shot, leaning closer to the bar so everyone can see me. "Well, since we're all toasting to bullshit, not anything that really *matters*—" I stress that last word before I continue, praying for a steady voice, "—to Luke." His eyes study my face with an apprehension I don't see often from him. He's not the kind of guy who gets easily unraveled, but I see it as he waits with parted lips.

I smile directly at him. "Fuck you. You broke my heart."

"And happy birthday to Reed!" Mia yells as I tip one, then the other shot back, shutting my eyes through my swallow.

I steal a quick glance at Luke, checking that I still have all his attention, but I break the contact almost immediately after I get it.

Mia spins on her stool to face in my direction, hopping down with help from Ben. "We're going to go play some pool. You two want in?" She directs the question at Mason and me.

"Who's we?" I ask, letting my eyes meet the blazing intensity of Luke's as he watches me from over top the beer he's drinking. The sleeve of his shirt rides up his forearm, and I swallow as his ink is revealed.

Damn it.

"Everyone but you two," she replies. Her belly nudges against my elbow, forcing her to take a step back. She looks down. "I have no idea how I'm going to physically pull this off. Maybe I'll just keep score."

"You two playing?" Ben asks, dropping his chin on Mia's

shoulder as his arms wrap around her.

I watch as Luke and Reed walk across the bar to the back corner where the pool tables are lined up.

"No," I answer, just as Mason stands from his stool with a "Yeah, sure."

"You don't want to?" he asks me, lowering himself back down. His eyes glance behind me, and reasoning washes over his face. He looks at Ben. "No thanks, mate. We're going to pass on this one."

Mia and Ben walk away to join the others.

"I'm sorry," I say quietly, turning my body once more so that it faces him. "If you really want to play, we can play."

A small crease sets in between his eyebrows as he grabs his beer. "I'm good sitting here with you." He brings the bottle to his lips as the annoying vibration in my lap starts up again. This time, he notices, dropping his eyes to the source.

"Fucking jerk-off," I mumble through gritted teeth as my hand flattens against the phone.

"You can answer that."

"No, it's fine. It's not important."

He sets his beer down, his other hand coming up and scratching the stubble on his cheek. "So, are you going to be coming to any more of my classes?"

I try and bite back the automatic wince at the thought of enduring more yoga, but it breaks through, tearing a loud laugh out of Mason.

"Not really your thing, huh?" he asks with a raised eyebrow.

I shake my head animatedly, sending my hair flailing about, brushing across my shoulders and the sides of my face.

His blue eyes grow bigger as he leans in to rub a strand of my hair between his fingers. "I really like your hair."

"Thanks. I really like yours." My hand is inches away from the blond strand darting out from behind his ear when my lap vibrates. I curse, cranking my neck around and glaring over my shoulder.

Luke is leaning against the wall, cue stick in one hand, his other dropped beside him to no doubt hide the phone he's holding. His eyes slowly meet mine, and he tilts his head expectantly. *Answer it. Stop fighting me.*

I fumble with the phone in my lap as I turn back around.

I have to look. It's killing me not to.

"I'm sorry. Just give me one second," I say hopefully to Mason, if he's still next to me. To be honest, I wouldn't have any idea. I'm too focused on my thumb as it slides eagerly across the screen.

"No worries. Want another beer?"

I shake my head as I scroll back to the first message I ignored.

> *Luke: He'll never see that part of you, Tessa.*

I'm immediately confused, until I read his previous texts about how beautiful I am when I come. I guess now he's deciding what guys I'll sleep with. How sweet. I go to scroll to the next message, but my unwanted impatience nearly causes me to drop my phone.

"Shit."

"Sorry?" Mason asks.

"Nothing, be right with you." My eyes narrow in on the block letters.

> *Luke: He'll never see that you're just as desperate for him as he is for you.*

I try to swallow, but I can't. Instead, I let my mouth hang

open as I read the first real confession Luke's ever given me that pertains to his feelings. I read it again, then once more, as the words become almost illegible through the tears filling my eyes. I have one more message to read, and I can't get to it fast enough.

> *Luke: Read this next line slowly, so it sinks in. It was never just about sex. Go back and read it again. Again, Tessa. Do it.*

A laugh bubbles up in my throat as I re-read that line three times before I continue with the rest of the text.

Just in case you're being stubborn, because you are stubborn, I'll type it out again. It was never just about sex. Not even the other night when you kept me out. I wanted to be with you because it's the only time I see how much you need me. And I don't feel completely alone anymore.

My breath hitches as my hand covers my mouth, holding in the sob that's begging to escape.

"Tessa?"

I hop off my stool, practically falling into Mason as I slam my phone on the bar next to my clutch. "I'm sorry. I need a minute." The words come out like a desperate plea before I turn and push through the crowd of people in the direction of the bathrooms. I know the layout of McGill's well; I know the long hallway that leads to the restrooms and the privacy it holds. I also know that I don't need to look in Luke's direction to signal him to follow me. I *know* he'll follow me, and it's confirmed when a hand grabs my elbow, halting me halfway to my destination.

"Hey."

That little word is the only thing I allow him to say before I open my mouth.

"You asshole! You can't send me texts like that. It's too

late! You're too fucking late, Luke." My hands shove against his broad chest, hard enough my elbows strain not to bend. He could fight against me easily if he wanted to, but the only resistance I meet is the wall behind him that's unwilling to give.

I ignore the way my hands mold to his body. How my fingers reflexively seek anchor in the defined ridges of his muscles. It's my body's natural response to his. To grab a hold of any part of him I can.

I take in a constricted breath, my lungs burning as the air fills them. "You're desperate for me? You *need* me? Where the hell was all this when I needed to hear it? Huh? When I begged you . . ." A sob breaks apart my voice, followed by more tears.

I push and push, wanting some sort of fight from him. Words, a hand holding me back, something—anything. I don't want this to be easy. We have *never* been easy. I need a reaction from him and at this point, I don't care what all I tell him.

How can this hurt any more than it already does?

"How did I fall in love with you?" I blink, sending the tears down my face. His lips part as a rushed breath escapes him, and for the first time since I pushed him up against this wall, he leans into me, causing my elbows to collapse under the pressure. I keep the distance between us with one hand flat against his chest, and he waits for more, studying my mouth as if he'll be able to read the words I'm about to say.

"I wanted so much more than you ever gave me. I cried over you, every time you kept me out, but I still loved you. When you broke my heart . . . again and again, I loved you. A year ago . . . and yesterday, I loved you."

"Do you love me today?" he asks, and I suddenly realize how close we are now. I don't know when his hand formed to my hip, or his other to my cheek, but I'm too shattered to protest it.

I close my eyes with a heavy swallow. "In any universe, any version of you I could get, I would find you, and I would love you." He moves in, his lips sealing against mine with the gentlest of kisses. "But I can't love you today."

At the feel of him leaning back, my eyes flash open, meeting the wounded look in his.

"Tessa."

"No." His hands drop away as I slide out of his grip. "I won't, Luke. Not today."

I leave him standing in the hallway, forcing my feet to move to get me out of there. I can't see him like that, exactly how I've always felt when he's pulled away from me—heartbroken and destroyed. It's his turn to feel it now. Not just me.

The bar noise hits me as the room opens up, and I spot Mason bending over to take his shot at the pool table. Mia frowns as I step up to join the group, and I give her a weak smile, hoping to hide my misery.

"Hey, everything all right?" Mason asks, leaning his pool cue against the table. He looks over my shoulder, and I watch his eyes move with someone, following them.

I look to my right and catch the back of Luke as he exits the bar.

"Do you want to get out of here?" Mason's voice brings my attention back to him, and I tilt my head up, expecting to see the look that's normally paired with that line. I've heard variations of it, hell, I've used it myself, but I don't get that shameless lust that's usually burning behind the eyes of the person who's delivered it. Mason only looks at me with kindness, the way a concerned friend comforts you when you're too far gone to ask for help.

I know the smile I give him in response isn't much, but he takes it as if it is. He spins around, his hand reaching for something on the pool table. Seconds later, my clutch is being held out in front of me.

"I put your phone in there," he says, handing it over in the most casual way, as if being incredibly thoughtful is a trait every man carries.

"Thank you," I reply.

"Are you two leaving? I was going to get another round of shots," Reed says from the other side of the pool table. A leggy brunette rubs her hand along the front of his polo shirt, teasing the two buttons at the collar.

"You seem good," I shoot back at him, and he lifts his nose out of the girl's hair and winks at me. "Happy birthday."

"Thanks."

Mia places her hand on my arm and frowns. "Do you want to talk about it?"

"No, not right now. I'll call you later."

She kisses my cheek and waves at Mason. Ben says his goodbyes, shaking Mason's hand and wrapping his arms around me.

"Do I need to beat his ass?" he asks quietly into my hair.

I shake my head, snaking my arms around his back and squeezing him tighter. I love hugging my brother, the way I disappear the second his arms envelope me. He's slightly taller than Luke, but has the same build, and I swear his arms could rip a tree right out of the ground without any effort.

"He cares about you. He may never say it, but that doesn't mean it's not true."

"What if Mia never told you she loved you?" I ask, letting my arms drop to my side as he releases me.

He looks pained at the very thought of what I've just said. With a quick shrug, he drops his eyes to Mia as she joins his side. "I'd probably still be waiting for it."

"Waiting for what?" she asks, leaning against his arm.

Ben kisses the top of her head. "Nothing, angel."

Mason and I say our final goodbyes to the group before I let him lead me out of the bar. I feel drained, emotionally shattered. I don't know why they call it heartbreak when every bone in your body seems affected. The pain isn't stagnant in the center of my chest. It radiates out, then back in, pulsing at an unforgiving rhythm. I feel like I'm barely moving of my own accord, but I make it to the passenger side of Mason's Denali without too much difficulty.

"I thought we would just go for a drive," he says, opening my door for me. "I like to do that when I'm having a hard time with things. It helps me think."

"I've done enough thinking," I reply, strapping the seatbelt across my lap. My curt response has me pinching my eyes shut.

Asshole, Tessa. You're an asshole.

Mason doesn't have to do anything for me. He could just take me home and end what has to be the worst date of his life. I turn my head, nodding at his suggestion with a small grin. "I like going for rides."

His smile is immediate, lighting up his entire face. "Me too, and my sisters tell me I'm like a chick when it comes to listening to someone else's problems, so feel free to talk my ear off."

I laugh as he shuts my door, and ask my question as soon as he opens his. "How many sisters do you have?"

"Seven," he answers, strapping on his seatbelt and pulling out onto the road.

"Seven? Holy shit. Do you have any brothers?"

He shakes his head, giving me a quick glance. "No, just me, and I'm the youngest, so they used to use me as their own personal doll to dress up. The pictures are mortifying."

I cover my mouth with my hand, muffling my laugh. "Aww, you poor thing. Did they put you in dresses?"

"Yep."

"Makeup?"

"Yep."

I let my head flop back against the seat with my chuckle. "Is that why you left Australia? To reclaim your manhood?"

He keeps one hand on the wheel, resting his other in his lap. Leaning forward, he checks for traffic through my window, then his, before pulling onto a back road.

His fingers scratch along his chin before he speaks. "Following a woman to another country who didn't ask me to move with her sounds like the opposite, if you ask me."

"Was she your girlfriend?"

"I always saw her as that. She didn't, which I tried to be okay with. But that's not me. I get attached really easily, and I'm upfront about it. I don't hide my feelings or play stupid games. I'm almost thirty years old. I want something that's real." He looks over at me. "Not many blokes are like that, I guess."

"Not a lot that I've met."

He fixates his gaze on the dark road in front of us. "I realized how pathetic I looked after I uprooted my life, but I didn't want to go back home. I needed something new. So I left her in Texas and drove until I didn't feel like driving anymore."

I cross one leg over the other, angling my body toward him. "She sounds like a C-word. If some guy followed me thousands of miles away, I'd probably ask him to marry me."

The car comes to a stop at a red light, and he looks over at me, confusion creasing his brow. "C-word?"

"Cunt."

His eyes go wide, and I can tell I've just embarrassed him a bit. "Wow."

I give an apologetic shrug while my fingers begin nervously twisting the ends of my hair. "Sorry. My mouth doesn't have much of a filter."

"No need to apologize. I like your mouth."

I glance over at him, forcing down an uncomfortable swallow. "Mason, I don't think I'm . . ."

"I know you're not ready, Tessa," he interrupts with a kind smile. "I think I knew something was up when I asked for your number. You went from flirting with me pretty hard to being almost uncomfortable."

"I'm sorry."

"Don't be sorry. I still had a good time tonight."

I drop my hand into my lap, letting my eyes focus on the dashboard. "He said things to me tonight I've been waiting to hear from him, and I told him it was too late." I reach up and wipe the tear off my cheek as a small whimper slips past my lips. "Do you think he believed me?"

Mason squeezes my hand. "I don't know. Did you look like this when you said it?" I shake my head before dropping it into my hands. His arms pull me against his side, and he rubs my back gently. "Shh," he says into my hair as I cry against him. "It'll be okay."

I don't know how long we sit there for, but Mason never rushes me. He never once pulls me away from him, not even to check the state of his shirt, which I'm rubbing my face against. When I've finally calmed myself down, he hands me a wad of napkins he keeps in the glove compartment and smiles at me, like I've given him one of the best dates he's ever had.

This guy will seriously ruin a very lucky girl.

I climb the stairs leading up to my apartment, gripping my clutch with one hand while my other slides along the railing. When I reach the top, my heart slams against my ribs at the sight of Luke, sitting with his back against my door, knees bent and his head hanging low between his shoulders. I stand motionless, but he senses me and lifts his eyes to meet mine.

We both move at the same time, me slowly inching forward toward my door, and him pushing off the ground and straightening up. He tucks his hands into his pockets, looking unsure of himself, as I come up beside him.

"How long have you been here?" I ask, pulling my keys out of my clutch. My nervous fingers drop them, and I curse as I bend over, picking them off the ground.

"I came straight here from the bar. I didn't think you'd be that long." His voice comes from close behind me as I try and steady my hand enough to shove the key into the top lock. It's not working, and I nearly drop them again. I let out a rushed breath when he reaches around me, covering my hand with his, and unlocks the door.

"Please let me in," he says into my hair, sending a chill down my back. His hand moves, twisting both of ours together, continuing the motion with the rest of the locks until the last one is unlatched.

I stare at the door, not pushing it open yet, while his hand remains on mine, holding the key in the bottom lock.

"Please. I'm not here for . . ." He pauses, moving closer until his lips press against my ear. I close my eyes. "I won't touch you if you don't want me to, Tessa. Just let me be here. Please."

I turn my head, prompting him to lean back so he can look at me. "If I say no, are you going to leave?"

"Probably not." His eyes soften, and I watch his neck roll with a hard swallow as he stares at my mouth, waiting for the words he needs to hear.

I make a decision, one that I might regret tomorrow, but it's done. I push open the door and walk inside.

luke

TURN IT. PLEASE, *let me in.*

Her eyes are reddened, heavy with uncertainty. She blinks slowly as she contemplates this decision, and I want to rush her, to decide for her, but I don't. I won't force myself inside if she doesn't want me, but there's no way in hell I'm leaving.

Her lips part, and with a soft exhale her wrist finally turns, opening the door.

I wait, not wanting to push my way in if she doesn't want this. My fingers curl around the wood of the doorframe as I keep my body braced, ready to enter. She looks back at me after taking a few steps inside, raising her eyebrows expectantly, and that's all I need.

I shut the door behind me, clicking the locks in place as I try and keep the blinding relief coursing through me hidden.

But, fuck, I want to kiss her just for looking back at me.

Waiting outside her door, not knowing what she was doing with that guy has left my nerves fused together, coiled in a tight bundle in the center of my chest. I've heard of panic attacks, and I damn near had one, thinking she wasn't going to come home.

I would've waited. She could've been out all night, and I would've fucking waited.

Seeing her like that at the bar messed my shit up. I never

needed Tessa to admit her feelings to me. What we had, what she gave me was always enough, but hearing her say it, that she's loved me all this time, that . . . fuck, I don't know how I ever lived without hearing it.

Tessa watches me over her shoulder as the fifth lock is latched, then drops her purse and keys on the kitchen table.

"I'm going to get changed, if you want to watch TV or something." She avoids my eyes, but gestures in the direction of the couch before walking toward the hallway leading to the bedroom.

Fuck watching TV. The only thing I want to watch is her. Tessa can do whatever the hell she wants tonight, but my eyes will be on her the second she comes back out here.

I need a distraction to keep myself from walking to her bedroom, so I open the refrigerator, leaning down to peer inside. I grab the packet of cookie dough squares off the top shelf and tear across the top, breaking the seal. As I pop one of the squares into my mouth, I notice the tea-kettle on the back burner. Tessa loves drinking that green herbal shit at night. She used to try and get me to drink some when she said I needed to relax. I never did. It looks awful, and it smells worse, but she likes it.

I fill the kettle with warm water and turn the burner on high. The low whistle begins to sound as I'm chewing up my third cookie dough square. Setting the pack down, I turn off the burner and pour the water over the tea bag, filling the cup. The aroma seeps out from the top and hits me in the face.

I lean away, setting the kettle down. "Fuck. How do you drink this?"

"How do I drink what?"

I look over my shoulder to see Tessa standing on the other side of the small island attached to the kitchen counter. Her face is flushed, stripped of all makeup like I prefer. Her hair is pulled up out of her face into one of those messy knots she always does, and she's wearing my T-shirt from the other day.

I set the cup down on the island in front of her, placing the bottle of honey from the cabinet next to it. "Here. I wasn't sure how much you usually put in there. I didn't want to mess it up."

She steps forward with caution, rising a few inches on her toes to peer down into the mug. A strand of her hair falls into her face, and I make a fist to keep myself from guiding it back behind her ear. Her head stays turned down, then her lips part before her eyes slowly lift to mine. "You made me tea?"

I slide a spoon across the island. "Yeah. I know how much you like it."

It takes her several seconds to blink, maybe a full minute, but when she does, she focuses back on her cup. "Thank you," she says quietly, popping the lid off the honey and drizzling some into the mug. She looks up at me when she hears the cookie dough package opening with the force of my hand.

I freeze, leaning my back against the counter with my fingers ready to pull out another square. I don't know what makes me say it. I never talk about this, even when it's heavy on my mind. Maybe it's the confession Tessa gave me earlier that has me needing to give her some part of me, but whatever it is, the words come out of my mouth before I can think to swallow them down.

"My mom used to buy these all the time when I was a kid. She never baked them. She just kept them in the fridge for a snack." I look down at the package in my hand, turning it over to look at the cooking instructions. "I've never actually had baked chocolate chip cookies before." After examining the information I've never bothered to look at, I glance up and meet Tessa's wide-eyed stare.

She blinks several times, focuses on her mug, and then lifts her head again. "I want to ask you about her, but if you don't want me to, what you've just said is okay."

"You can ask me," I quickly reply, the words rushing out of my mouth as if they can't escape fast enough.

She nods, lifting her mug and blowing across the top. "How did she die?" Her eyes fall to a space between us immediately after her question.

I seal the top of the package and slip it back into the fridge. My hand flattens against the side of my face, sliding down roughly, as I take a minute before I respond.

"I'm sorry," she says. She looks regretful as she sets her mug down.

I step closer to the counter separating us. "It's all right. I told you, you could ask me. I'm just not used to talking about it." My shoulders sag as I tuck my hands into my pockets, needing somewhere to put them. "She was driving into town to go to some store or something, and while she was at a red light, this guy came up to her window and asked for some money." I look down, picturing how I've always imagined it in my head. "Once she rolled her window down, he pulled a gun on her and told her to get out of the car. I think she would've listened to him if he would've waited two fucking seconds, but he didn't. When the cops pulled him over in the next county, he told them he'd shot her as soon as she'd looked at the gun."

Arms wrap around my waist from behind, and her head presses against my back as she flattens herself against me. "How old were you?" she asks in a gentle voice.

"Fifteen."

"Is that why you became a cop? Because of what happened

to her?"

I stare down at her fingers as they grab the bottom of my shirt, curling around the material. "Yeah, I guess."

She breathes against me, in then out. "I'm so sorry. I can't imagine losing somebody like that. Were you really close with her?"

The second I feel her finger run along the skin of my stomach, I pull my hands out of my pockets and grab her wrists, gripping them with a warning. "Don't do that."

"Don't do what?" she asks, but doesn't resist my hold on her.

I take in two calming breaths while my reaction to her stirs wildly in my blood. "You know what. Don't play with me, Tessa. I'm not here for that."

"I'm not playing with you. I was just . . ." She sighs loudly before something thuds against my back. "I was just trying to comfort you. I wasn't going to go any lower."

I turn around, breaking her hold on me, and stare down into her eyes. She looks pained by my rejection, also slightly embarrassed, and I tilt her chin up with my finger when she tries to avoid me. "You don't need to comfort me. I just want to be near you."

"But your mom. That's so sad, Luke. I don't know how you do it. I just . . ." Her bottom lip begins to tremble seconds before she crashes against me, wrapping me into the strongest hug of my life. My back hits the hard edge of the counter and I wince through a groan. "Please let me just do this for a little while. I won't go under your clothes. I promise." She sniffs and wipes her face against my shirt. "I love that you got her name tattooed on you. I bet she would love it too."

I press my mouth to her hair as the ache in my back numbs out. "I doubt it. She hated my dad's tattoos."

"But yours is different, and the fact that you only eat cookies the way she ate them . . . Can we go lay down in my bed?"

Fuck no. Is she crazy?

"No."

She tilts her head up, blinking the tears away. "Just to do this. I promise. I won't do anything besides what I'm doing now. No more touching than this."

I set my jaw as I try and come up with at least one reason why this is a bad idea. But every reason, good or bad, escapes me when her full lips mouth a desperate *please.*

I tilt my head down, staring at the front of the T-shirt she's wearing. "With clothes on. I know what you normally wear in that bed, and I can't handle that right now. Okay?"

She steps back, letting her hands fall away from me. "Okay," she echoes before moving in the direction of the bedroom. Halfway down the hallway, she glances back to make sure I'm following her.

Where the fuck else would I be going?

I wait for the moment to hit me, the sudden clarity that should move my ass away from anything that'll put Tessa in a horizontal position, but it never comes.

She shoves something into the drawer of her nightstand as I enter the room before tugging at the blue tie in her hair. With her free hand, she motions toward the bed.

I stand there, wondering what the fuck I'm about to do right now. Tessa has always thought what we had was based solely on sex. It never was, not for me, and I've spelled that out for her already, but I know how she is when we're in bed together. There's never any space between us. Having her touch me in any way makes me crave her, and I'm trying to prove what I texted her earlier wasn't just some bullshit to get her away from that guy she was with.

She stares at me as her hair falls past her shoulders, waiting.

This is where I need to leave the room, or say I don't think this is a good idea, or even suggest the fucking couch instead of her bed.

"Please," she says, taking a step closer. "I'm tired, and I just want to talk, and maybe fall asleep with you. That's it."

I look at the bed, then back at her. "I meant what I texted you earlier. I meant every fucking word of it."

She tucks her hair behind her ear, looking up at me from underneath her lashes, and I catch the slight tremble in her hand before she drops it to her side. "Okay," she replies in the softest voice I've ever heard her use.

I settle on my back in the center of the bed, tucking my hand underneath my pillow to boost myself up.

"Were you really close with her?" she asks as she climbs onto the bed, resting her head on my chest. Her arm wraps around me, then her leg, until I'm completely blanketed by her tiny body.

We don't need to talk. The only thing I need from her right now is this. She has no idea what this does to me, what this has always done to me.

I look down the length of my body, staring at the top of her head. "Yeah, I guess."

"I can't imagine going through that. Losing a parent in any way is so unbelievably sad. It was devastating to Mia, but she at least knew her mom was sick, and there was always that chance something could happen to her. But with you . . ." She squeezes me harder. "How did you handle it?"

I look up at the ceiling, concentrating on the steady rhythm of her heartbeat against my side. It's crazy how much that soothes me. The feel of her, breathing, living—having her right here like this.

She sniffs, and I know she's crying again as she nuzzles closer. "Luke?"

I remember her question, shifting my body underneath hers a bit so her leg stops brushing against my cock. "I don't know. I was forced to handle it, so I did. What else was I gonna do?"

"I don't know what I would've done. And your dad, oh God, was he devastated?" Her head tilts up and she rests her chin on my chest. "He must've been heartbroken."

"I don't want to talk about him," I reply, watching her eyes dilate behind the tears in them. "And don't call him my dad. He stopped being that a long time ago."

"What happened between you two?"

"Tessa, what the fuck?" I practically shout, startling her. Her hold on me tightens as she sucks in a breath, and I can tell she's regretting pushing this shit. Her mouth falls open, the tears still spilling down her face. I slide out from underneath her and sit on the edge of the bed, resting my elbows on my knees and dropping my head. I'm no longer calm. I'm fucking tense, anxious like I was sitting outside her door.

The bed dips behind me, but I don't turn around to look at her.

"I'm sorry," she whispers, brushing her body against my back.

I cup my hands together and rest my chin against them, staring blankly at the wall. "I don't talk about shit I don't give a damn about anymore. Yeah, he was heartbroken and devastated, but while he turned to getting piss-drunk every day, I was left with nobody. I had to deal with that and the shit he put me through alone, and I will always deal with it by myself. It's my fucking burden, no one else's."

She sniffs again, louder this time, as her hands flatten against my chest from behind. "I just . . . I want to be there for you. You don't have to do this alone anymore. Whatever it is, we can handle it together."

"Why can't what I've given you be enough?" I ask. I look over my shoulder, connecting with her tear-filled eyes. I'm beginning to feel as shattered as she looks right now, because I know she'll never be content with just this. But that doesn't stop me from telling her I will.

"Just being with you has always been enough for me," I say, turning my body until she's next to my side. I hold her face with both my hands, sliding my thumbs along her skin. "I don't know what it is about you, Tessa, but you make all that bad shit go away."

She starts full-on crying now, and I pull her into my lap, really holding her for the first time in days.

"I don't want to let go of you," she whispers against my neck, pressing kisses there.

I close my eyes, dropping my head to her shoulder. I savor the breath I take in, the scent of her, as if it's my last. My lips touch her neck, then her ear. "Do you want your tea?"

She laughs softly, leaning back to look at me. Her hand touches my cheek, then a finger traces the line of my jaw. She always used to do that. "I forgot about it. Will you get it for me?" she asks through a yawn as I wipe the tears from her face.

I watch her settle under the covers before I walk out of the bedroom. I need to take a piss first, and as I'm finishing up in the bathroom, I hear the faint echo of Tessa's ringtone, sounding from the direction of the kitchen. It starts up again just before I reach the counter where her mug was placed. I walk over to her purse and pull out the cell phone, my face hardening at the name flashing on the screen.

"Yeah," I answer, more as a demand than a question, because I'm really not fucking interested in what this guy wants right now.

"Uh, this is Tessa's phone, correct?"

"Yeah, it is, and she's busy."

I hear a faint laugh. "Right, mate, sorry. Luke, is it?" He pauses, and my silence is the only response he's going to get. I roll my shoulders back, trying to loosen up as I wait for him to hurry the fuck up with this so I can give Tessa her tea.

"I'll take that as a yes. Listen, I was just calling to see if she was okay. She was pretty upset when I dropped her off."

"She's fine," I grunt out, trying to keep my voice low as I lean against the table.

"Yeah? That's good. I've seen some pretty sad women before. My sisters like to dump their man problems on me 'cause I'm a good listener, but I don't think I've seen any of them cry like Tessa did. She was pretty heartbroken, mate."

I know what that looks like. I know too damn well, and just picturing it kills me. If it were any other guy making her upset, I'd find out who it was and beat the shit out of them.

But it's me. She'll never stop crying over me.

"Do you like her?" I ask, hearing the fear in my voice as my free hand wraps around the edge of the table.

"Uh . . . yeah, mate. Sure, I like her, but—"

"She'll love you, and it'll be the best damn thing you've ever felt. Nobody loves the way Tessa does, and she deserves somebody to give her that." I swallow hard, closing my eyes. "Are you sticking around here?"

"Yeah, for a while, at least. I like it here."

"Good." I hang up the phone and push it back into her purse.

After re-heating the tea in the microwave, I carry it into

her bedroom and set it on the nightstand.

"It's really hot, so be careful," I say as I take a seat on the edge of the bed.

I stare at the wall, letting my eyes lose focus.

I know what I have to do.

"You changed my life the second I saw you getting out of Ben's truck. It was fucking crazy. I've never felt like I needed somebody before, but I needed you, and I knew it. Then I had you, and . . . I'll never need anybody again. I know that. I hate keeping you out, but you're so good, Tessa, and I don't want you affected by this shit. It's dirty, and ugly, and everything you're not, and what I'm about to do is going to fucking kill me, but this is what I can give you."

My heart thunders in my chest, trying to break its way out before I destroy it.

"That guy can be good for you. He seems decent, and he'll give you things I can't." I drop my head, keeping the shaky breath I take in quiet. "You'll always be mine, Tessa. In a couple years after you've forgotten about me, you'll still be mine. You're going to hate me for doing this, but I need you to be happy, and I think this guy can help with that."

I wipe my hands down my face, drying the wetness there before turning sideways to look at her. She's in a deep sleep, her heavy, even breathing escaping the small opening between her lips.

I lay my hand on hers, memorizing the feel of her skin. "I love you. Those words are yours. I'll never say them to anyone else."

I bend down, pressing my lips to hers. A gentle kiss that she'll never know about.

The last one I'll ever have.

I pull my phone out of my pocket as I walk to my truck.

The call connects after three rings.

"Yeah? Hello?" a gruff voice answers.

"Captain Kennedy, this is Luke Evans. I'm sorry to be calling this late, Sir."

"Luke. That's all right. Hadn't meant to fall asleep. I'm hoping you're about to give me some good news."

I open the door of my truck, looking over my shoulder one last time at the apartment building. "Yes, Sir. I'd like to accept the position."

I KNOCK ON the door, trying to be as quiet as I can in case the kid's asleep. My efforts to be discreet either failed or wouldn't have mattered as the door opens and Nolan pops his head around the side.

He focuses on me through heavy eyelids, then the excitement pours out of him as he shoves the door open all the way, stabbing it with his sword.

"Uncle Wuke! Check this out!" He produces a small airplane from the pocket of his dragon-covered pajamas and soars it above his head. "I got to climb on one of these with Daddy. It was so cool, Uncle Wuke! Mommy didn't want me to because she said I could get hurwt, but . . ." He looks behind him back into the house, then steps closer to me. "But Daddy let me do it, and I didn't get hurwt. Don't tell Mommy, okay?" he whispers, bringing me down to his level. His eyebrows pinch together as he studies the airplane in his hand. "My dwagon keeps trying to eat this."

I muffle my laugh, reaching up and rubbing a hand over his wild hair. "Listen, Nolan, I'm not going to be around too much anymore. But you're going to be a really awesome big brother, you know that?"

He drops his hand down to his side, plane in one hand and sword in the other, as his big gray eyes study me. "Arwe you going to fight bad guys?"

I nod. "Yeah. I'm going to go fight bad guys. But I need you to do me a favor, okay? Can you do something for me?"

He bobs his head up and down, eagerly.

"Your Aunt Tessa might be a little sad when I'm gone. Do you think you could give her a lot of hugs for me?"

Nolan's mouth turns up into a crooked grin. "I wike hugging Aunt Tessa. She smells like stawberries." He puts his hand up to the side of his mouth and leans close to my ear. "And she lets me have cookies when Mommy says I can't have any."

"Nolan, what . . ." Mia enters the doorway, dropping the frown on her face when she sees the two of us. "Oh, hey, Luke."

"Hey," I say through my laugh.

She puts her hand on her hip and looks down at Nolan. "What did your daddy and I tell you about answering the door without us?"

Nolan turns around to face her, and I straighten up. "But it was Uncle Wuke."

"Did you know it was Uncle Luke before you opened the door?"

He shakes his head, then drops it with a sigh. "No."

She waves him toward her. "Come on. You should already be asleep by now. It's way past your bedtime."

Nolan steps into the house, but turns around before he gets too far. He wraps a hand around Mia's leg and looks up at me. "Uncle Wuke, do you want my dwagon? He could help you with the bad guys."

I force a smile through the pain I'm feeling, noticing the peculiar look on Mia's face before shaking my head. "No, that's okay, buddy."

He raises the hand holding the airplane and rubs his knuckle against his eye. "But he keeps eating my airwplane."

Mia places her hand on his shoulder, gently directing him in the direction she wants him to go while I drop my head, laughing under my breath.

"Sorry," she says, smiling as I look up at her. She steps aside and holds the door open. "Are you going to come in?"

"No, I just wanted to talk to Ben real quick. Can you send him out?"

She pinches her lips together, but gives me a tentative nod. "Yeah. He was just getting out of the shower. Let me grab him."

I don't say goodbye to Mia, because I don't want her getting too worked up right now. Ben says she's extra sensitive about stuff with the pregnancy, and the last thing I want is to upset her.

I lean against the side of my truck, sticking my hands into my pockets and staring at the dirt. Ben walks out and gives me a nod as he pulls his T-shirt on.

"What's up? Why do you have Max with you?" He walks up to the truck and pets Max's head as it sticks out the window. He tilts his head, peering into the backseat. "All your shit's in there. What the fuck, man?"

"I accepted that job," I tell him, stepping back as he lets his hand fall to his side. I see the emotion wash over him like a wave, the kind that takes you under and lets you know just how fucking powerful it is.

"You what?" he asks sternly.

"I'm leaving tonight. Right now, actually. Captain Kennedy is letting me stay at his guest house until I can get something set up there."

Hands fist my T-shirt, and before I know it, I'm being shoved up against my truck. "What the fuck is wrong with you? Did you tell her? Does she know?" he yells, and I let him. I don't fight him off in any way.

"I'm doing this for her. I don't want to leave her, you fucking know I don't, but I can't keep hurting her like this. She'll understand eventually."

He leans in close, gripping my shirt hard enough I think he's about to shred it. I watch his nostrils flare with rage, and the whites of his eyes glaze over. After several breaths, he backs off with a final shove. He points at my face. "She'll never understand this. You're making a huge fucking mistake, and I think you know that. You're just scared. You think all this stuff with your dad is going to push her away. That's why you keep her out, and it's bullshit. Tessa can handle anything."

"You don't know that."

"I know she loves you, and this shit you're doing is going to kill her."

I hold my arms out by my sides, as if my hand is being forced and this choice isn't even mine, because that's how it feels.

"It's done, man. I'm leaving," I say. "Don't make this harder for me. You know I don't want to do this."

His eyes pinch closed before he runs both hands down his face. When he looks back at me again, I see the defeat sag his shoulders. Heavy and unforgiving. "You fucking suck, asshole," he says with a shake of his head as he steps closer to me. He holds his hand out, nodding harshly for me to take it, and I do, not expecting the hug he pulls me into.

"Jesus," I say through a grunt, giving him a hug in return.

"Fuck you. I was banking on getting rid of Jacobs. Now I'll be stuck with that dipshit, and a new fucking partner I don't feel like getting used to."

We release each other, a bit awkwardly, and I nod toward the house. "Tell Mia I said bye, all right? I didn't want to upset her."

"Yeah, thanks. I'll tell her in the morning."

"And don't tell Tessa where I am. I don't want her coming for me."

He looks like he wants to say more, or possibly beat the shit out of me for making him feel like this, but he simply drops his head before turning toward the house. He gives me a final look over his shoulder when he reaches the door, and I think I see the understanding there, but the look is too fleeting to be certain.

One more stop before I can leave all this behind me.

"SIR, VISITING HOURS ended at 8:00 p.m. You'll have to come back tomorrow if you want to see him."

I stare at my dad through the window of his hospital room. I've never been here this late before. It seems almost eerie how quiet the entire building is. Even the temperature seems colder. The chill of death, maybe, which is a morbid thought, but this is a hospital. People die. My mother would've died here if she hadn't coded in the ambulance. This is where they were taking her.

"Sir?"

I turn my head, connecting with the older nurse standing next to me. She's gripping a clipboard tightly, her pen tucked behind her ear.

I nod toward the window. "I won't bother him. I just wanted to give him something really quick before I leave town."

She purses her lips. "Sir, hospital rules. No visitors after 8:00 p.m."

"Please," I beg, sounding desperate. "I'm not going to see him again. He's my dad; just let me say goodbye. I'll be one minute."

She looks conflicted, glancing around us before letting out a heavy breath. "One minute," she echoes, and I know she isn't playing. She'll drag me out of this room as soon as those sixty seconds are up.

I won't even need half that time.

I step into the room and move to the end of the bed. I take the bronze coin out of my pocket, the ten years sober AA chip I stole out of my father's cigar box when I was fifteen, and look at the inscription on it one last time.

"To thine own self be true," I read, turning the coin over in my hand. "What the fuck does that even mean? It should say something like you have a son who needs you, or don't be a fucking coward and deal with your shit like a man." I toss the coin onto the bed, watching it land on the white sheet. "I don't know if you ever knew I took that. I think I always kept it 'cause I had hope I'd be giving it back to you at some bullshit ceremony, but I don't have any hope for you anymore."

The nurse enters the doorway, pointing at the clock on the wall and indicating with a finger that my time is nearly up.

I look back at my dad, watching his smooth breathing lift the white hospital blanket with the rise of his chest.

"I don't just miss Mom. I miss a lot of shit. But I won't stay here and watch you die. You made your choice, and I'm making mine."

After my final words to him, I leave, brushing past the nurse who studies me with a curious frown.

The hospital seems even colder now. The dead silence surrounds me.

I wish I felt better about this. I wish this decision came

with some sort of clarity, a sense of calm, or even reassurance that I'm doing the right thing.

But nothing comforts me as I leave Ruxton and everyone I've ever cared about.

I KNOW I'M alone before I open my eyes, because I can't feel Luke. My body would normally be touching some part of his, most likely all of it, or as much as I could wrap myself around if he'd stayed the night. So when I feel the cool satin of the pillow against my cheek instead of Luke's warm body, I don't even want to confirm what I know to be true.

He's gone.

Because you pushed, Tessa. You always push him too far.

I cling to the pillow, burying my face in it to try and pick up some of his scent.

What I get isn't enough. It's never enough.

He gave me so much last night, more than he's ever given me, and I still pried for that last piece of him. I should've held on and kept my mouth shut. Showed him how good it could be, having someone there for you when shit gets too heavy. A silent support. Then maybe he would've opened up more, or at least stayed.

The reason why I'm alone in this bed is my own damn fault. Not his.

Even though I know he isn't here, I still walk through my apartment with that tiny shred of hope that he's beaten me to the coffee maker. My naïve optimism fades the second I turn the Keurig on, and I stare at the dark liquid as it seeps into my mug, watching it mingle with the cream sitting at the bottom. I'm reminded of last night the second my hands wrap around the warm mug.

My tea.

I remember Luke leaving the bedroom to get it for me, but I don't remember him coming back.

Did he come back? Or was that when he left?

I walk down the hallway, spotting my neglected tea on the nightstand by the bed. I carry the mug out into the kitchen and pour the contents down the drain, hating myself for missing that last second with him. I decide right then as the sink clears, his sweet gesture disappearing as if it didn't happen, that I'm done pushing Luke for more. It's moments like the one he gave me last night that matter; when we're just together. Just us. Not the shit he's trying to deal with on his own.

I love him. That's enough. That will always be enough.

It's daunting how easy that decision comes to me, like it's been on reserve all this time. It feels right, and good. The way love should feel.

Everyone has something they're afraid of. I never thought men like Luke, or my brother, men who risk their lives for others, who make it their job to protect people they don't even know, would be afraid of anything. Luke said I made him feel things he never wanted to feel. Maybe that's what he's afraid of. If he lets himself love me, if he gives me every part of him, leaving himself vulnerable and I can't take it, he could lose someone else.

Me.

I won't let that happen. He'll never be alone again.

I shower and get dressed as quickly as possible, not even bothering to put on any makeup. After downing my coffee, I grab my keys and purse off the table. My phone has half its battery life still, even though I didn't charge it last night, and as I'm walking out the door, I notice the last call I received.

Mason.

After securing the fifth lock on the door, I stare down at the phone in my hand, thinking back to last night. I didn't talk to Mason after he dropped me off. I may not remember Luke bringing me my tea, but I'd remember having a two-minute-and-forty-seven-second conversation on the phone.

Did Luke talk to him? Is that why he left? *Shit. Shit, shit, shit.* Does he think Mason and I are together?

Well, you did go on a fucking date with him, dumbass.

"Ugh!" I yell out, looking up at the sky as I press the heel of my hand against my forehead. I rush down the stairs to the ground floor, practically sprinting to my car. My thumb glides along the screen of my phone as my other hand inserts the keys into the ignition.

His voicemail picks up, and I decide against leaving a message. This should be said in person, and if he's at the precinct, I'll be able to tell him everything face to face. If he's on patrol, I might be shit out of luck until tonight.

My phone rings in my hand as I inch out of my parking space, startling me. I slam my foot on the brake and watch Mia's name flash across the screen.

"Hey," I answer, easing on the gas and pulling out of the parking lot.

She sniffs into the phone. "Oh, God. Are you okay? You sound okay. Are you in shock right now? Do you need me to come over?"

"What the hell are you talking about?" I ask, switching to speaker-phone so I can concentrate on the road in front of me. "Are you in the middle of some pregnancy hormone overload or something?"

I hear commotion in the background, recognizing Nolan's

voice. "Nolan, not right now. In a minute, baby." A door closes, followed by a few more sniffles from Mia. "God, sweetie, I can be over there in five minutes if you need me to. Your mom might be able to watch Nolan for me today and we can just hang out. I'm sure she won't mind."

I'm thoroughly confused, glancing down at the phone in my cup holder with what I'm certain is my most baffled expression. "You've lost me, Mia. Am I supposed to be upset about something?"

"How are you so strong right now? I've been crying all morning, just thinking about what this is probably doing to you. I know you love him, Tessa. Everybody does. Why are you okay with this?"

The strangest feeling washes over me, stealing my breath, and I wrap my hands around the wheel until my palms ache. "Mia?" I whisper, hearing the sheer terror coat my throat, thickening my voice until I'm practically choking on that single word.

"Oh, God," she pleads, gasping through the phone. "You don't know, do you?"

Several things happen at once as I concentrate on continuing to breathe. Mia's voice becomes distant, unrecognizable, as I let the car come to a complete stop in the middle of the road. Drivers blare their horns as they speed by me, but I'm numb, too numb to care, or move, or do anything besides listen to my lungs struggle for air. A quick gasp, followed by another. Not enough air. Another breath in, deeper this time, but still not enough. White spots blur my vision, and the sweat beads up on my body, pooling between my breasts. Mia's words circle over and over again, in my head.

He said he did it for you. He doesn't want to hurt you anymore.

My nails claw at the material of my shirt, then up around

my neck, gripping, digging into my skin. I gag on a breath and my stomach rolls, lurching me forward against the wheel. I barely get the door open before the bile rises in my throat, burning my esophagus like acid on concrete.

Vomit splatters on the asphalt as I hold onto the door, using all the strength I have left in me to keep myself in the car. My body shakes with another violent spasm, ejecting the contents of my stomach. I wipe the back of my hand along my mouth when I think it's over, settling back into my seat and pulling the door closed.

The loss sinks in, settling deep inside my soul. Rooting itself there like a splinter.

Luke left me. He left. How could he . . .

No. I refuse to accept this. This isn't how today was supposed to play out. This isn't how my life is supposed to go. He's mine, and I'm his, and it's enough. What he can give me is enough. This shit isn't over. It'll never be over.

"Tessa? Tessa, are you there?"

I look down at the phone, hearing Mia's voice as clear as if she were sitting right here next to me.

The driver behind me lays on his horn, his voice getting drowned out by the blaring noise. As soon as I hear him yell the word "bitch" in between two long beeps, I react.

I roll my window down, stick my head out, and glare back in his direction. "Hey, douchebag! Pull the dildo out of your ass, and go the fuck around me!"

"Move your car!"

"Suck my dick!"

"What is going on?" Mia asks through the phone I've neglected.

I flip the limp-dick off as he pulls around me, making sure everyone on this Goddamned street sees it, in case anyone else wants to ask me so politely to move before I'm ready.

"Tessa?"

"Nothing," I choke out, a whimper catching in my throat. I grab a day-old water bottle off the floor behind the passenger seat and take a swig, spitting it out my window after washing my mouth.

"Do you need me to come get you? Or meet you somewhere?"

I step my foot onto the gas pedal and continue moving in the original direction I was headed. "No. Is Ben at the precinct? I need to find out where Luke is."

"Yeah, last time I checked."

"All right. I gotta go."

"Tessa, wait," Mia pleads, her voice wavering a bit. "I don't think he wants you to find him."

I grip the wheel harder, digging my teeth into my lip until I taste blood.

"I'm sorry," she says softly. "I'm so sorry."

I disconnect the call before she can hear my sobs.

SPEEDING INTO THE parking lot of the police precinct probably isn't the best idea I've ever had, but right now, a ticket is the last thing on my mind.

I spot Ben immediately, standing at his patrol car near the far end of the lot.

"Where is he?" I ask, throwing the door open before the car comes to a complete stop. Ben looks up, turning his body toward me, and takes a few steps in my direction with wide eyes. I slam the door shut, blinking the tears out of my eyes before I move to get to my brother.

"Where. Is. He?" I repeat.

Ben shakes his head, looking at me with concern. There's a deep crease in his forehead, and he has heavy, worry-filled eyes. "He's gone, Tessa. He took another job."

I jab a finger into the center of his chest. "I know that. What I'm asking you is where the fuck did he go?" Looking up into Ben's eyes, I see the sadness there hidden behind his tough exterior, as he wraps his big hand around my wrist, holding me ever so gently.

He shakes his head, and his lips part slightly to speak, but he doesn't give me any words.

"You're going to tell me where he is, right now. Right fucking now, Ben!"

"No, I'm not."

His defiance knocks the wind out of me.

He knows. He knows, and he isn't going to tell me? How could he keep this from me?

I resort to begging. I'll do anything at this point.

"Ben," I faintly whisper, as my heart struggles to keep beating. "Please. Please just tell me where he is. I can't . . . I love him. *Please.*" I cry harder, fisting his shirt. "Please."

His eyes fall into a heavy blink, but the accustomed shake of his head comes again before the grayest eyes I've ever seen regard me. "He's gone. I'm sorry, Tessa. I know this hurts, but he doesn't want you to come after him."

I no longer have any strength left in me to keep my head raised, so I drop it against his chest with a heavy thud. His arms wrap around me in an embrace, but I don't feel the comfort he's trying to give me.

I don't feel anything.

The tears roll down my cheeks, wetting my neck, a continual stream of agony leaving my body.

"I'll wait for him," I say to myself, to Ben, to Luke, if

there's some chance he can hear me. I press the side of my face against Ben's uniform. "You said you'd wait for Mia. You said you'd still be waiting. I can do that. I can wait. He'll come back. He has to come back."

Warm breath blows across the top of my head. "I will always wait for her, but I would've never left Mia. Never." His hands hold my face as he guides my head up to look at him.

I don't want to. I fight it, trying to keep my eyes clamped shut, to block out the words I know he's about to say.

This is going to kill me. I love him, and it's going to kill me.

"Tessa."

I shake my head against Ben's hands, trying to break free, but the second I glance up at him, he takes the opportunity he's given, and tells me what I'm dreading to hear.

"You need to let him go. Let him go."

I cover my face with my hands as I silently reply.

I can't.

THERE ISN'T MUCH resemblance. The sharp angle in his jaw, maybe, and his size. He's definitely built like Luke, but he might have a bit more muscle, and he appears taller, even in the hospital bed.

His arms are covered in ink, but his tattoos aren't as beautiful as the ones I've studied. The ones I can picture when I close my eyes.

"If you're looking for Luke, he ain't here, darlin'."

My eyes flash open, connecting with the pair staring back at me, amber, almost golden in color.

Just like Luke's.

I step closer to the foot of the bed, slightly embarrassed about being in here, gazing at a man I never met.

He leans his head back against the pillow, smiling. "He's talked about you."

I feel my eyes take up the majority of my face as I step closer, placing my hand on the footboard. "What?"

He lets out a slow breath before continuing. "I don't think he knows I'm listening, but I hear . . . I hear a lot."

"Not enough though," I say, my anger consuming me. "I doubt Luke hid his pain from you, if you're the reason behind it."

He frowns. "No, he didn't. But my pain was greater than his."

"I don't believe that," I counter. He lifts his brows in response. "I'm sorry you lost your wife. I can't imagine what that pain must feel like, but Luke was a kid when his mom died, and the only thing's he's told me is that he had to deal with it alone. I'd ask where the hell you were, but I think I know the answer to that." I reach into my back pocket, pulling out the folded pamphlets I had slid into my nightstand last night. "Maybe I'm way off with this, but I overheard a few things the other day when I was here. There are programs available through this hospital for people like you. Free programs, with support." His eyes follow the pamphlets as I toss them onto the bed. "Your pain will never be greater than his, because Luke lost everything that day. Not just his mom. He lost the only other person who could understand how he was feeling. I don't feel sorry for you. I don't feel sorry for a man who makes his son go through something like that alone. Be the father he needs and get your shit together."

I'm out the door before he can give me a response, but I don't need one. Not from him. The only voice I want to hear comes to me in a recording as I hold my phone up to my ear.

"Leave a message."

I nearly stumble at those three words before I give him my own. "How could you leave me? How could leave us, Luke? You couldn't even tell me goodbye, and I'm supposed to move on, and forget you, and be okay with this, but I can't. I won't let you go. Do you hear me? I'm not letting you go."

I disconnect the call and step out of the hospital.

"SSHOOOOO. SSHOOOO."

"Nolan, get that airplane off Aunt Tessa's head."

Nolan stands on the couch, leaning his body into me as he skims the airplane down my neck and onto my shoulder. I'd normally get annoyed that he keeps getting that thing tangled in my hair, but for the past three days, nothing has gotten a reaction out of me.

Not the asshole that banged his car door against the side of mine, leaving a very noticeable dent.

Not the shit weather we've had, the constant slow drizzle that makes it impossible to pick a damn windshield wiper speed.

Not even the looks I've been getting from Ben, Mia, Reed, my parents . . . okay, practically everyone in this entire fucking town. The sympathetic stares. The knowing head tilts, paired with a silent "it'll all be okay". I don't want to hear it from anyone, but I don't react. I keep my head down and let a four-year-old get airplanes tangled in my hair.

"Hey, what did I say?" Mia asks, coming up to stand in front of the two of us.

Nolan quickly removes his airplane off my shoulder. "But Aunt Tessa said I could pway." The couch cushion shifts beside me as his little body moves closer. Suddenly, his head pops up in front of mine, big gray eyes filling my vision.

My eyes focus for the first time in an hour, and I glance up at Mia. "I don't care if he does that. It's fine."

"Do you want something to drink? Some tea?" she asks.

I shake my head. I can't have tea. "No thanks."

"Uh-oh," Nolan says, falling back against his cushion. He clutches his airplane to his chest as Mia leans down.

"What's the matter, baby?" Mia asks, trailing her finger down this nose.

They always do that. The three of them. It was something Ben and Nolan did before Mia came into the picture, and now it's something they share.

Nolan looks over at me with a deep frown. "Arwe you sad, Aunt Tessa?"

Mia straightens up, quickly turning away from me and heading back to the kitchen. I hear her quiet sniffles as I nod at Nolan. "Yeah, buddy. I'm really sad."

A tiny line forms between his eyebrows, and I watch him move quickly, scrambling into my lap and wrapping his arms around my neck.

He squeezes me with all his strength, I know it, and I gently hold him against me, wincing as I remove his knee that's digging into the sensitive spot on my hip.

"I'm supposed to give you hugs when you'wre sad. I forwgot."

"Who told you to give me hugs?" I ask, closing my eyes as this tiny hug gives me more comfort than I ever thought it could. He smells like the detergent Mia uses. Lavender, and that distinct little boy smell. Like he's been playing in the dirt all day.

He shifts in my lap, flattening his cheek against my chest. "Uncle Wuke. He told me to give you lots of hugs. Are you still sad?"

I press my lips against the top of his head. "Yeah, buddy. I think I'll be sad for a while."

"I think Uncle Wuke is sad too."

I take in a deep breath, opening my eyes at the sound of something in front of me. Mia sets a mug down on the coffee table and falls back onto the cushion beside me, both hands flattening against her belly.

"Nolan, why don't you go play in your room for a little while. Daddy said we'll go out for pizza later if you want."

"Pizza!" Nolan darts off my lap and scrambles in the direction of the stairs leading up to the second level.

I drop my head against Mia's shoulder. "I said I didn't want any tea."

"I know."

"You made me some anyway."

"It was either that or ice cream, and we only have Cherry Garcia."

"Sick."

She laughs. "Tell me about it. I don't know how Ben can eat that flavor." Her head leans into mine. "What's going on with you and Mason?"

"Nothing. We're just friends."

"He's such a sweet guy."

"Mia," I warn. "I can't be with anybody else. I can't."

"I know that. I'm just saying he's a sweet guy, but once you're friend-zoned, that's it."

"Not for you," I say through a small laugh, one paired with my first smile in what feels like a month.

"Definitely not for me," she agrees with a chuckle. She holds her hand out, palm up on her lap, and I place mine in hers. "I'll make Ben stop for ice cream on our way home from getting pizza. What kind do you want?"

"Cookie Dough."

"Okay."

"And the one with the waffle cones crushed up in it. Whatever that's called."

"I think that's . . . No, that one has potato chips."

"Don't get that one."

She laughs again, and so do I.

"You can stay here as long as you want. You know that, right?" she asks.

I nod against her shoulder.

"It won't always hurt this bad. Give it some time."

"Grab that salted caramel one too, while you're at it, Miss Chatty. If you keep saying shit like that, I'm going to need an army of Ben & Jerry's to numb out my heartache."

She gently squeezes my hand. "Sorry."

"It's fine. I'm really hungry anyway."

"Me too."

I tilt my head, eyeing up her monstrosity of a belly. "I can't imagine why. At least your binge-fest is warranted."

She squeezes my hand. "So is yours."

I let my eyes fall closed, and we both sit there until Nolan calls out for Mia sometime after I've almost fallen asleep. When I'm finally left alone, I slip my phone out of my pocket and tuck myself into a ball.

"Leave a message."

I hang up three times, needing to hear those three words again, then again, before I give him my own.

"You sound so pissed off on your recording. I love it. Is it weird that I love it? I can picture you, all annoyed and ready to break your phone 'cause you have to leave a greeting. I'm really glad you left one.

"I think that's the only thing keeping me going right

now. Sometimes I listen to it twenty times before I leave you a message, which actually sounds kinda stalkerish, now that I've heard it out loud." I laugh softly into the phone. "I'd totally stalk you if I could. But I know you don't want me to know where you are." I turn around as the sound of footsteps on the stairs alerts me of Nolan's presence. "I love you today. I really wish you were here to ask me."

I disconnect the call and shove my phone back into my pocket.

HER NAME FLASHES across my screen with another incoming call. I ignore it like I always do, like I have to do, letting it go to voicemail. I don't listen to those either. I can't. Hearing Tessa's voice isn't something I can handle right now. She's racked up eighteen voicemails, one a day, and I've let them sit there. Maybe in a couple of months I'll be able to listen to the soft, raspy sound that rumbles in the back of her throat, teasing every syllable, but not now. She could scream at me for leaving her, or beg me to come back. It wouldn't matter. I'd hear the pain I've caused her and it would fucking destroy me.

I swipe my thumb across the screen to clear the call and the voicemail waiting for me, pulling up all my text messages to Ben. The ones that prick is doing a damn good job at ignoring, for the most part.

I can't talk to Tessa, or listen to her voice, but I need to know she's okay. I need someone to tell me I've done the right thing by getting out of her life, but my asshole best friend won't give me shit.

I go to the first one I sent him the day after I left, and begin scrolling through.

Me: How is she? Is she okay?

Nothing. I'd tried again the next day.

Me: Have you seen her today? Is she any better? She likes that disgusting green tea shit. Make that for her. It might help.

Again, nothing. I'd kept trying.

Me: She keeps calling me. Is she talking to you? Is she talking to anybody? Mia? I'm about to start texting Reed if you don't give me something. I haven't answered any of her calls, but I need to know she's okay.

Me: Reed is a dick. He won't answer me either. I'll fucking call Mia if you don't start answering.

I'd never call Mia, 'cause it would upset her. And this fucker knows it.

Me: I'm going fucking crazy. Just tell me she's breathing, asshole. I need something before I start ripping shit apart.

That finally triggered him.

Ben: She's great. She's completely forgotten about you. Her and that Aussie are picking out engagement rings and shit.

Me: What the fuck, man?

Ben: What the fuck, nothing. You want to know how she is so badly? Get your ass here and find out.

I scroll through the rest of the texts, all different versions of me begging, and Ben giving me bullshit responses.

Ben: She's great.

Ben: She's moving to France to study Art History.

Ben: She got a life-sized cutout made of you and ran it over with her car.

That one I actually believed.

Reed finally removed his fingers out of some chick's pussy to text me back, four days after I sent him a message. His response almost had me driving back to Ruxton to choke him out.

Reed: Did you move or something?

Eighteen fucking days of this shit. I feel like I'm losing my mind, which seems appropriate, considering I've lost everything else. All I want—besides Tessa, because she's still everything I want—is for her to be okay, and happy. That's it. I know the happy part might take a while, but I need someone to tell me she's okay, and I needed to hear it seventeen days ago.

"Hey, Evans. There's some guy here to see you."

I look up from my phone at Harding, my new partner, as he stands behind my desk. He's only about ten years older than me, but the stress of the job has left him with a full head of gray hair, and deep lines etched into his skin.

He takes a sip of his coffee and motions in the direction of the double doors.

"Who?" I ask, closing the folder in front of me than getting to my feet, tucking my phone into the inside pocket of my jacket. I try to peer out the small window in the door, but I can't make out anybody at this distance.

"I don't know. Big guy. Tattoos."

Ben?

"Is he a cop?"

Harding smiles through a swallow. "Not with that haircut, man. You finished with that paperwork yet?"

Fuck. What the hell is he doing here?

"Yeah, it's in the folder." I point in the general direction of my desk as I begin walking toward the double doors.

He's sitting alone in the last chair lined up along the wall, head down, elbows resting on his knees with his flannel shirt rolled up to mid forearm, exposing his ink. His hair is pulled back out of his face, which turns up at the sound of my entrance.

The first thing I notice is how rested he looks. I'd even go so far as to use the word *healthy*. His eyes aren't bloodshot, there's color to his face, and he appears steady on his feet as he stands, greeting me with a drop of his head.

"Son."

"What are you doing here?" I ask, ignoring the bullshit title he's just given me. I do a quick take of the waiting room to make sure we're alone. If I have to lay into this asshole, I don't want anyone else to hear it.

His eyes trail down the front of me, and he smiles. "You're in a suit. It's been a long time since I saw you dressed up."

"Yeah. Twelve years at Mom's funeral. I'm surprised you even looked at me that day."

"I looked at you, Son," he replies, lifting his chin and squaring off with me. "I just couldn't deal with your pain and mine at the same time."

"What do you want?" I'm losing my patience, and it's evident in my tone as I try and hurry this conversation along.

He sticks his hand into the front pocket of his shirt and retrieves something, which he flips at me. I catch it out of instinct, letting my fingers fall open to reveal the blue chip.

"Ten days sober," he says proudly. "I know it ain't much, but it's more than I've had in a long time."

I study the chip, letting my thumb glide over the engravings, rolling it between my fingers like I did with the one I took from his cigar box. I don't realize he's moved closer to me until I feel a hand on my shoulder.

"I'm not gonna lie. That doctor scared the shit outta me. After you left when he told us both I needed to stop drinking or I'd kill myself, I kept thinking about your mom and how she would've looked at me. How she would've hated me for what I was doing."

"I've told you that for years," I grunt out, shrugging his hand off my shoulder and looking up at him with nothing but resentment. All the shit he put me through, and all it took was hearing from a fucking doctor that he was going to end up drinking himself to death for him to listen? "You never even flinched when I brought it up."

"Drunks can't be reasoned with, Son. We care about one thing, and one thing only. Anything you tried to say to me when I was drinking?" He shakes his head with a grimace. "Waste of your time."

I toss the chip at his chest. "You know what else is a waste of time? You, driving six hours to show me you've finally decided to man up to your shit. You're too late. I don't care what you do anymore."

"I didn't just come here to show you that. I came to give you this too." His hand not clutching the chip produces a set of keys out of his pocket. He forces them into my hand, and I look down, recognizing them immediately.

"Your house keys?"

"It's hard for me to be there," he explains, his voice shifting into a tone I haven't heard him use since I was a kid. "I want to drink, every day. Right now, I want to drink, and it'll always be like that. That shit doesn't go away, and being in that house doesn't help me. My sobriety has to be number one. I found a small apartment in town. I'm gonna stay there. The house is yours if you want to sell it, or do whatever you want with it."

I look up at him. "I thought you were already selling it 'cause you needed money for booze?"

"Booze? No. I left you a message telling you why I was selling it. Didn't you listen to it?"

I shrug. "Few seconds of it."

He tucks the blue chip into his pocket, giving the panel a gentle pat. A smile twists across his mouth. "You know I can't work computers for shit. Your mom was always better at that stuff." His eyes fall to a space between us. "The first rehab center I found online was gonna cost me fifty grand. I figured they all cost that much these days, and I don't have that kind of money. I've dipped into your mom's life insurance policy a bit, but the rest of it I put away for you."

My eyes widen.

He studies my response with a steady look of assurance. "I've known I've had a problem for a long time. I made it so I couldn't touch that money, sober or not. It's yours when you want it. I called a realtor to put the house up for sale to pay for that rehab center, but then that little spit-fire of yours came to see me."

There's a lot of information I should be taking in right now. My dad's sober, I'm holding keys to the house I never thought I'd step foot in again, but that last thing he just said to me seems to be the only thing I've heard.

"What are you talking about?" I ask, wanting for the first time in years to hear what he has to say.

His smile grows to a full on grin now. "The redhead. She's a feisty thing. Reminded me of your mom a bit."

My heart knocks against my ribs, hard enough to crack several. "Tessa? She came to see you? When?" I feel myself moving closer, needing this information more than I need to breathe. "Hello? Fucking talk!"

He backs up, holding his hands up in surrender with a laugh. "Jesus. Relax, will ya? She came by . . ." He looks up at the ceiling for a few seconds, and I think I might actually die before he figures this out. I'm so close to beating the information out of him, but what the hell good would that do me?

He nods decisively, and a loud gush of air leaves my lungs as he comes to his conclusion.

"The day after you gave me my chip back, she came to see me. I'm not really sure what brought her there, but she had these pamphlets with her. Treatment programs for addicts that are run through the hospital. It's great, and it's free. I have a ton of support. I can meet with doctors if I'm having problems . . ."

"Yeah, yeah, that's great. What did she say?"

He chuckles through his grin, reaching up and scratching along his jaw. "She laid into me a little bit. A lot, actually. Said some shit you've said to me, but it felt different coming from her. It was like she was protecting you or something."

My mouth goes dry, making swallowing near impossible. "I don't understand why she would bring you anything. She doesn't know you. I never talked about you with her."

He shoves his hands into his pockets, his smile fading. "That doesn't surprise me. I can't say anything I've done over the past twelve years deserved to be talked about, and I get keeping her out of all that. I do. But women, they figure shit out on their own, Son. Your mom was the same way. When they're determined, good fucking luck keeping them in the dark about stuff." He shakes his head through a laugh. "That girl of yours, I like her. She doesn't take no shit. That's a good quality to have in a woman."

"I don't have her anymore," I reply.

"Then that's your choice, not hers. 'Cause she sure as hell didn't come to that hospital for me." He pulls his hands out of his pockets, and grabs my shoulders, firmly holding my attention. I see the regret weighing heavy on his face, deepening his frown.

"I should've been better. You deserved better."

"It's a little late for an apology," I say, trying to step back out of his grasp. His hands tighten their hold, and he steps closer.

"I'm not here to tell you I'm sorry. I'm not sure it would mean anything."

"It wouldn't," I agree. "It wouldn't mean a damn thing."

He smiles. "Good. 'Cause you deserve a lot more than a bullshit sorry." His arms pull me into a hug so quickly, I can't think fast enough to protest it. I keep my hands at my side, not reciprocating, but not pushing away either.

"There are a lot of things I wish I could take back, but I can't, and if you want to hate me, if you never want to see me again, I'll understand that. What's done is done. You're a good man, Luke, and you're more than I ever deserved to have in a son. I'm proud of you. I'll always be proud of you."

His arms release me suddenly, and he keeps his head down as he pushes open the doors that lead to the parking lot. He's gone before I can even think of a response to what he's just said. The only thing I'm able to do is stand there, holding the keys to the house he's just given me.

I'M RESTLESS, AND it's pissing Max off.

That poor dog has been following me around the guest-house we've been staying in since I walked in the door three hours ago. I've moved from the kitchen, to the living room, to the bedroom, back to the living room, where I'm currently trying to keep my mind off the phone charging on my dresser. The game's on, but I'm not interested.

Not when I have eighteen messages waiting for me.

Not when I want to get in my car and drive all night to get to her.

Not when I'm thinking I've made the biggest mistake of my life.

I toss the remote onto the coffee table and drop my head into my hands. Max nudges me with his wet nose, sniffing behind my ear.

"I'm gonna listen to one. Just one." I raise my head and he gets up on all fours on the cushion, his tail wagging excitedly behind him. "You want to listen to one too, don't you? You miss her? You miss Tessa?"

He reacts exactly how I'd react if someone asked me the same thing right now. By jumping around like a fucking lunatic, knocking shit off the coffee table. His head nudges the back of my legs as I move down the hallway, urging me faster. I rip the cord out of the bottom of my cell phone and sit on the edge of the bed with it.

I dial my voicemail, ignoring the way my heart pounds, the heavy pulse of it surging back to life. I hit the speaker-phone button as Max settles next to me on the bed, dropping his head into my lap. After skipping seven messages, 'cause I figure after a week of me being gone, she's probably more likely to cuss me out then cry, I wait for the eighth message to begin playing.

"Hey, it's me," she whispers, and I raise the phone up to my ear, keeping it on speaker. "I have to be really quiet. Nolan fell asleep on me." I count her breaths, six full inhales and exhales, and fuck, just hearing her living does something to me.

I breathe faster, heavier, matching her rhythm. I think maybe she's fallen asleep until I hear a soft sigh. "I'm pretending you're here with me, and I don't have to say anything. We're just together. Just you and me, and it's . . ." Her voice breaks into a whimper, and she shudders an exhale before continuing. "It's so perfect, Luke. Do you remember? I'm not crazy, right? It was kinda perfect, what we had.

"I wasn't—I know I wasn't perfect for you. I'm stubborn. I yell, and I like to push you, and we argue about the dumbest shit, but you're the only person I want to sit on a couch and do absolutely nothing with. *You* are what makes it perfect. And I miss it. I miss just being with you, so I'm going to sit here, and pretend that's what I'm doing."

I wipe my hand down my face and shift Max off me so I can lie down, dropping the phone on my chest. Max settles at my feet, resting his chin on my leg while I stare at the phone. The soft sounds of her pain fade out, and it's just her breathing, filling my ears, my bedroom, and my soul. I watch the seconds tick away on the screen, and when it reaches ten minutes, the message abruptly cuts out. I cue it up again, letting my eyes fall closed so I can picture her with me.

I miss you, and it was perfect.

I was planning on listening to a few of her messages tonight, but this one, this is the only one I want to hear.

It kills me; her, thinking she's not enough. That she wasn't exactly what I needed, all the time.

I'm halfway through my fifth listen, when a beep cuts into the message, breaking apart one of the best sounds I've ever heard. I tilt my phone to see the screen, and the name I read has me sitting up and kicking Max off my legs.

> *Mia: Hey, Luke. Nolan wanted to send you a text. I'm handing him the phone now.*

I smile, watching the bubbles float as he types. I'm not sure what to expect. He's four, so I think he should be able to spell out some words.

> *Mia: Nolan Nolan Nolan dragon jfksnen kskeiju qio l ☺ jfks hi ☺ Unkle Luke hi*

I get a good laugh out of that, reading it several times to try and figure out if the random letters are meant to say something. My phone beeps again, and I'm expecting more smiley faces and names.

> *Mia: Hey, it's me. Sorry. He's been asking me every day if he can call you, and I didn't want him telling Tessa he talked to you. I can't imagine how sad that would make her.*

My fingers begin moving at their own volition. Thank fuck for spell check picking up what I'm meaning to get across instead of the nonsense I type out.

> *Me: How is she?*

> *Mia: She's sad, Luke. She's really sad. You destroyed my best friend, and your dumbass is the only one who can fix it, so I need you to get back here. Now. I don't know how much more of this she can take. I've never seen her like this.*

Sweat builds on my palm as I grip the phone, staring, re-reading the words again, and again. I've destroyed her. I need to fix it.

> *Mia: I'm going behind Ben's back to talk to you right now. I hope you know how shitty I feel doing this, but I don't think you made the right choice. I did at first. I understood why you left when Ben told me, and I wanted to hug you for choosing Tessa's feelings over your own.*

Mia: I know you love her even if you've never said it, and I know you've never said it, because Tessa would've told me. But you screwed up. It's not supposed to be like this. Every couple has shit they have to go through. But you work it out. Together.

Mia: I swear to God. Sometimes you men are complete idiots. We love you, and you just screw everything up.

Mia: I'm getting worked up, so I'm going to go fold something. I love you and I miss you, but I will straight up nut punch you if you don't fix this.

Nut punch me? What the fuck?

I toss the phone on the bed next to me and lie back. My head feels heavier when it hits the pillow, my indecision weighing on my mind.

What do I do? What the fuck do I do?

If I go back, I'll have to let Tessa in. She knows some shit, but she doesn't know all of it. Not the stuff that pulls me out of bed at night. The ugliness I've kept her away from.

He's sober. He could stay that way, but there's a greater chance he won't.

Bottom line? I'm scared. I'm fucking scared she'll be the one who pulls away.

The phone rings, startling me, and I grab it expecting Harding, since we're on call twenty-four hours a day. Ben's name flashes on my screen.

"Fuck!"

Max barks, jumping off the bed and darting down the hall to go hide in the bathroom. I hear the rustling of plastic, confirming he's now in my shower, and let out a heavy sigh before I answer this call.

I bring the phone up to my ear as I try and make myself comfortable. It doesn't work.

"She texted me, man. I swear to God, I wouldn't . . ."

"Get your ass here, Godfather. Mia's water just broke."

"SWEETHEART, DO YOU want me to take him?"

My eyes blink open several times, adjusting to the fluorescent light of the waiting room at the sound of my dad's voice. I lift my head from the tiny pocket of warmth Nolan's sleeping body created against mine, and look up.

"What time is it?" I ask, stretching out my neck from side to side.

"A little after 2:00 a.m." He reaches down and lifts Nolan into his arms, holding him against his chest.

"Ben hasn't come out yet? Mia's been in labor for like, five hours." I look across the row of chairs, spotting my mom, fighting sleep with little drops of her head.

My dad sits down next to me, taking the stuffed dragon out of my hand and tucking it next to Nolan. "These things take a while sometimes. You kept your mother in labor for over twelve hours before you were ready."

I drop my chin, giving him a teasing glare. "That number seems to get bigger every time I hear that story." I cover my mouth to stifle my yawn as it breaks apart the end of my sentence.

"Why don't you go back to sleep? I'll wake you when someone comes out." He slides down the seat a bit, letting Nolan rest more on his chest.

"No, I need to stay up in case Mia needs me. I really didn't mean to fall asleep." I stand from the chair, patting the pocket of my jeans to feel for my money. "I'm going to grab some coffee. Do you want some?"

My dad smiles with a light shake of his head. "No thanks, sweetheart."

I walk around the corner to the row of vending machines, eyeing up my candy choices. If I am going to stay awake, I need caffeine and chocolate, preferably injected straight into my veins. I probably would've been fine if it wasn't for Nolan falling asleep on me. That kid is just too damn snuggly for words.

I should know. He's been attached to me for the past nineteen days, giving me hugs whenever he thinks I need them, which apparently, is every five minutes.

I do need them. I need them because Luke told him to give them to me, and in my warped mind, it's his arms around me, not Nolan's. It's Luke who sees my pain and stops everything he's doing to comfort me.

That's the only thing getting me through each day. Knowing he cared enough to make sure I'd have someone.

I pop a peanut M&M into my mouth as I wait for my coffee to dispense out of the machine. As I'm walking back around the corner, holding onto the nearly overflowing cup with both hands, while my teeth secure the bag of candy between them, I spot Nolan, moving around on my dad's lap, awake and alert. He looks over at me, wide-eyed, but gets distracted when my dad points at something, or someone, across the room. Nolan's jaw hits the floor, and his feet quickly follow.

"Uncle Wuke!"

I gasp, releasing the bag from my tightly clenched jaw. M&M'S scatter along the tiled floor at my feet, rolling underneath the waiting room chairs. I glance up at my dad, then my mom, who is now standing and awake, looking at me with a deep frown. My eyes drop to Nolan just as he tilts his head almost completely upside-down to watch the candy roll about.

"Whoa! That's awesome. Uncle Wuke! Look at all dis candy!"

I see someone. No, not someone. *Him.* I see him, out of the corner of my eye, but I can't turn my head, or shift my gaze in his direction. I'm frozen in place, my body stiff. I can't do anything besides look between the three members of my family. The ones who have seen me at my worst lately.

He's here. He's here. Luke. Oh, God. Breathe, Tessa. Just breathe. Don't fucking pass out right now. Or puke. Jesus Christ, don't puke.

He moves into my line of sight, which hasn't wavered at all, and our eyes meet.

Briefly, but God, I feel it.

My body reacts as if he's just reached into the ocean I've been drowning in and pulled me out.

This is what it feels like to have your heart beating the way it's supposed to. I've been surviving on twitches, tiny spasms against my sternum, just enough to say, "You're alive, Tessa. Barely alive."

My dad steps forward, extending his hand with a smile. "Luke, nice to see you."

"You too, Mr. Kelly." Luke's dark T-shirt stretches across the muscles in his back as he grips my father's hand. My mouth goes dry, and I could quench it with the coffee that I'm miraculously still holding, but I need ice-cold, frigid water. Thrown on me, preferably. I swallow as the ink on his bicep moves with his muscle, some of the shadows becoming more evident, while others roll to the parts of his arm I can't see from this angle.

Damn it. I want to see. All of him.

"Nolan, those are dirty. Don't touch them," my mom scolds, grabbing Nolan by his shoulders and moving him away from a pile of M&M'S that's collected under a chair close by. She gives Luke a warm smile, devoid of any resentment.

"Uncle Wuke!" Nolan yells again, letting go of the candy diversion and re-focusing all his excitement. "You'wre hewre!"

Luke bends down, places a hand on Nolan's shoulder, and leans in close to whisper something in his ear.

Nolan moves back and nods proudly, training his eyes on me. His crooked grin appears, smearing across his face as if he's in on some big secret.

I want that secret.

The doors leading out to the main hospital burst open, gaining everyone's attention. Luke straightens up, spinning around toward the noise and Nolan squeezes between his legs to peer through.

"Daddy!"

I follow Nolan's body as he runs straight at Ben, who quickly wraps him up into a hug. He carries Nolan over to the group. Well, the group, minus me. I'm still glued to the floor about ten feet away from everyone.

"You made it." Ben walks up to Luke, shifting Nolan in his arms to shake Luke's hand.

I know Ben wasn't happy about Luke leaving either. He wouldn't talk about him, and if he heard Nolan bring him up, he'd quickly change the subject and scold Nolan for doing it. Plus, he'd turned into Mr. Broody as of lately, edgy and always on the attack. The only person he seemed to have any patience for was Mia. But you wouldn't know he was affected at all by the way he's looking at Luke.

"I knocked an hour off my time, doing eighty all the way

here," Luke replies, dropping his hand to his side. "I figured if I got a ticket, I'd just make you pay it."

Ben laughs, hearty and genuine, moving Nolan again when he starts to wiggle. "You're the one pulling in detective pay. I should send you this hospital bill."

"Son," my dad says, stepping closer to the men, "how is Mia? What's the update?"

Luke turns his head, brushing his gaze over me. My hands grip the paper cup tighter as I lock my knees, keeping myself upright. He looks at me almost the way he's always looked at me, but there's something different about it this time. There's nothing gentle about the way Luke looks at you. He's cocky and self-possessed at all times, baiting you to make that move toward him. Owning you before you even know it. There's a hidden promise behind his eyes. A quiet threat.

No one else will exist to you after me.

But something's different. He doesn't hold my stare the way I'm accustomed to. There's no danger lying dormant, sparking my curiosity with an assurance of something I'll never forget. What has my skin ignited into a slow burn is the tender caress his eyes are giving me. Like he's examining my soul for any signs of trauma, silently whispering to me while he moves over my body.

I did this, and I'm sorry. I'm so fucking sorry.

I don't know how I do it, but I break the contact and look over at my brother. Mainly because I can't handle a gentle Luke right now, a Luke who looks as broken as I feel.

Ben smiles, his two dimples sucking in prominently as he looks between the four of us. "You guys ready to meet him?"

I finally move, my legs remembering why I've been in this hospital all night. I drop my cup into the trashcan I walk past and keep my attention on Ben. "Is Mia okay?"

His cheeks hollow out even more as he looks unashamedly awestruck. "Yeah, she's perfect. She was amazing, but she's completely wiped out. This visit needs to be quick so she can get some rest."

Nobody argues with Ben. He'll always do what's best for Mia, and I love that about him.

Luke hangs back as my parents move through the doors behind Ben. I go to follow, but Luke halts me with a hand on my arm.

"Tessa."

"Not now." I pull out of his reach, my skin tingling with the loss of contact. Our eyes lock. "I'm here for Mia, and the baby. I can't."

He nods his understanding, but his eyes burn with conflict, and regret, so much that it steals the breath right out of my lungs.

I force myself to keep moving, going against every fiber in my being that wants me to stay still with Luke. I focus on Mia, and Chase, burying my pain deep down, creating a deeper hole inside me. Luke stays by my side, walking with me in silence, but his thoughts are so loud the sound seems to echo off the walls around us. My body begins to pulse with a reaction I haven't yet acknowledged. I've been too numb to feel anything besides empty, but this flares to life inside me, curling my hands into fists.

Anger. There you are.

"You left me," I spit through gritted teeth. His response comes to me in the form of a sharp inhale, seething into a hiss. I keep my eyes straight ahead, focused on what I'm here for. He doesn't get my glare, fueled with resentment, or the punch I'm ready to throw.

But he is about to get my mouth.

"I had to," he quietly replies.

My control breaks, snapping completely in two. "No, you didn't!" I stop in the middle of the hallway as Luke stumbles to a halt, eyes wide and wild, on me. We're only a foot apart, and I quickly close the gap, stealing his personal space out from under him. I get as close to his face as my tiptoes allow me, and I don't hold anything back.

"Don't you dare act like you didn't have a choice! You left me because you wanted to! You chose this, and you were a fucking coward about it because you didn't even tell me goodbye. You knew . . . you *knew* I wouldn't let you leave. You should've stayed and fought for us, Luke! I will always fight for us."

He leans down, scowling, giving me his own neglected anger. "You broke up with me, remember? Who was fighting for us then?"

"I did that because you didn't want a family with me. I wanted that!"

"I will always want anything that gives me you!"

I suck in a breath so fast I start to feel light-headed. Blinking into focus, I read him for any signs of dishonesty, but Luke isn't avoiding my scrutiny with little-to-no eye contact. He's giving me just the opposite.

"I fucked up, okay?" he says, bringing his voice down so that it's just us in this conversation, and not everyone in the state of Alabama. "You think leaving you didn't kill me? Because it did." He jabs a finger at his chest. "I'm a dead man, Tessa. There's nothing in here anymore. This part of me died when I left. But I did it because I was trying to protect you."

My eyes well up with tears, but I don't blink. I won't give him that.

I take a step back, and he moves with me until I hold my

hand up. "I never asked you to protect me, Luke. I asked you to love me." I let my hand fall. "That's it. That's all I've ever wanted from you, and you left me because you couldn't do that."

He moves in front of me when I try and continue down the hallway. "Wait."

"Did you even listen to any of my messages? I called you, every day, sometimes more, just to hear that stupid voicemail recording."

He blinks, then swallows. "I listened to one, last night. I think six times, or something. The one where you just wanted to pretend we were together."

"That's it? That's the only one you listened to?"

His eyes widen at my question, glazing over with guilt. "Yeah."

"Give me your phone." I move into him and hold out my hand, palm up. He hesitates, but only briefly, and produces it from the side pocket of his shorts. I take it from him and dial his voicemail, entering the code, and ignoring the look he gives me because I know it.

He's so close to me I can smell the shampoo he uses, the faint hint of his cologne. He's freshly showered and I probably look like death run over.

Fucking awesome.

I hit the speaker-phone button, and begin sliding my thumb along the bar to get to the end of a message. I know what I want him to hear. The only important thing I ever said on these messages.

"I love you today. I wish you were here to ask me."

His eyes shift from my face to my hand, back to my face. Blinking, as if he can't believe that phone, the very one he's had with him all this time, had those words hidden inside it. I go to another message, and another, letting him hear seventeen versions of that sentence.

"Tessa," he whispers, reaching up and pulling me into an embrace. One hand grips the back of my neck while the other secures around my waist.

I don't fight it. I don't want to. There will never be a part of me that doesn't need him, vital and desperate like this.

He drops his forehead to mine. "Tessa," he repeats, even softer, as his eyes close.

"Ask me."

I see the slight shake of his head. The hesitation.

His eyes flash open when I lay my hand on his cheek. "Ask me. Please, ask me."

He waits, shifting his hand on the back of my neck to get a better hold. As if I'll run, and the thought terrifies him.

"Do you love me today?"

I nod, sending the tears down my face. My *yes* blows across his lips as he slides his mouth along mine. It's unexpected, and perfect, and I'm done. I'm so done for with that kiss. He moves from one corner of my mouth to another. Pressing, pressing harder, until I'm being pushed up against the wall. His hands hold my face, guiding me with a tilt so he can kiss along my jaw, my cheek to my ear, where he whispers, "Ask me."

I don't breathe as my eyes open to meet his. He smirks. The asshole actually smirks, and it's beautiful.

"Not here," I say, and he looks wounded until I run my hands around his neck, pulling him back against me. His lips tease mine, then his tongue, and I know he's doing it to get what he wants right now.

"God, I fucking missed you," he softly presses against my mouth. "Missed this so much."

"Hey, if you two want to see Chase, knock that shit off

and get in here."

We both turn our heads, locking onto a very amused looking Ben. Luke grabs my hand and pulls me off the wall, moving us in the direction we need to be going.

Ben raises an eyebrow as he looks between the two of us. "Are we happy now?"

"Yes," I answer, blending with Luke's teasing, "Fuck off."

We follow behind Ben as he walks into one of the birthing suites. My dad and mom are standing beside the bed, looking down at Mia and the tiny baby in her arms. Nolan is sitting next to her, perched on his knees and leaning to get closer.

Mia looks up at the sound of our entrance, glances between Luke and I, and smiles. "Hey, you made it."

"I wouldn't miss it," Luke replies, walking with me to the side of the bed. Ben walks to the other side and sits on the edge behind Nolan.

My hand curls around the bedrail as we both look down at Chase.

"He's really small. Is that normal?" Luke asks, concern softening his voice.

"He's perfect. I was only six pounds when I was born, but he's a healthy seven," Mia replies, shifting Chase so he's now on her chest. "Do you want to hold him?"

I'm expecting Luke to decline. Most guys aren't into holding babies unless it's their own.

"Yeah, I would," he says, extending his arms and leaning over the bed to allow Mia an easy transfer.

"Just make sure you support his head. Like this." She adjusts Luke's elbow, tucking it closer to his body. "There you go."

He straightens up slowly, releasing his breath on a soft exhale. His lips tease into a smile and he drops his chin, running his nose along the top of Chase's head.

Goodbye, ovaries.

"Dude, did you just sniff my kid?" Ben asks.

Everyone in the room laughs, while Luke shrugs unapologetically. "He smells good. Better than you."

A hand touches mine, and I drag my gaze off Luke to look down at Mia.

You okay? she mouths.

I let my smile answer for me, and she rests her head back, her eyes misting over.

A knock on the door alerts everyone of company, seconds before Reed and Mason step into the room, quietly arguing about something.

Reed tosses up a mini football into the air and catches it again, looking behind his shoulder at Mason. "Whatever, man. She was clearly looking at me. If you had opened your mouth, and said something in that accent of yours, I'd give it to you."

Mason lowers the giant gift basket he's holding to see in front of him. "You wouldn't even know what to do with a woman like that."

"Oh, I'd know exactly what to do with her," Reed counters.

"Did you two idiots forget you walked into a room?" Ben asks, standing from the bed.

Reed doesn't seem fazed by that, but Mason tenses.

"Sorry, mate." He hands over the gift basket to Ben, slapping a hand on his back. "Congratulations."

"Thanks. Good God. What all is in here?" Ben holds the basket up and begins examining the contents through the cellophane.

"Candy!" Nolan yells, scrambling off the bed. "Can I have a pop, Daddy?" He jumps up and down, trying to poke the bottom of the basket with his finger.

"Here, Nolan. Look what I brought you." Reed bends down, reaches into his back pocket, and produces a small airplane. "It's a fighter jet. My granddad used to fly these."

Nolan snatches it out of Reed's hands. "Cool! Daddy, look! Look what Uncle Weed bwought me!"

"Uncle *Weed* is awesome," Ben teases. "He should be legalized."

"Benjamin," my mother scolds with a glare. "You're in law enforcement, for Christ's sake."

"How did you guys get back here past Nurse Ratchet?" Mia asks through a yawn. She drops her head back on the pillow, looking half ready to pass out. "I thought only family was allowed in here this late."

"I sweet-talked her. Didn't take much," Reed says, shooting her his familiar flirty smile. He points to his face. "*This* will get me in anywhere."

I suddenly realize Luke's attention is fixated on Mason, and Mason only. I remember Mason telling me what Luke had said to him on the phone the night before he left. How he was basically giving Mason permission to be with me, to let me love him instead of Luke, and the tension wrinkling his brow begins to make sense.

I give Luke's arm a gentle squeeze, gaining his attention. "We're just friends," I say for only him to hear.

"Hey, good to see ya, mate," Mason greets Luke with a friendly smile.

Luke's shoulders drop, and he shifts Chase against his chest so he can shake Mason's hand. "You too," he replies, sincerity in his voice.

Chase gets passed around the room, spending a little more time in my hands than anyone else's. He is small, but so was Nolan, and I doubt a guy like Ben, massive and built like a brick house, could produce anything that wouldn't rival him in size eventually. He has Ben's dimples, which I point out when I see Chase slip his thumb into his mouth. Mia immediately starts crying when she hears that. They hadn't known if he had Ben's dimples or not, and even though she says they are happy tears, Ben still kicks everyone out of the room so she can get some rest.

"Tessa, can I talk to you for a minute?" Mason asks when we all reach the parking lot.

I wave at my parents as they walk to their car before turning my head up at Luke. "Give me a minute?" I ask, releasing his hand.

He looks at Mason, nodding. "All right." They exchange another handshake, and Luke walks off with Reed toward their trucks.

"What's up?" I ask.

"I'm moving."

I frown, crossing my arms disapprovingly. "Back to Australia? But you just got here."

His hand swipes up and brushes back the hair that fell into his eye. "I've been here for five months. I never really planned on staying in one place that long. I like to travel, and there's a lot I want to see in this beautiful country of yours."

"So, you're what? Becoming a gypsy?"

He shakes his head with a chuckle as his finger flips his keys back and forth. "No, not quite. There's a business opportunity for me in Chicago. A buddy of mine I met at the gym told me about it. His cousin lives out there and he's in real estate. I could open up my own yoga studio."

"Chicago? Why can't you open up one here?" I ask.

"Who knows how long I'd be waiting for that? Owning my own business has always been a dream of mine. I might not get a chance like this again. The building is apparently in a really hip neighborhood. I could do well there, and I've always wanted to go to Chicago." He smiles. "I hear they have good pizza."

I cut my smile with a pout. "I'll kinda miss you, mate."

I actually think if I begged Mason to stay, he's the type of guy who would. We're only friends, we've really only ever been friends, but just in the way he's looking at me, like he's afraid to disappoint me by this decision, I know he'd stay.

I would never ask him to give up a dream like that. And who knows? Maybe he'll find someone in Chicago who's worthy of such an amazing guy.

"I'm really happy for you," I state, nothing but pure honesty in my voice.

He motions with his head in the direction behind me. "Is he sticking around?"

I turn and spot Luke, leaning against his truck, hands in his pockets, and staring directly at us. My heart constricts when I think about him leaving. "I don't know. We haven't talked about anything yet." I look back at Mason. "But I think he loves me."

"I *know* he loves you," he says, tilting his head with a smirk as the heat burns my cheeks.

I give Mason a hug goodbye, wishing him luck, and threatening to remove his manhood if he doesn't stay in touch.

Luke pushes off his truck when I approach and wraps his arms around me. His lips brush against the shell of my ear. "What was that about?"

I close my eyes, pulling him closer, ducking my head under his chin.

Don't leave me.

"He's moving to Chicago. He wanted to say goodbye."

"Was he good to you?"

I look up at him, running my finger along his jaw as his amber eyes study me. "Yeah. He was a really good friend."

"Good." He presses his lips against the top of my head, breathing me in.

"Come home with me?" I ask, and maybe it shouldn't be there, but the worry, the fear of him leaving floods my voice with doubt.

His finger lifts my chin. "Is that what you want?"

"Yes," I answer, immediately, adamantly, and so fucking sure, it's as if he just asked me if I wanted to continue breathing.

His lips press against mine, smooth and full, answering my yes with a kiss that melts away everything that doesn't matter, that whispers the answer to Mason's question against my mouth.

He's staying.

LUKE'S WAITING FOR me outside my apartment door, his back leaning against it, and I know he's smirking when he sees me step onto the landing. Even in the darkness, I know.

"You beat me." I insert my key into the top lock, clicking the latch open, as my mouth stretches into a yawn. I work my way down the five deadbolts as his body presses to my back.

"Tired?" he asks against my hair, placing his hand on top of mine and twisting the doorknob.

I break into a squeal when he spins me around and lifts me, securing my legs around his waist.

I smile against his lips, giggling, as his foot kicks the door closed. "Not anymore."

"What you did for my dad," he says, and my smile

disappears as quickly as it came on. I'm tempted to squirm free of his hold, beat him to my bedroom, and lock myself away until he forgets all about my ballsy attempt to help him.

"I'm sor—"

He silences me with a finger to my lips. "He's sober. I don't know if it'll last, and if it doesn't, you will not see him like that. If I have to go get him, I do that alone."

"You're never doing anything alone again." I draw his face closer to mine as he stops dead in the hallway, his shoulders lifting with tension. "If you have to go deal with him, you can go, but I will know where you're going. No more leaving me in the middle of the night and not telling me why."

"I don't want you affected by this."

"Well, too fucking bad."

His laugh warms my face before he drops his head against mine. "It's ugly, Tessa. I don't like who I become when I deal with him."

I unhook my legs from around his waist and slide down to my feet. "You think I won't like it?" I ask, reaching up and flattening my hand over his chest.

He grabs the back of my neck, his other hand gripping my hip, sealing our bodies together again. "I. Can't. Lose. You." The emphasis he puts on those four words wrecks me, his honestly staggering. This is it. This is why he keeps me out.

"If this is too much for you, and you pull away from me . . ." His eyes close on a heavy blink. "Tessa, you're the only thing that keeps me still."

I mold my hand to his cheek, the weight of his head falling into my palm. "I'm not going anywhere. Your dad may stay sober; he may not. If he doesn't, we'll deal with it together. No more doing this alone."

I see the struggle in his eyes, the battle he's waging against himself.

I turn his head and move my lips over his ear. "Let me in, Luke. I'll make it *so* good for you."

His hands tighten on my body, rooting into my skin.

I drop back onto my heels, nearly stumbling at the sight of his tongue teasing his bottom lip. "Are you trying to bait me with sex to get me to agree to this?" he asks, his tone firm, but he can't hide the playful glint in his eye.

I step out of his grasp, tugging at the top button of my blouse. "I'll use whatever means necessary to get what I want." I pop the next button. "And I want you." Pop. "All. Of. You. Every inch." I hold the last button between my fingers, waiting for him to make his move.

He pulls at his belt, snapping it off and tossing it onto the floor. "What do you want to do with *all of me*?" he asks, moving his hands to his shorts.

My blouse falls to the floor, and his gaze drops, widening at the sight of my breasts. "Love you." I wait for his eyes to reach mine. It happens immediately. "Is that okay with you?"

"Fuck yeah, it is." Fabric rustles as he lowers his shorts, but I can't look anywhere but his eyes right now, the hungry shift in them pinning me in place, and willing my fingers to snap open the button of my jeans. His forearm flexes, and that gets my attention immediately, because I know exactly what's causing those beautiful muscles in his arm to roll.

He's working his cock at a painfully slow pace. Pulling the skin, teasing the head with a slide of this thumb. "Take them off," he orders, dropping a nod as he stares at my waist.

"You take them off."

"Are you going to work this for me?" he asks, his hand stagnant on his cock.

"Depends," I run my finger over the seam of my jeans, teasing my pussy.

"Fuck," he groans.

"Me," I add, and he moves like lightning, forcing me with two firm hands on my waist down the hallway. My back hits the bed and his hands rip my jeans off in one swift motion.

He pumps his cock while his eyes burn down my body, leaving scorch marks on my skin. His gaze stops abruptly at my left hip, just above my panty line, and he hauls my body closer with a firm hand on my thigh.

"Tessa, did you . . ." His finger runs over the sensitive skin, tracing the letter. The script, matching my initial on him perfectly, but twisted into the shape of an *L*. He doesn't look up at me, which I'm expecting. Instead his tongue wets his lips, and he presses them into my tattoo.

"Luke," I pant, arching off the bed, forcing a firmer seal of his mouth on my body.

"Flip," he orders with a hand on my waist, moving me himself before my body agrees to it.

Not that it wouldn't. I know exactly what he wants to do, and my thighs are practically trembling just thinking about it.

I look over my shoulder at him after I'm positioned on my hands and knees. He reaches back with a hand, grips his T-shirt, and pulls it off, tossing it, as his gaze remains locked between my legs. He guides my panties down to my knees, runs his finger up my length, and I fist the sheet with both hands, dropping my head when he bites the skin of my ass.

"Ask me," he says between long, torturously slow licks up and down my pussy.

I moan against the lip I have tightly secured between my teeth, trying not to scream out, as not one, but *fuck*, two fingers enter me. He pushes between my thighs and sucks on my clit.

"Ask me," he repeats, blowing against my heated flesh.

My body trembles, the pleasure becoming too intense,

too much, too perfect.

His fingers fuck me in a teasing rhythm, slowing down when I tighten around them to prolong my pleasure.

I gasp through a moan when he runs his tongue up my spine.

"Ask me, Tessa. Now." He's at my ear, leaning over me, grinding his rigid cock against my flesh.

"Do you love me today?" I ask as he tilts my head to taste the skin of my neck. My eyes fall closed when he pushes inside me, filling me, owning me.

My name breaks apart the moan that rumbles in his throat. "Yes," he answers, pressing the word into my cheek. "I love you. Every day."

I shudder, reacting to his response and the way he's slowly fucking me. His thick cock slides between my legs, wetting my lips, my thighs, gliding over the skin of my ass.

He enters me again, this time greedy, lust driven, rocking my body with punishing thrusts.

"Fuck, yeah, babe." He groans behind me, sliding his hand up my back.

My elbows give out under his power, bowing my back to him, forcing him deeper, and oh, God, he's so deep.

"Luke, I'm gonna come."

"I want you how I used to have you," he says, slowing down the drag of his cock, prolonging his release. "Fuuuck, Tessa, please."

I remember his words to me at the hospital, and my decision is made.

"Come in me."

He knows how to get me there with him; all too well, he knows it. A shift of his hips, the way he hungrily digs his skillful fingers into my skin. I stretch my arms out in front of me as his thrusts become frenzied, as my body burns up from the inside out, and I feel it, the second he breaks, when all control is lost, and it happens the very moment I call out his name.

"Luke!"

"Tessa, oh fuck, yeah, squeeze my dick, babe." He pumps into me, whispering dirty words against my ear, rooting himself deep until his cock stops twitching.

I whimper when he kisses my shoulder, running his lips along the line that leads to my neck. He nuzzles me, breathes me in, and sighs.

He fucking *sighs*.

Nothing could make me happier right now. Nothing.

"Ask me," he whispers against my ear.

I smile.

Well, almost nothing.

luke

I HAVE MANY ugly memories of this place. Ones that outweigh, or make me forget all the good ones.

When my mom died, this house became cold, and desolate. My father was like a dark cloud hovering over every room, shadowing all the light my mother had left behind. I hated being here with him, especially during this time of year.

Holidays were always harder. I didn't need the added bonus of watching him stumble around the house, reacting violently to the loss of her one minute, then collapsing on the floor in a sobbing pile of misery the next. While other families were partaking in traditions I grew up with, I was making sure my father fell asleep on his side, in case he started vomiting in the middle of the night. I spent a lot of Christmases alone, not knowing where my father was, not bothering with putting up a tree, because who the fuck would care if we even had one? We were the only house on the street not decorated with multi-colored lights, but I got to the point where I didn't give a damn. I let myself forget about all the things my mom used to do around this time of year. The decorating, how she used to spend hours in the kitchen, presents.

Yeah. No presents. I forgot what those were.

I was alone. Everything I did, I did alone.

Not anymore.

Tessa bangs away in the kitchen as I straighten out that

damn star on the top of the tree. That shit has been crooked since she put it up there, but she was so damn cute, adamant she didn't need my help, while her height clearly made the task difficult. That thing has been dropping to the left so far that it's beginning to resemble a candy cane.

After I right it so the branch isn't stressed anymore, I step through the doorway leading into the kitchen, admiring my view.

My amazing, un-fucking-believably hot view.

Tessa, bent over to check the cookies she's been baking all day in the oven. Her jeans form a damn second skin to that ass I can't get enough of. The one I'm obsessed with. The one covered in bite marks.

I lean against the counter, watching as she pulls two baking sheets out of the oven and places them on top of the stove. It smells amazing in here. The whole damn house smells amazing, and it's decorated for the first time in twelve years.

Tessa wants everything to be perfect. Every decoration she pulled out of the boxes I had packed away twelve years ago was held up and asked where my mom used to like it. The house looks exactly like it did when I was a kid. And my girl did that.

We moved in together a few weeks after Chase was born. I had to go get all my stuff from Port Deposit and give enough notice to leave that job without screwing myself out of any future employment. Jacobs took it, a win-win for everyone, and since Ben hadn't been set up with a partner to replace me while I was gone, I slid back into my old position.

I press my lips against her shoulder, along her neck, while my hands wrap around her chest, pulling her back against me.

"Hey." She turns her head and kisses my jaw. "Did you put up all the lights?"

"Yeah."

"All of them worked?"

"Nope."

She chuckles. "Well, they were crazy old. I told you we should've probably bought new ones."

"The house looks fine with only half of them lit."

She spins in my arms, hitting me with an alarming look. "Half of the lights? Are you kidding? That probably looks so tacky."

I lift the bottom of her shirt to run my thumb along her hipbone, tracing the tattoo. I do that a lot, and the smile she always gives me keeps me doing it.

"Kidding, babe. The whole damn thing is lit up. We look like that house from that movie you made me watch."

"*Christmas Vacation*!" she beams. "The little lights aren't twinkling, Clark."

I laugh, dropping a kiss to her forehead. "They're twinkling." My eyes strain over the top of her, looking down at the counter covered in trays of cookies. "Jesus, woman."

"What?" She looks over her shoulder. "Oh, well, you're supposed to bake a lot of cookies at Christmas. And I wanted to make a bunch for your dad to take home when he stops by later." She steps back and gestures at one of the trays. "You said his favorite is snickerdoodle, right?"

I nod, remembering my mom baking them for him every year. "Yeah."

She tilts her head with a sweet grin. "Five months is a big deal. You should be really proud of him."

"I am," I affirm, stepping up to the stove and looking down at the cookies.

Her hand touches my shoulder, gently squeezing. "I left out three raw squares. You don't have to try the baked ones if you don't want to. I'm perfectly capable of throwing these back by myself."

I pick up one of the warm chocolate chip cookies that have been cooling on a wire rack, lift it to my mouth, and bite into half of it. She moves in front of me, watching my mouth with tentative eyes. Her fingers begin twirling a strand of her hair as her lip becomes trapped between her teeth.

She relaxes when I smile.

"Good?" she asks.

My hand wraps around her waist and pulls her against me. I brush my lips across hers, feeling the vibration of her moan. "I'm going to ask you to marry me," I say quietly, and she goes perfectly still in my arms.

Her breath blows against my mouth in sharp bursts. "Umm . . ." She swallows. "Are you . . . ?"

"You're going to say yes, right? When I ask you?"

She closes her eyes with a nod. "Yes."

"Good." I give her ass a quick smack, reaching behind her for two more cookies before I walk away.

When I look over my shoulder, her expression is perfect. Shocked, but so fucking happy.

The End

Read on for a bonus scene from

ben & mia

Mia: Oh my God, I'm so excited! I feel like I haven't been with you in years!

Mia: Hurry up. Is he asleep? Just lay him down. He'll be okay. Actually no, don't do that. He'll scream, and then I'll feel guilty.

Mia: Shit, I'm so horny right now. I might start without you. But I won't . . . but I might.

Mia: Ben, HURRY UP.

I SMILE DOWN at the phone in my hand as Chase rubs his face against my shirt.

"Buddy, you are really screwing me here fighting sleep. Your mommy is in the other room, and she is *ready*. I gotta wait for you though, little man, and the longer you take to pass out, the slimmer my chances are to get up in that pussy. And do you know how long it's been? Do you know how old you are?"

Chase coos against me.

"You are six weeks old today, Chase. Six weeks. I know that doesn't mean anything to you right now, but when you're older, and you've gone that long without being inside your woman, you'll understand how serious this situation is. Your daddy is dying here."

He brings his fingers up to his mouth, and a wave of relief washes over me. I know that sign. Shouldn't be long now.

> *Me: Give me five more minutes. He's sucking on his fingers now. Funny, I'll be doing the same thing after I make you ride mine.*

> *Mia: You're KILLING me . . .*

I wind up the mobile when the sound fades out and settle back into the glider, rocking Chase slowly the way he likes. He's so different from Nolan. Chase needs constant movement to fall asleep, and noise. Any kind works for him. It doesn't have to be his mobile. He'll fall asleep in a crowd of people at the mall as long as you're moving him around. But Nolan, when he was a baby, you couldn't do anything with him. He needed to be still, and he needed silence. That took forever to figure out. I thought all babies liked listening to those annoying nursery rhymes when they were in their cribs. But not Nolan. I'd pace around with him, trying to get him to fall asleep while that damn mobile played in the background, and that just made it worse. It wasn't until I was exhausted from almost two weeks of him fighting me every night when I sat down on the couch with him against my chest and shut my eyes. I wasn't trying to fall asleep. I'd never do that while holding a baby, but I was fucking drained. Angie was God-fucking-knows where, and I just needed a break. Even if she was around, she wouldn't want to deal with him. I put him to bed every night. I played both parents while she did whatever the fuck she wanted. I never complained because I loved my son, and I wanted every second with him. But fuck, I was tired from being up all night constantly. I just wanted to sit for a minute and shut my eyes. Not even thirty seconds after I got comfortable on the couch, he fell asleep. It was dark. It was quiet. And I wasn't moving. The next night, and every night after that when he was with me, I sat down with Nolan in my living room, and almost immediately, he'd close his eyes. If I pulled that shit with Chase tonight, I'd never get laid.

And I'm getting fucking laid.

After winding up the mobile one more time, I slip out of Chase's nursery once he's fast asleep in his crib. I get to my bed- room door, palm the knob, and twist it to push the door open.

"Daddy?"

My head hits the still closed door with a soft thud. *So fucking close.*

Oh, God. What does she look like in there? Is she naked? Is my dirty little angel pumping her fingers in and out of that sweet pussy just thinking about my cock?

"Dadddyyy."

My hand drops from the doorknob and presses against my hard-on.

"Yeah?" I turn my head, keeping my temple on the door, and spot Nolan standing at the end of the hallway with his stuffed dragon in his arms.

"I can't sweep. My bwain wants to watch TV and eat a snack."

I scoop Nolan up in my arms and step into his room. "It's too late to watch TV and eat a snack. You should've been asleep over an hour ago." I lay him down on his pillow, and his hands fist my T-shirt, refusing to let me straighten up. "Nolan . . ."

"Can you way down with me? Pwease, Daddy?"

My hands flatten on the bed, and I stare down at my son. His big gray eyes are heavy, eyelids slightly swollen with sleep. His hair is a wild mess, and his mouth opens to allow the ear of his dragon to slip inside for him to suck on. He reaches up and runs his finger down my nose, and fuck, he has me. He's smiling big behind that dragon because he knows he has me when he pulls that shit. I repeat the gesture and climb in next to him, tucking him in with the hand that isn't braced behind my head.

"Daddy?

"Hmm?

"Why don't I go over Mommy's house anymorwe?"

My chest tightens, making breathing difficult.

We haven't talked about this. Nolan rarely asks about Angie, other than the times he's wondered if he was going to see her again. And I've given him a one word answer, yes, and changed the subject, because I don't know what the fuck to say. I don't want him to see her again, but when she does get out of jail eventually, I'm sure I'll have to deal with that shit. She'll probably serve a few more years for the DUI she got arrested for. The one that could've killed my son. If I had any say in it, that cunt would rot in jail for the rest of her life. But I don't. I can't do shit about her getting out some day, but I can protect Nolan.

He's mine. Mia is his mommy now, and Angie can go fuck herself if she thinks she's taking him away from us.

"Daddy?"

I look down into Nolan's tired eyes. "Your mommy, your first mommy, had to go away somewhere, because she couldn't be a good Mommy to you. But she loved you very much, and she wanted you to have the best Mommy in the whole world. So me and her, we went looking for a princess, because we knew a princess would be the best Mommy to you."

He smiles, letting the dragon ear fall out of his mouth. "I wove Pwincess Mia, Daddy. She's the best Mommy evewr."

"And she loves you very much, buddy."

"Did my firwst Mommy weawy love me?"

I nod before I have a chance to hesitate, because I don't fucking know the answer to this. And this shit fucking kills me.

What kid should have to question this? What the fuck kind of person makes their own child doubt whether or not they love them?

Running my hand along his cheek, I feel him lean into it as he brings the dragon back to his mouth. "She loved you, buddy. She just couldn't love you like a princess could."

Nolan closes his eyes and scoots closer, nuzzling against my shirt. "Is Chasey going to be wittle fowrever?"

"No, buddy. He'll get bigger just like you."

"Wiwl he wike dwagons too?"

"Probably."

He makes a soft grunting sound.

"I won't let him take you," he whispers into the darkness of his bedroom.

I turn my head away from him, keeping my amused reaction to what he's just said silent. Only Nolan would comfort his stuffed animal. Only my son would think about some inanimate object's feelings after touching on his own so profoundly.

Nolan yawns, then says quietly, "Wove you, Daddy." His voice muffled against his dragon.

"Love you, buddy."

I press a kiss to his forehead, then slide out of the bed, not moving toward the door in case Nolan protests it. I wouldn't be surprised if he did. But as I stand there in the dark, his breathing changes, becomes heavier, more relaxed. I wait a good minute before I move, because I'm not getting hard again and shutting that shit down. Pulling my cell out of my pocket, I hit the power button and light up the screen.

11:24 p.m. Fuck. FUCK.

I texted Mia over an hour ago saying five minutes. And she hasn't texted me since, which can only mean one thing.

As I push my bedroom door open, my eyes find Mia's body like there's nothing else in the room to focus on. The glow from several illuminated candles casts over her, showing my angel in the light I always see her in. Eyes closed, she's on her back in an outfit I can't even fucking stare at right now without busting a nut in my shorts.

Black. Lace. Those fucking stockings I found in her dresser last week that she refused to put on for me.

Jesus fucking Christ. I'm going to come before I touch her.

I strip and wrap my hand around the base of my cock, willing it to chill the fuck out for a second. I'm so amped right now, there's a good chance I'll embarrass the hell out of myself if I do exactly what I want to do, fuck her awake. So I go with option two. The second best thing to sliding inside her tight pussy. The thing she'll chose over anything else, except my cock. The thing she'll beg me for.

I should make her beg right now for teasing me with this outfit.

Dirty, dirty Mia. You're going to scream so fucking loud for me.

I don't waste any time. I can't tease her tonight unless I feel like coming all over this mattress. Dropping my head, I nuzzle my mouth against her pussy, throw her legs over my shoulder, and wait until she slides her hand into my hair before I run my tongue over her clit.

"Mmm . . . I thought I was dreaming."

I grab a handful of her tit overtop the lace, squeezing a

gasp past her lips. "Not dreaming, pretty girl. You touch this pussy without me?"

She shakes her head through a moan.

"You sure?" I ask, biting down on her clit and holding her down when she squirms.

"No, no I . . . Oh, Ben, please."

"Better make sure you're not lying." I pull her hand off my head and slip her two favorite fingers into my mouth. She watches me, mouth open and tongue rolling along her bottom lip as I suck. "You waited for me," I conclude, turning my head to plant a kiss in her open palm.

"I told you I did," she says, her voice throaty from sleep. She cups my jaw. "Are the boys okay?"

"Mia, please leave them out of this room tonight. I need to fuck my wife, and I can't do that if you start asking me about other men."

She laughs as I lay my head on her thigh and run my thumb between her lips. "I need you to fuck your wife, too. But you can't do it if you're down there."

"I want to eat your pussy first."

"*Ben*," she pleads. Her head lifts from the pillow to see me better as both hands grab my face, forcing my attention up her body. "It's been six weeks. Please. Fuck me already."

I crawl up her so fast, she squeals underneath me, giggling into the skin of my neck. My cock lays heavy against her thigh as her hands roam all over my back, then her nails mark my skin with an urgency that has me shaking as I press the tip of my cock against her clit.

"Oh, my God. Yes."

"Tits out, angel. I might consider fucking them first, `cause I will lose my mind the second your clamp down on me." I release a rough exhale, gripping the base of my cock until it's almost painful. "Fuck, Mia. I'm dying here."

Her eager hands free her breasts, bunching the material of her lingerie between us at her waist. Then her hand is covering mine, sliding my cock along her slick pussy and coating me with what my mouth should still be savoring.

My head falls back with a groan, my muscles straining as I rock forward on my knees. "Mia," I rasp, moaning when her hand cups my balls. My resistance breaks. No, it doesn't break. It fucking shatters.

No longer able to hold off, and I grab her hand that's fondling me like she fucking owns me, secure it above her head with a firm grip, and brace my other hand next to her head as I slide into her, slowly, taking what's mine, burying myself so deep inside her, she'll never stop feeling me.

Her face contorts, eyebrows pinched together and lips pursed as she throws her head back onto the pillow.

Shit. It's been six weeks since I've been inside her. And now I'm fucking hurting her.

"You okay?" I ask, bringing my hand to the side of her face. I release her wrist and lean on both elbows to stare down at her, watching her eyes close through a deep breath. Her chest shudders against mine. "Talk to me, pretty girl. Tell me what you're feeling."

Eyes still closed, she wets her lips before whispering, "Ben."

I drop my head next to hers as my heart lodges somewhere in my throat. I can't stand hurting Mia. I should just pull out right now and go back to worshipping her pussy with my tongue.

But then her lips brush against my ear, stilling everything inside me.

"Fuck me," she begs, hitching her legs around my waist,

tilting her pelvis so I slide in the last insanely perfect inch.

"Yeah?" I ask, leaning back to look at her. "You want it hard, angel?"

She nods, keeping her eyes on mine. "I want it hard."

"I'll come," I warn her.

"Me too."

She smiles, and fuck, I'm so gone for this woman. Screw every motherfucker out there who thinks they've loved more than any other man on this planet. Who thinks they've found the perfect chick. Nobody will ever come close to having what I have, to feeling what I feel every time my wife looks at me.

To this. Right here.

I've taken my wife a lot of ways, but when she wants it hard, I will never hold back with her. I'll give her exactly what she needs, because it's always exactly how I need it. When I take her slow and worship her body with more than just my cock, it's perfect. And when I take her hard, showing her how desperate I am for what she gives me, it's perfect. It's always fucking perfect, and right now as I push her legs against her chest and fuck her until I can't breathe, it's perfect.

"Mia," I groan, as the sweat drips off my temple and onto her chest. "Mia."

She runs her finger above my hip, and without looking down, I know she's tracing her name. One of my newer tattoos, besides Chase's name which blends into the design on my arm. Mia closes her eyes through a groan and presses against her favorite mark. Embedding herself deeper into me. I don't know why, but that sends me over the edge. Knowing how permanent she will always be. Knowing how badly she wants that.

I dig in deeper, fuck her harder. "Get there, Mia." I bite her bottom lip, swallowing her gasp. "Fucking *get there*."

"Ben!" She claws at my skin, bites on my tongue, and comes so tightly around me, it nearly blows my head off. I fuck her until I collapse, our bodies a tangled mess as she rolls me onto my back. Sweat sticks to her skin, and I run my hand between her tits when she straddles my waist.

"Angel, I need a minute," I tell her, thinking her mind's set on riding me until I can't see straight. She flattens her body on top of mine, buries her face in my neck, and sucks on my skin as her heartbeat thunders against my chest.

"I love you, Benjamin Kelly. I love you, and your giant cock."

I press my lips to her hair, muffling my laugh as my arms engulf her. "It's not giant."

"It's huge. And perfect. And so very mine."

"That's not all of me that's yours."

She's silent for several seconds, and I think maybe I've said something wrong, or maybe she's passed back out. Until she lifts her head, sealing our mouths together with a gentle kiss.

"I'm yours, too."

"I know," I tell her, wiggling a hand between us to cup the only pussy I'll ever drop down on my knees for. "I think I'll fuck you slow this time."

She smiles, all big and beautiful.

All Mia. All mine.

acknowledgements

MR. DANIELS, THANK you for being supportive of my dream. For taking care of things while I'm locked away in my writing den, for smiling at me from across the room when I peek up from my laptop, and for being my Reese, Ben, Luke, and every other hero I think up in my head. I love you more than cupcakes, and I LOVE cupcakes.

My badass betas, thank you for telling me I could write this story. For having faith in my ability, when I doubted myself, and for helping me give Luke and Tessa the love story they deserved. Beth and Lisa, I couldn't have done this without you.

To all the bloggers who have helped me on my journey, thank you for reading my books, promoting my books, and helping me reach more readers than I could have ever imagined. There are too many of you for me to list, but I love you all. Please know that. My girls over at Give Me Books for everything you have done for me. Kylie, you are amazing. Just amazing.

R.J. Lewis, for being the first person to ever take a chance on me. I will never forget you.

Elle Keating, for the gerbil story. Thank you for letting me use your horrible dating experience for my Tessa.

To my readers, I never imagined anyone wanting to read my stories. The love you have shown me is staggering, and I can't thank you enough for your support.

Thank you all again,

J

books by
J. DANIELS

SWEET ADDICTION SERIES

Sweet Addiction

Sweet Possession

Sweet Obsession

Sweet Love (Coming Soon)

ALABAMA SUMMER SERIES

Where I Belong

All I Want

When I Fall

Where We Belong

What I Need

So Much More (Halloween Novella)

All We Want

Say I'm Yours (Coming Soon)

DIRTY DEEDS SERIES

Four Letter Word

Hit the Spot

Bad for You

Down too Deep (Coming Soon)

about the author

J DANIELS IS THE *New York Times* and *USA Today* bestselling author of the Sweet Addiction series, the Alabama Summer series, and the Dirty Deeds series.

She would rather bake than cook, she listens to music entirely too loud, and loves writing stories her children will never read. Her husband and children are her greatest loves, with cupcakes coming in at a close second.

J grew up in Baltimore and resides in Maryland with her family.

follow J at:

www.authorjdaniels.com

Facebook

www.facebook.com/jdanielsauthor

Twitter—@JDanielsbooks

Instagram—authorjdaniels

Goodreads

http://bit.ly/JDanielsGoodreads

Join her reader's group for the first look at upcoming projects, special giveaways, and loads of fun!

www.facebook.com/groups/JsSweeties

Sign up to receive her newsletter and get special offers and exclusive release info.

www.authorjdaniels.com/newsletter

CPSIA information can be obtained
at www.ICGtesting.com
Printed in the USA
JSHW021100030223
37163JS00001B/35

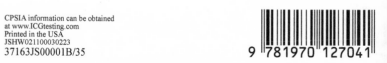

9 781970 127041